Jason Franks writes comics, prose and source code. His first novel, BLOODYWATERS, was short-listed for the 2012 Aurealis Award for Best Horror Novel.

He is the writer of the THE SIXSMITHS graphic novels (a Ledger Awards finalist) and the comic series LEFT HAND PATH (also short-listed for an Aurealis Award), as well as numerous short stories in prose and comics. A collection of his mainstream short stories was collected in UNGENRED by Black House Comics.

Franks has published work in most genres, but he is most comfortable in the darker reaches of speculative fiction, although his writing is often humorous. His protagonists are likely to be villains or anti-heroes and the Devil is a recurring figure in his work.

Franks has lived in South Africa, the USA and Japan. He currently resides in Melbourne, Australia.

Faerie Apocalypse

BY
Jason Franks

Faerie Apocalypse

ISBN-13: 978-0-646-59588-7

V1.0

Printed in Palatino Linotype Chocolate Box, and Chocolate Box Decorative

IFWG Publishing International
Melbourne

www.ifwgaustralia.com

Acknowledgements

A great many people have helped me to bring Faerie Apocalypse into the world. In roughly chronological order:

Thanks to Erin Marcon, Karen Jacobson, David Richardson and Frank Curigliano, who gave feedback on the very earliest fragments of this project. Without your encouragement I would never have written past the opening scene.

Merci beaucoup to Celia Franca, for housing her vagrant grand-nephew while he wrote the second and third chapters, as well as providing encouragement and criticism. I still miss you, GAC.

Domo arigato to James Johnson, AD Silverman, Edwin Rydberg, Rhoda Franks, David Franks, Glenn Mafodda and Denh Lay, for their assistance in helping me to grind down the style and the story for those early attempts to sell it. You told me where the book would fail, and you were right.

Cheers to Jason Fischer, who helped me get up when I thought I was finished. Danke schoen to Angela Slatter, who lent me the use of her good name despite the fact she had never even communicated with me before.

Muchas gracias to Marta Salek for her painstaking assistance with drafts 7,054,356-7,054,363. Bayalalaa to Kirstyn McDermott, who vouched for me after I had fled the scene.

Fangyouverramuch to Stephen Ormsby, who took on my crazy broken project when nobody else would. While it didn't work out as we might have hoped, I will always be grateful for your support.

Toda raba to Gillian Polack, for showing me how to solve the final puzzle. I would never have gotten there without your insight. Shkoyach.

Dankie, Stephen McCracken, for opening the final door, and bedanken to Gerry Huntman, for letting me through it. I will try not to eat all the soup.

Jason Franks

Melbourne, 2017

For Sarah and Ed

Book 1
Lovers, Poets and Madmen

1. The Tree

For weeks he wandered alone amongst the trees, living off the land; breathing and eating and sleeping, and searching. The birds overhead sang to him, but he spoke no reply. The creatures in the brush came uncomplaining to his traps, though he did not thank them. The tread of his scuffed old army boots and the sweeping of his stick said all that he had to say.

When he had sojourned long enough a path revealed itself to him. The mortal slung on his rucksack, scratched his new beard, and set upon the way.

Night had fallen by the time he came to the clearing where a tree of indeterminate species grew from the naked bedrock. The withered grey moon hung directly above it, so low that it seemed to be resting in the tree's highest branches.

The mortal negotiated the circumference of the tree. It was wider around than the terraced house in Southend that he had haunted in the years before he had taken to traveling.

Two more circuits revealed a small opening at the base of the tree, where the two roots had split the trunk around a spur of rock. He bent down and peered inside, but he could see only darkness. The mortal reached his hand towards the aperture, then hesitated. Instead, he poked it with his stick.

Something squealed inside the Tree of Indeterminate Species. The mortal jerked his hand away as it snatched the stick from his grasp. Another scream issued from the aperture, followed by a spray of wood-shards. Then, there were no more sounds.

The mortal considered the aperture from a safe distance, suddenly glad that it was not bigger. He wiped his hands on his dirt-stained jeans, adjusted his rucksack, and looked for a low-hanging tree limb.

Thus, the mortal climbed the Tree of Indeterminate Species, moving up and around its knotted trunk until he was high in the canopy of the forest. By the time he could see through the foliage, the moon had rotated out of view. The rocky clearing below had filled with shadow. From his new vantage, it seemed as though he had climbed out of a well.

The sky looked flat, as though it had been skinned from the universe and drawn taut upon a wire frame. The stars shone unflickering and intense. The mortal did not recognise any of the fixed constellations, but the scenes they depicted were detailed and vivid.

At the top of the tree he discovered a new opening in the trunk. Inside was a golden slippery-dip, which twisted down into the darkness.

The mortal laughed. His voice rang clear, though he had not used it for weeks. He climbed onto the chute and gravity spiralled him down into the tree on the seat of his pants.

2. The Moon Above, the Star Below

The mortal was deposited into a vast, dark chamber. He picked himself up and fumbled open his rucksack for his SureFire torch. He swung the flashlight about, but it would not shine. The mortal put the SureFire away and instead struck a flame from a small, silver lighter.

The cavity inside the tree was far wider than the globe of illumination cast by the lighter's tiny flame. His boots clocking softly on the bare rock, he set forth in what he hoped was a straight line.

The mortal walked until he reached a rough-cut wall, wet with sap and ridged with capillaries. If he followed the tree-wall for long enough he would surely find an exit.

In minutes or hours or days he came to a breach in the tree-wall, where two roots had split the trunk around a spur of rock. Just inside the aperture lay the skeleton of a creature that was a bit like a sloth, or perhaps a badger. The badger-sloth's ribs had been stoved staved-in by some blunt instrument. There were shards of wood in its serrated jaws.

The mortal nudged the little corpse with his boot. He snapped shut his lighter and bent down and picked up the skull. He wrapped it carefully in an old t-shirt and put it in his rucksack.

When the mortal turned his back on the aperture, he found that he was unable to strike a new flame from his lighter, though there was still fluid in its reservoir. He tried it again and again, until even the flint refused to spark.

He put the lighter away and sat down with his back against the tree wall. His legs ached. His heart pained him. His eyes hurt, so he closed them. He was trapped; he would never escape. He would fall asleep, there inside the tree, and never awaken.

The mortal opened his eyes. He could see a blue-white radiance in the distance. He blinked hard, but it would not go away. The more he looked at it, the more it came to resemble a star. The star had five rounded points, like an asterisk.

The mortal set off towards it, and the asterisk retreated before him, leading him deep inside the tree. He rushed after it, but walk, run or stumble, he could not close the distance. His feet became entangled and he fell.

When the mortal picked himself up, the star had vanished. Ahead, he could see the breach in the side of the tree. The asterisk had led him in a circle.

The mortal sighed and trudged towards the aperture. It grew as he approached it, and, by the time he reached the gap, he found that it was large enough to let him pass. He ducked his head and eased through, pulling his rucksack after him.

3. The Spinning Compass

The mortal emerged into daylight. Grassy meadowlands sloped away in all directions. Close by was a river, blue and fast and clean. In the distance he could see a forest of bare, black-skinned trees.

This was not a real place; he knew that immediately. Here, every sensation felt more vibrant, more meaningful than those in the world from which he had come, but only because his senses were not acting in their proper accord. The air had a distinct flavour on his tongue, but he did not feel it in his nose. The horizon receded as he approached it, but the vanishing point seemed to vary in order to provide him with the most pleasing view.

The illusion of perspective operated across all of his senses, not to mention his reduced capacity to think logically. In this place he might sleep, but he would have no dreams.

The needle of his compass spun erratically in one direction, then the other. He snorted and put it away. The black forest seemed a dangerous place, but the river would surely lead to some kind of habitation. He set out towards it, rolling his shoulders and his neck as if to slough off the grimness of the real world, like a snake shedding an old skin. He had not bathed for days, but he felt cleansed and renewed.

This was the place he had sought and he felt lucky, if not blessed, to have found it.

Only three kinds of mortal were permitted entry into the

Realms of the Faerie—lovers, poets, and madmen—and he was most certainly to be counted amongst their number. He, who sought the most beautiful thing in the world.

4. High in a Tower

Far away, on the perimeter of a Realm that had no borders, there stood a dark and jagged tower.

So dark was the tower that it stained the very skies it broached. So thick was the slime of evil coating its shaft that it left a residue upon the eyes of any who looked upon it.

The tower had not been built from stone and wood and mortar. It had been cast whole from rune and ritual and will…and the magus who had willed it dwelled there yet.

The magus sat in the top room with his back to the window, his shadow upon the tomes and scrolls spread open before him. After a time, he looked up from his texts. The magus rose and went to his instruments.

Symbols flashed across his scrying mirror, written in an alphabet that no other wise-man might recognise. Patterns that no other seer might discern were revealed to him when he shook the pan of divining bones.

"Ah ha."

The magus shed his robes and donned instead the vestments he had worn in the days before he had raised the tower. He gathered to him weapons he had not borne for innumerable years, and smiled a smile his lips had not borne for longer still.

Another of his kind had come to the Realms, and it would be impolite not to welcome him properly.

5. The Village

At twilight, the mortal made camp on the western bank of the river. He had nothing left to eat, but he was too tired to hunt or forage, so he retired without supper. He rested until dawn, though he did not sleep. He was no longer hungry when he broke camp.

At noon, he came upon a village: threescore low buildings, crouched in a valley that the river had cut between two small hills. Some of the dwellings were round and some were angular; some were flat-roofed and some were thatched. Some were made of stone, some of mud. Others were constructed of wood or iron or glass. None of the buildings were aligned the same way. There did not appear to be any roads running amongst them, besides the main thoroughfare.

It was a market day, and the single avenue was lined with carts and stalls and tents. Bright-dyed fabrics and colourfully painted signs declared the vendors and their goods in dozens of languages, few of which were familiar to the mortal.

The village folk were generally shorter and slighter than the mortal's kind, though some were broader and taller than any man. Some were gnarled and deformed, others were straight-backed and handsome. Some had furry hides, while others were knobbed or silken or glassy. The villagers' dress was as varied as their skins—if they wore clothing at all.

The mortal felt strange as he walked amongst the folk, ungainly in size and uncouth in his manufactured clothing.

This did not discourage merchants from propositioning him everywhere he went, in his own language and in many others. They offered him jewels and refreshments and spells and weapons, animals and fortunes and maps. The mortal only smiled, and shook his head, and kept on walking. He knew that anything purchased in the open marketplace was likely to be ephemeral…and if it was not, it was probably cursed. Any price he agreed to would be far dearer than the one he thought to pay.

But one merchant was not easily dissuaded. It scurried about the mortal, tugging at his garments; wheedling and whining and imploring him to stop. When it became clear that the merchant would rather be trampled to death than allow him to proceed unhindered, the mortal acquiesced.

The merchant was a slight creature, dressed in robes of blue and green silk. Gold sparkled at its neck and upon its wrists. Its face was long and fine-boned; its ears were pointed; its eyes were narrow. The merchant's left hand was made from steel-sprung glass.

"Anything you desire, sirrah," said the merchant. Its breath smelled of cinnamon and sulphur. "I can give you anything, an you meet my price."

Most of the wares in the merchant's stall were sealed in small containers inscribed with arcane script. A mangy white terrier with faint brown markings was tethered to a cabinet. A lustrously plumed black falcon was chained to the awning.

"If you can provide me with anything I could name," the mortal replied, "what need have you for my price?"

The merchant bobbed its head. "There are prices that you alone can pay. There are things of value that cannot be taken unless they are first given."

"I have nothing of worth."

"You are wrong, sirrah," said the merchant. "You have power."

He shook his head. "I'm no sorcerer."

"Not all magic is sorcery," said the merchant. "But all power is magic."

"Perhaps that's true," the mortal replied, "But it has the ring of nonsense to my ear. In any case, if I could purchase what I desire, I would no longer desire it."

"Name a thing you would have and I will find a way to make you a deal. I swear it."

"Alright." The mortal replied slowly, having formulated a bargain to which the merchant could not possibly agree. "I want everything that you possess. In exchange, you must accept nothing more than the words I have spoken."

A pallor spread across the merchant's face and it collapsed at the mortal's feet. Among the possessions he had forced the merchant to relinquish was its immortal life.

The glamour the merchant had laid upon his stall shimmered away, and his wares were rendered true for the mortal to see: bottles of withered flowers; shards of stone wrapped in twine; empty jars made of cracked, unvarnished clay. The fabrics adorning the stall were stained and patched. The robe the merchant wore was threadbare and ragged.

The marketplace fell silent. A hundred pairs of eyes turned upon the mortal: slitted or goggled, coloured or blank, rheumy or sharp. The terrier growled. The falcon hopped and swayed on its perch.

The mortal raised his hands. "I didn't know," he said. "I didn't mean it."

One by one, the merchants and patrons returned to their business or pleasure, though a sense of unease lingered.

The glass hand was all that remained of the merchant, lying quiescent amongst the pile of ragged clothing. Its fingers twitched on their springs when the mortal picked it up. He wrapped it in another t-shirt and put it in his rucksack.

"Sir," said a coarse voice. The speaker was a muscular, two-legged being that stood tethered to the stall in place of the terrier. It had a wet, upturned nose, dark eyes, and a lipless mouth that was filled with a carnivore's teeth. The dog-man was shorter than the mortal, though it was bulkier. It was dressed in the uncured hides of some fair-skinned, hairless beast. A dagger hung from its belt and a cutlass was secured to its back.

"Sir," said the dog-man, allowing the falcon to hop onto its arm, "We were bound in servitude to the merchant, who is no more. Now we are bound to you."

The falcon screeched its assent.

"No," the mortal replied. "Now you're free."

The falcon hopped from foot to foot and screeched again. The dog-man inclined its head, listened, nodded. Still grinning, it said, "My comrade begs you to lift the enchantment binding it to its present form."

The mortal frowned at the dog-man. "How is it that your enchantment is broken, yet the falcon's is not?"

"Mine is no enchantment," said the dog-man. "I am a shape-shifter."

The mortal shook his head and looked away. "I have not the means," he said. "I'm no sorcerer."

"Then we shall trouble you no more." The dog-man set about freeing itself from its tether with its dagger. The falcon fluttered its wings uselessly and cried its pain.

The mortal spied a plain stone building in a laneway that was barely visible from the main thoroughfare. He could not read the sign that hung above it, but the door was open and it had the look of the kind of place he sought, so he went inside.

The dry goods store smelled variously of damp earth and treated wood and metal polish, but, the mortal noticed, the odours did not comingle. All manner of ordinary items crowded the shelves, hung from the ceiling, or were stacked upon the floor: oil-lamps, ropes, axes, cook-pots, and of course, dry goods.

The storekeeper was grey-haired and straight-backed, with eyebrows that grew into its sideburns. It wore trousers, a loose white shirt, a leather waistcoat, and pince-nez spectacles.

"I need some things," the mortal said.

"Name them, and I will name the price," the storekeeper replied. Its voice was smooth and without accent.

"I have only the currency of the mortal realm."

"Good," said the storekeeper. "Then I know your coin is true."

The mortal bought a length of rope, tent pegs, soap, a straight razor, a whetstone, a flint, candles and some dried meat that the storekeeper told him was goat. He paid fourteen pounds sterling for the goods. The storekeeper accepted notes as well as coins.

"What do you seek here?" it asked, when the transaction was done.

"I have everything I need, thank you."

"Here in the Realms of the Land."

The mortal considered the storekeeper again. Seeing no harm in the telling, he said: "I seek the most beautiful thing in the world."

"Aye, indeed? Can you identify this object?"

"She is the Queen of the Faerie."

"Which Queen would that be?"

"The Queen of the Faerie," the mortal repeated. He had not expected scepticism from a creature of the Realms.

"There are many Realms in this Land," said the storekeeper. "And many Queens. Can you name the one you seek?"

"The only name I know is Titania."

The storekeeper shook its head. "I have not heard of that one."

The mortal gave it some thought. "If there are many Queens, which among them is known to be the fairest?"

The storekeeper shrugged. "Opinions differ. The judgment must be yours to make."

"Fair enough," said the mortal, and quit the store.

6. A King Rides Forth

Far away, a king took the goblet from his lips and tilted his head to hear an exchange spoken many leagues distant. His smile faded as the words sounded in his ear. His court ceased their merriment and looked to him in askance.

The king stood up from his throne. He dismissed his court and summoned his squires to help him into his smoked-silver armour. He buckled on his swords and, barefoot, mounted his burnt-gold stallion. Then he took up his battered wooden lance, and he rode forth in anger.

Someone was seeking his Queen.

7. The Dog-Man and the Not-Falcon

The mortal followed the river out of the village and through the hills. As twilight fell he considered his fortune so far. The episode with the merchant disturbed him, but he felt good about the slaves he had freed from servitude. He had not made any progress towards his goal, but he had learned something about the nature of the place in which he sought it, and it seemed to him that was a pretty good start. If he remained patient and cautious he would find his queen eventually.

In the distance he spied a fire. It was dark, now, and some other traveller had made camp amidst a stand of trees by the riverbank. He went towards it as quietly as he could; knowing that he would not find what he sought by avoiding company, but wary of strangers in this strangest of lands.

The dog-man from the marketplace sat cross-legged before the flames, turning a strange and unappetizing bird on a spit. It looked up at him and nodded, though he had not yet announced his presence.

"How did you get here ahead of me?" asked the mortal. Now that his eyes were adjusting to the firelight, he noticed black feathers scattered all around the campsite.

The dog-man grinned. "The direct way."

This did not answer his question, but the mortal was not going to ask twice. "You killed the not-falcon," he said.

"Aye," said the dog-man, turning the bird. "It was, as you

say, not truly a falcon, though it wore a falcon's shape. It couldn't fly, or hunt."

The mortal sat down beside the fire. "And it could not have escaped you."

"Aye," said the dog-man.

When the dog-man removed the charred carcass from the fire it did not offer the mortal any, for the portion was scant. The mortal took some goat jerky from his rucksack and they ate in silence.

"Tell me, mortal man, how did you find passage into the Realms of the Land?" asked the dog-man, when the meal was done. "There are few of your kind who venture here now, and I fear the Ways that once led here have turned back on themselves."

"There was a tree," replied the mortal.

"What sort of a tree?"

"A tree of…indeterminate species," he replied.

"The Worldtree." The dog-man seemed impressed.

"I prefer my own name for it," the mortal replied, smiling.

"If the Worldtree manifested for you, you must have some important purpose here," said the dog-man, leaning close enough that he could smell its carrion breath. It was panting. "Some quest of terrible import."

"I am looking for the most beautiful thing in the world," the mortal said. "The Queen of the Faerie."

"Ah," said the dog-man, making a man's grin with its dog's teeth. "A lover-man, looking for someone to love."

"I seek the Queen of the Faerie," the mortal said again.

"There are many Queens," said the dog-man, "And they are all beautiful."

"So I have been told," said the mortal, displeased with the news. He had hoped the storekeeper was mistaken, or had perhaps been trying to discourage him by magnifying his task, but he did not believe the dog-man to be capable of such deception.

"But do you know which Queen to seek?"

"The only Queen I know by name is Titania," said the

mortal. "In my world, she is the most famous of Faerie Queens."

"That means only that she is careless with her name, and meddles beyond her own borders."

"Perhaps," the mortal replied, "but I have nothing else to go on. Unless you can name me the fairest Queen?"

The dog-man gave it some thought. "You will only consider bipedal queens?"

"Yes."

"Then to my eye, Zelioliah is the fairest. But I have not beheld all of the Queens. I have not seen your Titania."

"Zelioliah? Is she, too, incautious with her name?"

"She is the Queen of the Warriors, and has little fear of its misuse."

"Well, I don't care about names. I will know the one I seek only when I lay my eyes upon her."

"I hope so," said the dog-man. "No other can know for you." It turned its back and curled up, and became once again the scarred and mangy terrier.

They rose with the dawn and ate their respective breakfasts. The mortal filled his canteen from the river, upstream from where the dog-man lapped its thirst away.

"Tell me, mortal," said the dog-man, "what will you do, when you find this Queen that you seek?"

"I will kiss her, and make her mine."

"And what if she refuses you?" said the dog-man.

"She won't refuse."

The dog-man's frown creased its nose as well as its brows. "I make no claims to understanding of how such congresses are arranged among your folk," it said, "but here in the Realms it is usually more complicated than that."

"There is no reason for it to be so," replied the mortal. "I will know her when I see her, and she will know me."

"Even if that were true," said the dog-man, "I do not believe that Faerie Queens will consort with any common mortal—if that is indeed what you are."

"I have been many things in my life, but I am no prince," he replied. "If that is what you are asking. I have been a soldier and a husband and a traveller and a beggar. I am as low-born as any man."

"Even the lowest born man is higher than a dog," said the dog-man. It did not appear to find this situation of concern.

"In my experience, a dog may be just as noble as any man, or as base," said the mortal.

"That is good to know," said the dog-man.

"Now tell me," the mortal said, "Which Realm is closest to here?"

"The closest Realm, or the closest Queen?" asked the dog-man. "Some Realms have no Queens, just as some Queens have no Nations...and some Nations have no territories."

"You haven't answered my question."

"In this Land it pays to be careful how you ask questions, and how you answer them. Falsehood will destroy you; truth will devour your bones."

The mortal sighed. "Where is the court of closest Faerie Queen?" He considered the dog-man's advice, and so added: "The closest *bipedal* Queen."

"This year, in this cycle, the Sea City on the Plains is near to our present location," said the dog-man. It sketched a map in the ashes of the falcon's cook-pyre. "I will take you there, an you will it."

The mortal shook his head. "I began this alone, and so I must end it."

"It's no bother," said the dog-man.

"Thank you, but no."

"Please?"

"I cannot."

"Please," said the dog-man. "A dog with a master has honour and purpose. A wild dog is but a beast."

"I'm sorry. I cannot."

"Very well," said the dog-man, trying to keep the whine from its voice.

"Perhaps we will meet again," the mortal said.

The dog-man barked, or laughed. Made a sound that was both at once. "We have met twice already," it said. "In this Land, you can be certain that will eventually become thrice."

8. A Queen Upon Her Throne

Far away, a velvet-furred page in black and crimson livery scampered up to its Queen. It hauled itself up onto the arm of her black and crimson chair and whispered in her ear.

The Black and Crimson Queen wasted no time in summoning her guard, who came forth with her black and crimson banners waving from their black and crimson armour. Their weapons were forged of shadowsteel: black, like shadows sopped with blood.

Bearers in black and crimson tunics made of the throne a palanquin; and thus, the Queen and her war party marched from the territory in which her black and crimson nation was currently encamped.

Someone had named a Faerie Queen fairest, and the name they had spoken had not been hers.

9. In the Pass

As the dog-man's dirt map had suggested, the mortal followed the river through the hills until they became mountains and the grassy soil abraded to sand and scree. During the day, the sky was golden behind the clouds. At night it was black.

After some days' travel, the mortal found a pass that led between the tallest and shortest of the mountains, as the dog-man had said he would. The way steepened, and the rock walls rose on either side of him until the sky was a narrow ribbon far above. That night, the mortal slept sitting upright in a shallow crevasse. He had no fire, for there was no wood to burn.

When the golden ribbon of sky reappeared above him, he rose and set out again, rubbing his arms against the chill. He drank sparingly from his canteen and wondered if he had enough water to last him.

Around noontime, a noise stopped him in his tracks. He was not sure if it was a voice or a landslide, but either prospect terrified him. There was no shelter to be had in the pass, and there was nowhere to run.

A sheet of stone detached itself from the escarpment. It spun like a dancer *en pointe*, shivering and compressing its mass. The creature's true shape was insectoid and feminine, though its back was ridged with jagged stone. Its newly exposed underbelly showed psychedelic patterns in all the colours of a rainbow.

"Greetings," it said. Its voice was soft, like diamonds falling onto a fold of velvet. Its face was as chitinous as its torso and limbs, but configured into recognisably human features.

"Hello," said the mortal.

The rock–thing looked him over. "Where are you from?"

"I've come from the village, over the hills."

"Yes," it said, "But you are not from there, nor from any of the Realms."

"The Realms are wide and varied," he said. "Surely you cannot know them all."

"This is true," said the rock-thing, with delight. "But one need not have seen all the Realms of the Land to be able to identify those who are not indigenous to them."

"You have the right of it," he conceded. "I am a mortal."

"I don't know what that is."

"Something quite uninteresting, I fear."

The rock-thing smiled as seductively as an insect made of rocks could. "Yet your manner of speech is fair."

He smiled back. "One must ensure that one is understood."

"And yet some take pains to conceal the true meaning of their words," said the rock-thing.

A spear-blade as wide as the mortal's hand and as long as his forearm sprouted from the rock-thing's rainbow-breasted thorax. Its limbs twitched; its delicately armoured jaw worked. Fluids welled from the joints in its exoskeleton.

The wielder of the spear levered the corpse aside and let it crash to the ground. "I just saved your life, pig-fucker," she said.

The warrior stood five-and-a-half feet tall in frayed leather and ring-mail armour. She wore a short sword on her hip and an enormous bastard sword on her back. Daggers protruded from each of her boots; dirks were strapped to the insides of her forearms. A sickle attached to a length of chain was looped through her belt.

"I have never consorted with any kind of farmyard animal," replied the mortal. "Much less a pig."

"Had I not saved you, you may never have had the opportunity."

"I was not being menaced," he replied, angry at having been insulted twice in as many utterances. A week in the Realms and already he was unused to discourtesy.

The warrior snorted. "Not everything that smiles prettily means you well," she said. Her hair was brown, tied back in a ponytail and tucked inside the collar of her jerkin. Her eyes were brown. There was something unusual about her ears, but that was all that set her apart from the women of the mortal's own world. "I've been hunting that thing for weeks. It murdered and ate seven of my best fighters."

"Perhaps it was hungry," he replied.

"If it was hungry, it would have eaten rocks," the warrior replied. "It was a lithophage."

"I see." He felt angry. Angry at his own foolishness, and angry that she had called him on it.

"What are you doing here? This is not your place."

"I am seeking the most beautiful thing in the world."

"And that is?"

"A Queen of the Faerie folk," he said.

"Ah," she replied, with apparent disgust. "So you're a *poet* as well as a pig-fucker."

"I have no power over words," he replied.

"That is why you are a poet," she said. "The words have power over you."

The mortal shook his head, but she continued before he could speak his denial. "Tell me, *poet,* how do you know that the most beautiful thing in the world is a Queen of the Faerie? Could it not be a whore, or a flower, or a gem, or a sunset? Or a lithophage with a spear through its guts?"

"I just know it," said the mortal. "That's all."

"Go home," the warrior replied. "You know nothing. On this path you will find only death and sorrow."

The warrior turned on her heel and walked away. She vanished from his sight as stealthily as she had appeared, although he had tried to watch her every step.

10. The Sinewed Forest

The mortal straightened his rucksack on his shoulders and walked on, through the pass and out of the mountains. The landscape bent and slewed around him, and even the direction of gravity's pull canted to one side, forcing him to walk at an incline. Veins of mirrored glass and liquid flesh ran through the rock-face, and the stunted trees that grew from it were sinewy and bare. The birds that lit in their boughs were feathered with moss and squealed like swine.

He held out his hand and whistled, and one of the pig-birds turned to look down upon him. It cocked its head and, when he crooned to it again, it came gliding down and perched on his index finger. The pig-bird preened and grunted and, when he petted it with his free hand, it nuzzled his palm with a snout that was velvety and wet.

The mortal spread his fingers and the pig-bird flapped away, leaving a coil of black faeces on the back of his hands and a smile on his face.

He walked until gravity returned to its usual downward vector and the hills levelled off, giving way to a forest of the sinewy trees. He wondered if the bulbous, embryonic fruit they bore could be consumed, and if, were he hungry enough, he could bring himself to do so.

11. The Sea City on the Plains

Presently he came upon a river of some pale, opaque liquid, as the dog-man had said that he would. He followed it to the edge of the forest and then waded out into a sea of grass. In the distance, rising from that vast green ocean and sunken below the vaster blue sky, stood a great and luminous place that could only be the Sea City on the Plains. He struck out towards it.

Although it was quite dry, the city appeared to have grown in some briny deep. Its buildings were curved and gelatinous, with walls that breathed and fluoresced. The doorways and windows were valves and sphincters. Nettled members on the domed roofs waved lazily in the breeze.

The denizens of the Sea City were tall and narrow and soft-boned, with bleached white hair and pastel-hued skins. They moved with an easy grace and spoke amongst themselves in quiet, sibilant voices. The folk welcomed the mortal into their homes with unconditional love and undisguised curiosity, and they gave him refreshment and a place to rest. They bathed him and brushed the tangles from his hair and beard, and, when he felt he was ready, they took him to the palace to treat with their queen.

The throne room was vast and sumptuous. The walls of the chamber glowed pink, and the braziers that hung from the ceiling gave off a blue haze that was more fragrance than smoke. The guards were armed with halberds that appeared to be entirely ornamental.

The Queen of the Sea City was soft-featured and gentle. She was not so much dressed as swathed in feathers and silk. Her jewellery seemed to be as much a part of her flesh as her clothing. The throne upon which she reclined was as much divan as chair; as much a pet animal as a furnishing. It sighed and purred as it arranged itself beneath the Queen, accommodating her every shift in posture.

"You have sought an audience with us," said the Queen. The many rings she wore chimed as she fluttered her fingers. "It has been granted."

The mortal lowered his rucksack to the mother-of-pearl floor and went down onto one knee. "Thank you, Majesty," he said.

"Speak your plea. We are listening."

The mortal looked up without rising. "I have no plea, Majesty."

The Queen of the Sea City canted her head. "What purpose, then, this audience?"

"I had merely wished to behold you."

The Queen's smile broadened. "We are *delighted*," she said. "Why, pray tell, would one come all this way just to look upon us?"

"I am seeking the most beautiful thing in the world."

"What a *charming* notion!" said the Queen. "Are we, then, the fairest thing in the world?"

She was, he supposed, a perfect example of Rubenesque beauty...but to his eye, accustomed as it was to heroin-sapped supermodels and hunger-maddened actresses, she was simply fat.

"Your Majesty is fair indeed," he said.

The Queen's smile flickered and then faded. "Oh," she said. She frowned, and hunched, and withered. The fabrics that draped her abundant flesh fell in upon themselves, and the rings spilled from her fingers.

Without raising his head the mortal surveyed the room, looking to the courtiers and servants and guards. They stood around the divan on which their Queen had once reclined, tears gathering in their eyes and pooling at their feet. The

Queen's garments settled. Her throne slumped and shook.

Only one of the guards could meet his gaze. "Go," it said, its voice catching in its throat. The halberd hung useless and loose in its fingers. "Just go."

The mortal found that a ring made of purple metal had come to rest beside his rucksack. He put it in his pocket and took his leave.

12. The Magus

Though he thought himself trudging in a new direction, the mortal soon found himself back in the Sinewed Forest. The fleshy trees twitched and bled around him, and the pig-birds hid in the boughs. Gravity wavered drunkenly, and the milk-grey river frothed and surged when he came near to it. The vegetation itself seemed unwilling to touch him, receding to afford him passage.

After some hours, the river ran clear and the fluctuations in gravity became fewer and gentler. The flesh-trees gave way to elm and beech, oak and pine.

The mortal walked on, consuming the last of the goat-jerky as he went. He wondered where next he would find sustenance, in this Land where the strangeness of the vegetation and the unpredictable sentience of the beasts prevented him from foraging or trapping or hunting.

Night fell, and the mortal took shelter in the crook of a tree. He had known this Land would be a strange and dangerous place, but he had expected the danger would be such that he could overcome with wits and derring-do. He knew his quest would be tragical as well as comical. The mortal had believed that death and mayhem could not trouble his companions if he had none, and so he had made a point of traveling alone. But to this point he had found no opportunity for derring-do, and death and mayhem followed him yet.

He had seen death and mayhem before, of course, but

that was in wartime. Justified or not, it was expected and impersonal. The things he had seen and done in the theatre of conflict were, at least in part, the consequences of history and culture and politics, but here, walking the Land of his own volition, whatever befell those around him was solely his responsibility.

The mortal tried to banish such musings by imagining his goal. What would his chosen queen look like? Would she be dark or fair; short or tall? What colour her eyes? What fabric her dress? Would she be an earthy nature sprite, or an alien creature, glamorous beyond human comprehension?

The mortal could not find it in his imagination to picture her. All he could manage was a list of possible attributes, and when he combined them they always transformed into the image of his wife. His wife: so dowdy on their wedding day; so pale on the hospital bed where he had lost her, as well as their tiny, blue daughter.

The mortal awoke with the dawn, unrefreshed and sore from sleeping in the tree. He swung down and drank his breakfast from the river, for he had no more provisions.

He was filling his canteen when he noticed a stranger standing on the opposite riverbank.

The stranger was thin and weathered-looking, with slack blonde hair that fell to his shoulders. He was clad in torn jeans, work-boots, and a faded, tie-dyed Jimi Hendrix t-shirt. He wore a canvas kit bag slung over one shoulder.

"Welcome to Fairyland," the stranger called. He spoke with an Australian accent.

"Thanks," the mortal replied.

The Australian skidded carelessly down the embankment to the edge of the river and, without hesitation, stepped onto it. The flowing water hardened beneath his boots, footstep by footstep, and he negotiated the river with no more effort than he would have crossed a tarred roadway.

"Peculiar bloody place, this," said the Australian as he set his boots once more upon dry land.

"It is," replied the mortal.

The Australian shifted the kit bag on his shoulder and pretended to brush away the water, though his clothing was dry. "You're a Pom, then?"

"I'm an Englishman, yes."

"Thought so," said the Australian. "It's usually you Pommie bastards that come here. Most of the Gates are in your neck of the woods."

"I've heard there are several such portals," said the mortal. "Which did you use?"

"Made me own," said the Australian.

"You're a magician."

"No shit, Sherlock," said the magus. "Was it the walking on water or the trippy t-shirt that gave me away?"

"Have you been here long?"

"Yonks," said the magus. "Don't know, exactly. Time conversion's fucken complicated."

"When did you leave the…the real world?"

"November of nineteen-eighty."

"Twenty years. You must like it here." The magus did not appear to be much older than thirty.

"Nuh, not really," said the magus.

"Do you like the people?"

"Tell you the truth, I hate the fuckers."

"Why's that?"

"Well, bloody…look at them. Immortal, these fucken fairies, but they're so bloody *fragile*. So many fucken rules they have to follow. If they walk on the wrong grass or sing the wrong song, they just fall over and cark it."

"If you hate it here, why do you linger?"

The magus sneered. "Well, it's better than the old place, isn't it?"

"I see."

"So, anyway," said the magus, who was now rummaging

inside his kit bag, "I hate the fucken fairies, but you know what I hate worse?"

"No?"

"Tourists." The magus withdrew a dull metal object from his kit bag. He slid the magazine into its housing with a motion that was both practiced and loving.

"I don't know if you ever seen one of these before," the magus said. "You probably have ray guns or some shit by now. But in my day, young feller-me-lad, this was the best bit of blood and death that money could buy."

The mortal stood frozen as the magus swung the muzzle of the Uzi submachine gun towards him.

The mortal raised his hands. The magus was ten feet away; there was nothing else he could do.

The magus racked the Uzi and said, in a poor approximation of an American accent: "I know what you're thinking."

The mortal stepped towards the magus. "Please don't kill me."

The magus assumed a firing stance and drew a bead. "You're thinking, 'Does he know machines won't work in Fairyland, or does he think the gun will fire?'"

He took another step towards the magus.

"Well, seeing as how I'm a magus, and I know all kinds of magic, you gotta ask yourself a question: 'Do I feel lucky?'" The magus was having trouble maintaining the accent, in part because he couldn't restrain himself from snickering.

"Please. I've done you no harm."

"Well, do ya? Pom?"

"Hello, master," said a coarse voice from behind the magus. The Australian did not even have time to startle before a rusty cutlass blade separated his head from his neck. The head bounced onto the grass and rolled away.

The dog-man lowered its weapon and kicked over the magus' still-upright corpse. "Good morning," it said.

"Um, hi."

"I told you we'd meet again," said the dog-man.

"Indeed," replied the mortal, looking from the magus' corpse to the dog-man's blunt and dripping blade. "Did you follow me?"

"Of course."

"I asked you not to."

"No, you didn't," said the dog-man, "You forbade me to *accompany* you. Just as well, too."

"Just as well."

The dog-man grinned. "Well, my debt is paid."

"I annulled your debt when I freed you from the merchant."

"You annulled the debt of ownership," said the dog-man, "but in so doing, you instated a debt of honour."

"Well, anyway. Thank you."

"My pleasure." The dog-man looked at the corpse and licked its chops. "You want some of this? There's plenty for both of us."

"No, thank you."

"Oh, well. More for me." The dog-man rolled over the magus' corpse and spread its limbs. "You can tell me the plan while I butcher and dress the carcass."

"I will continue to seek what I desire to find."

"Of course," said the dog-man, lining up the blade of its cutlass with the joint of the magus' left shoulder.

"I'm sorry," said the mortal, "But I must continue alone."

The dog-man looked up at him.

"Thank you for your aid. You saved my life. But, as you said, your debt is now paid. Please be on your way, and I'll be on mine."

The dog-man's grin faded. If it had worn a tail in its upright form, it would have tucked it between its legs.

"Don't follow me again," said the mortal, as gently and firmly as he could.

The dog-man stared up at him, wide-eyed, mouth open. A barely audible whine escaped from between its thin, black lips.

The mortal slung the magus' abandoned weapon over his shoulder and turned away.

The dog-man did not speak a farewell.

13. The Inn

The mortal walked on, for days or weeks or months—he could not properly judge how much time passed. He tramped through the endless forest, keeping the river at his right hand. He did not hunger, and the river served to slake his occasional thirst.

When the weather changed it took him by surprise. He had become used to the constancy of the climate, to the unvaryingly fair days and the refreshingly cool nights. But now, as foliage thinned, the sky that showed through their bare limbs was pale and grey, and he felt a chill upon him. It began to drizzle, and, while it was not dangerously cold, his garments were soon wet through.

How long had it been since he had taken a hot bath? Since he had slept in a bed? He was filthy and soaking and, best-case scenario, he smelled like a football sock that had never been washed.

The mortal put his hands in his pocket and tried to walk faster in the hopes that it would warm him, but all he managed to do was to step into a puddle. The water soaked through his boot immediately and now the only part of him that was dry was a single foot.

"Bedraggled," said a bush, just a few feet beyond the puddle.

He stopped where he was and lowered his hands to his sides.

"You, sir, are bedraggled, if you don't mind my saying it."

"You will forgive my surprise," replied the mortal. "I have never been addressed by a shrub before. Or are you a bush?"

"Neither. I am a fox." The animal that emerged from the bush was indeed a fox: a fine, yellow-haired animal that stood with its two bushy tails erect and its nose high. "Tell me, mortal, what noble purpose brings you out in such miserable weather as this? What is it you seek?"

"Right now, the only thing I want is somewhere warm and dry to get out of the rain."

"Then come," said the fox, turning smartly and trotting away. The animal seemed to be dry enough, despite the sheen of moisture on its coat. "I know just the place."

The fox led him to an inn. It was a small, two-storey building, with a thatched and gabled roof. Smoke curled up from the chimney, and the glass in the windows shone with a welcoming yellow light.

"Come," said the fox. "They will be pleased to accommodate a traveller from the mortal realms. Dare I say it, they will not ask for any payment."

The fox trotted up to the door, where it stood up on its hind legs and operated the knocker with its forefeet. The mortal followed more carefully, the muddy ground sucking at his every step.

The door opened and the fox slipped through, ducking past a creature that was barely three feet tall in its skirts. "Come inside, come inside, mortal man," said the innkeeper. "Come stand by the hearth, before you take a chill."

He followed the innkeeper to the hearth. The fox did not tarry, but skipped away and disappeared through a door into what he assumed was the kitchen.

The mortal stood by the hearth and warmed his hands. By the time the chill was gone, his clothing had dried out, as well. His hair felt frizzy on his head, but otherwise he was warm and comfortable.

Including the innkeeper there were six tiny, wizened folk in the room, sitting upon the benches eating, or lounging near the fire. One of them wore a porter's hat. Another stood at the far corner of the room, tuning an instrument that was a bit like a fiddle. The room was smoky, as if the chimney was too narrow, but he could not smell the smoke unless he sniffed in search of its aroma.

Seeing him sniffing, the innkeeper came to him again. "Come, come, sit. I will bring you some dinner."

He sat at the table and presently the innkeeper returned, with a hunk of coarse bread and a chicken joint on a plate piled high with potatoes and vegetables. He thought it was chicken, anyway. It smelled delicious, and suddenly he realized he was famished. "Why, thank you," he said.

"Eat, eat," said the innkeeper, so he did. The food tasted as good as it smelled, and when he was done he covered his mouth and belched and sat back from the table. While his mind was on his belly the fiddler started to play, and though the tune was merry it made him feel drowsy with contentment.

He was feeling very comfortable now, and he closed his eyes and leaned back in his chair for a moment.

Hadn't he been sitting on a bench? He was no longer certain. He was definitely sitting in a chair now.

When he opened his eyes he was convinced, for a moment, that the other diners in the inn were not tiny people at all, but ferrets and polecats and stoats, staring at him with glistening black eyes. But when he blinked they were as before: diminutive folk, enjoying the warmth of the fire and good food and friendly company. The mortal knew that he could not trust his senses, but he was far too comfortable to be disturbed by the revelation.

A fellow across from him with a beard plaited into its hair raised a fine crystal decanter and said "Ho there, mortal, do you fancy a drink?"

"No thank you," he replied. "I cannot take wine."

"It is a very fine vintage," said another of his tablemates, a youthful one in dress that was both striped and spotted. "But if wine is not to your taste we have ale, do we not?"

"Oh, aye," said a third, chubby little imp dressed in dungarees and fold-down boots. "And all manner of spirits. We have whiskey and vodka and mescal. We have Wyvern's Kiss and Griffin's Claw. We have *shnkwer* and bourbon and shine distilled from the freshest of moonbeams."

"Name your tipple, mortal man," said the fiddler, sighting the mortal over the strings of his instrument. "I am certain we can provide it."

The mortal raised his hands, palms outward. "I thank you for the offer," he said, "But really, I cannot."

"Can't hold your liquor, then?" said the porter. "You are among friends here, but come the morning you will see none of us again. You need not fear embarrassment, mortal man. We do not judge."

"I have not partaken for years," he replied.

"Don't have a taste for it, then?" said the youthful one. She took a draught from a snifter of some yellow liqueur. "Perhaps a liqueur might be more to your fancy."

"You might even consider it a dessert," suggested the fellow with the plaited hair.

"I was a different man, when last I indulged in liquor," replied the mortal. "I have no desire to visit with him again." He stood up. "But for now, I am very tired. All I desire is a dry place to sleep. If my currency is not valid tender here I will be happy to pay in labour."

The room was silent then, and a look passed amongst the folk who occupied it with him. The fox was nowhere to be seen.

He could sense that a consensus had been reached, through the exchange of looks and fidgets and other signs that he could not discern.

"Let us not even discuss the matter of payment," said the

innkeeper. "It is an honour to have one of your kind as our guest. Come, come, I will show you to our finest room."

He followed the innkeeper up the stairs and she showed him to a room that was indeed fine, if small and windowless. There was a fresh bowl of water on the dresser, and a clean chamber pot under the bed, which was covered by many layers of blankets and sheets and eiderdowns. A cast iron tub stood in the corner gleaming from many hours of vigorous polishing.

"Please, take your ease," said the innkeeper. "I will send the porter to fill the bath for you.

"Thank you, madam," said the mortal, "but I am far too tired. I think I will go straight to bed. Please apologize to the others if my snoring is too loud."

The innkeeper bowed stiffly and backed out of the room. When it closed the door, he noticed there was no lock.

The mortal took off his boots and his socks, which were not only dry but also somehow clean. He washed his face and his hands and then lay down on the bed. His legs were too long for it and his knees hung over the sides, but it was high enough that his feet did not touch the floor, and the eiderdown was sufficiently long that it covered his feet. Still, he felt very comfortable, and he was indeed tired. He laid his head back on the pillow and went to sleep.

In the middle of the night he awoke. It was dark, but he thought the door was cracked open, and six pairs of glistening black eyes were regarding him through the gap.

A voice might have asked, "Is he awake?"

"I do not know," another might have replied.

"His eyes are closed." It was possible that a third voice had spoken.

"It said it would be snoring," a fourth voice may have cautioned. "But I hear no sounds."

Perhaps a fifth voice lamented, "We should have made it drink the spirits."

Their eyes continued to regard him for a few moments longer. Then the door closed silently--if it had ever been open.

The mortal awoke in the morning feeling refreshed and ravenous and very thirsty. He laced up his boots, collected his belongings, and made his way downstairs.

None of the weasel-folk from the evening before were in evidence. The only other person there was a black haired young woman whom he might have taken for human, were it not for the bushy yellow tails that were visible below the hem of her gown.

"Good morning, fox," he said.

"Good morning, mortal," the fox replied. "I have brought you some breakfast." She set down a half a loaf of bread upon the table, as well as a wheel of cheese and a pat of butter in a small dish.

"Why thank you, fox." He sat down to the table and began to slice the bread. "I did not expect such hospitality from you."

"It was the least I could do," the fox replied. "Given that our hosts have fled into the forest."

He smeared some butter upon the bread, and reached for the hunk of cheese. "Their plans have gone awry, then?"

"Indeed."

The mortal arranged the cheese on his sandwich and said, "I suspected a trap when they refused my payment."

"They refused to discuss payment with you," said the fox, "Because their intention was to extract it while you were asleep."

"I bear nothing of value," said the mortal. "I fear they would have been disappointed, had they succeeded in robbing me." He took a bite from his meal, and found it delicious, even if the bread had gone a little stale since the previous night.

"I fear they would not have been," said the fox. "Their

intention was to rob you of your liver, your kidneys, your heart, and your meat, and to line their den with your skin."

He swallowed a mouthful and said "And you, fox? What payment would you have won for your part in this endeavour?"

"Likely they would have given me your bones."

The mortal chewed his mouthful carefully, considering. "Why is it that you have not fled with the others?"

The fox shrugged. "I am not culpable in their scheme," it said. "I am just a guide. I delivered to you exactly what you asked of me. I even served you breakfast, while I have had none."

The mortal brushed the crumbs from his lips with the back of his hand. "Because I am still alive."

"Be that as it may," said the fox. "By my reckoning the ledgers are balanced."

"You are a wily one, fox," said the mortal. "But I am not fooled. You have remained here because you think to transact further business with me, now that your scheme with the weasel-folk has yielded nothing."

"As I mentioned, I am a guide," said the fox. "And you are a questing mortal. I may yet be of use to you. I am wily, as you say, but I am loyal to the one who employs me."

"I am not so ready to forgive as you imagine," said the mortal, "but I have suffered no harm, and I am feeling well, this morning. As a gesture of friendship, tell me in which direction I will find the nearest faerie queen, and in return I will forgive you for leading me into a trap."

The fox licked its lips while it considered his offer. He was not certain when it had resumed its fox-shape. The fox gave a shrug and said "Alright, then, mortal man. Perhaps it is best for all concerned if you continue to travel by yourself. Follow the river downstream and you will presently come to the Ore-lands. See if the Queen there is to your liking, or not."

He stood up from the table, and then cast one more look

down at the bread and cheese. "May I take this with me?" he asked.

"It does not belong to me," said the fox, grinning, "So I shall not make any effort to stop you."

When he left the house, he found that day was clear and bright, and the mud had started to dry.

14. The Queen of the Ore-lands

As the fox had suggested, he followed the river downstream. Soon he came to a place where a strange metal canoe lay beached upon the riverbank. A heavy iron paddle lay in the silt beside it.

Although it was scuffed and dented, the canoe seemed to be structurally sound, with not a spot of rust upon it. It had been crafted out of interlocking pieces of iron, without welds or rivets, and it was an impressive piece of work for all that it was impractical. The mortal pushed it down into the water, and was surprised to find that it was buoyant. He struggled into the canoe, doing his best to keep his belongings dry. The current picked up as soon as he was seated.

The river bore him out of the forest and into some arid new domain; a place that was cratered and barren, like the moon of the world he had come from. But this world was both stranger and simpler than his own. It contained neither satellites nor planets nor seas, just Land and Sky, subdivided into Realms according to whimsy, chance and hearsay. The moon here was usually a disk that hung fixed in the heavens at certain times of the day. Sometimes it was some other bauble, but it was an ornament, and nothing more.

As the canoe drifted down the river, the mortal noticed pits and scaffoldings and mounds of tailings scattered across the terrain, and he knew that folk who lived here mined the earth for ores. Before long, their city rose before him: a great metal edifice, jutting with gleaming spires and bulging with burnished domes. The buildings glowed with heat, and purged steam from pipes and regulator valves.

The mortal drove the canoe aground about half a mile from the city walls. He abandoned it there and continued towards the city on foot.

Inside its steel walls, the Ore City was entirely cast from metal. Every building was cut from sheets of brass or iron or bronze. Even the gutters in the streets were metal.

The only structure that the mortal laid eyes upon that was made of stone and bricks and wood was an old theatre. It had a ticket booth in the middle of its sweeping entrance, and the mortal was sure he could see a concession stand inside the darkened lobby. The billboard above the doors showed the title of the current production: A Fistful of Gold Coins. He thought that was funny, until he saw a playbill in the window advertising a coming attraction: The Mortal Josey Wales. Perhaps there was another magus here. He hurried on.

The folk who thronged the streets of the Ore City clanked and clattered as they went about their business, garbed as they were in clothing made entirely from metals. They grinned at him, and admired the Uzi slung over his shoulder. They asked him what it was, but scoffed when he told them it was a weapon.

Such technology would not operate in any of the Realms. Besides the raw forces of the elements and the pull of gravity, no power could be exerted upon this world unless by muscle and sinew. No work could be executed without a beast to labour at it, unless magic was invoked.

The mortal asked the Ore Folk if they had a queen, and they laughingly told him that they did. He asked if he might have an audience with her, and they laughed at him again. The queen's agents had been observing him since he had climbed into the canoe. She was expecting him at once.

The Ore Folk rushed him down the steel-riven streets and through the brushed-steel chambers of the chromed-metal palace. Before he had time to properly collect his wits, he found himself in the mirror-plated throne room.

The Queen of the Ore-lands was tall and slender and pale. Her raiment was cast from a dozen different metals, secured to her flesh with chains and welds and rivets. The skin of her cheeks had been peeled-back and secured with wire stitches, revealing too many rows of silver teeth.

The Queen shook out her iron-grey hair and rose from her throne. When she grinned, he could see her teeth from three orifices. "Mortal man, you have been granted audience." Her voice was like a hammer on an anvil.

The mortal put down his rucksack and bent to one knee. "Majesty."

The Queen's gauntleted hands clattered as she brought them together. "My time is valuable," she said. "What do you seek?"

"Majesty, I seek the most beautiful thing in the world," he said, keeping his gaze fixed on his bootlaces.

The Queen raised one ring-pierced, chain-threaded brow. "Indeed?"

"Indeed, Majesty."

"In what form, pray tell, do you expect to find this... object?"

"She is a Queen of the Faerie."

The Queen's smile did not waver. "Well? Have you found her?"

"The intricacy and skill of the work that has been wrought upon your Majesty is a marvel—"

"Answer the question," said the Queen, through her hideous grin. "Am I the most beautiful thing in the world?"

He looked right into her ball-bearing eyes and said: "I find your Majesty to be profoundly ugly."

The Queen threw her head back and laughed; so long and so loud that the walls of the throne room resonated in sympathy. Her minions smirked amongst themselves.

When she had recovered herself, the Queen of the Ore-lands brushed the hair from her eyes with a movement that was fetching in its economy. She licked her lips and shook her head and said: "I like you, mortal. Ask of me a boon, and I will grant it."

The mortal asked for directions to the court of the nearest queen, carefully stipulating that she still be living, and humanoid in shape. The Queen of the Ore-lands struck her armoured hands together and directed him to seek the Tree Queen. "She is no friend of mine," said the Ore Queen, "but I would not deny her the pleasure of your company."

The Ore Folk provisioned him with dry rations to last him for weeks, but the mortal refused their offer of a steed or an escort. He tramped along the hard-packed road that led amongst the mines until he came once more to the river. As he followed its course the skies lightened and the waters ran clearer. Eventually the grey earth became brown and fertile again, and the craters and pits gave way to grassy, rolling hills.

The Ore-lands were an ugly place, and their queen was cast to match, but the encounter gave him heart to continue his quest.

15. The Farm

Soon the mortal came to a fence behind which fields were tilled and beasts were penned. The farmers that cared for the crops and herds were small and quick, furry and strong, and altogether misshapen. They were not so deformed as to be grotesque, but it was a near thing.

The farmers took him into their homestead, where they laid out a meal prepared from the meats and vegetables they had cultivated. The mortal had been subsisting on the dry Ore-lands' rations for days and he had not felt hungry, but now, in the presence of fresh food, he found that he was ravenous. He ate every dish they set before him.

When he the meal was done and the children had been put to bed, the farmers gathered around the hearth. They sat him in the place of honour and plied him with wine (which he refused) and fruit and cheeses (which he did not). When he could eat no more the eldest among them asked him what it was that he sought.

"I seek the most beautiful thing in the world."

"What is that?" asked the elder.

"She is a Queen of the Faerie."

"The identity of this object is of no interest to me," said the elder, "but I would understand the property that attracts you to it."

"Beauty?"

"What is 'beauty'?"

"Beauty is the quality that makes something pleasing to

the senses and the intellect. To the ear and the skin and the nose and the tongue. To the mind, of course...but mostly to the eye."

The elder considered for a while. "What is pleasing to my nose and tongue is food spiced and cooked. What is pleasing to my skin is the heft of a hammer or an axe or a spade. My mind is pleased by my continued existence; my eye by the sight of crops harvested and beasts butchered." It scratched its chin, which protruded from the side of its skull. "A queen is not pleasing to me in this way. A queen has only soldiers with which to protect me and taxes with which to afflict me. How is this 'beauty'?"

"Beauty is independent of usefulness or worth," the mortal replied. "It is to be coveted for its own sake, though it can be appreciated without being possessed."

"Then what purpose in the seeking of it?" asked the elder. "The pursuit of beauty is bereft of meaning."

The elder shook its head. "I believe that I could learn to enumerate the qualities that 'beauty' denotes, though I do not possess the faculties to appreciate them in such a way."

"You are lucky," said the mortal.

The farm-folk muttered amongst themselves, but their interest in the mortal had finally waned. They sent him on his way with half a wheel of cheese, a loaf of bread and a quantity of dried meat.

The mortal turned his back upon the farmlands and headed down into a forest, where the trees twined together like dancers stopped in time. The shafts of golden sunlight that lanced through the canopy were too bright to look upon, and he avoided them for fear he would catch fire, like a fly under a magnifying glass.

16. The Black and Crimson Queen

For three days, the mortal wandered through the forest, finding his way by the sun, whose path through the skies was indicated by the Ore Queen's map. He saw no sign of the Tree Queen, but the forest was vaster than any Realm in the Land. He knew he would find her there, when the appropriate conditions had been met. Or, more likely, she would find him.

He was sitting down to his midday meal on the fourth day when the black and crimson host came upon him, with their black and crimson banners twitching in the still air and their shadowsteel weapons bared.

The mortal swallowed his mouthful, wiped his hands on his filthy jeans, and stood up. The black and crimson troops had him surrounded.

Bearers in black and crimson livery carried a palanquin into the circle and set it upon the ground. They drew back the black and crimson curtains, and the Black and Crimson Queen rose from her throne. A squire draped a black and crimson cloak across her shoulders.

The Black and Crimson Queen was short and slender. Her hair was long and red; her gown was long and black. A featureless oval mask cut from polished obsidian covered her face.

She turned that mask towards the mortal and spoke: "You are seeking faerie queens. Be it known that one has also sought you."

"I am honoured, Majesty."

"You have named a queen to be the fairest of all," said the Queen, "And the name you spoke was not my own."

(In unison, the black and crimson host said: "The name you spoke.")

"Begging Majesty's pardon," he said, "but the name I spoke was the only name I knew at the time. I would consider all queens of the Realms, that I may best determine which is the fairest."

"Am I, then, the fairest of queens?"

("You are fairest of Queens," said the host.)

"Majesty, I cannot see your face."

"Am I the fairest?"

("You are fairest of Queens," said the host.)

"Majesty, what I behold of you is fair indeed, but I cannot truly say if you will not reveal your face."

"The beauty you seek is of such magnitude that it should be apparent through any mask or veil."

("Of such magnitude," said the host.)

The mortal stayed silent.

"Plainly, you cannot perceive what lies behind my mask," said the Black and Crimson Queen. "Plainly, you are blind to true beauty."

("Plainly, he is blind," said the host.)

The Black and Crimson Queen extended her open hand. The circle of black and crimson soldiers advanced a single pace and raised their swords. "Plainly, you deserve a harsh and ignoble death."

("Death," said the host. "Death, death, death.")

The mortal found the magus' weapon where it hung behind him. He brought it about, keeping the muzzle pointed at the ground.

"Cut him down," said the Black and Crimson Queen.

The mortal racked the Uzi and looked up at the Queen. The host continued to advance. "Majesty, I beg you."

"You are scum from the mortal realm. My only regret

in slaying you will be poisoning the soil with your spilled blood."

The mortal raised the Uzi to a firing position, braced the stock against his shoulder, and thumbed the fire selector to full automatic. "Please, Majesty."

"No," said the Black and Crimson Queen.

The mortal squeezed the safety grip and pulled the trigger. The weapon issued a staccato bray. Bright-light runes flashed in the air amongst ejected shell casings.

Black and crimson troopers fell and died as he swept the submachine gun before him. The Queen exploded into a mist that was more red than black.

When the magazine was spent, the forest fell once more to silence. The survivors of the Black and Crimson host had already fled.

The mortal lowered the smoking gun and went to the place where the Black and Crimson Queen had fallen. Carefully, he bent to remove her mask. Though the obsidian oval was intact, her face beneath it had been burned and smashed by gunfire.

He could not tell if she had been fair or not.

17. The Tree Queen's Justice

Weeping, the mortal put the mask in his rucksack and fled into the forest. He staggered amongst the trees, the stink of powder harsh in his nose, his eyes raw from gun-smoke and tears. He shambled on, bumping into low-hanging limbs, tripping on the underbrush, stumbling and then rising and then stumbling again.

He did not get very far.

A band of soldiers in wooden armour fell upon him. Or perhaps it was the trees themselves that accosted him--his stinging vision made it difficult to be certain.

The mortal did not resist when they beat him down. He did not struggle when they bound him with vines as strong as electrical cables. He gave no fight when they hauled him away, dazed and battered, with his boots dragging in the dirt.

There were no buildings in the Tree City, for its denizens made their homes in the trees themselves. There were no roads or paths. Communal places were recessed in the hollows beneath trees or nestled up in the canopy, twisted together from limbs and foliage. Even the largest of these structures had been cultivated into its shape. No wood had been cut in the construction of the city.

The soldiers sealed the mortal and all of his possessions inside a hollow oak that was barely wider across than his shoulders. They left him there in darkness for a measure of time he could not fathom; upright, with his face pressed up against the rough-grained walls; bound hand and foot.

When the holding period was over, the oak released him and the soldiers dragged him away, parched and dazed and delirious.

The mortal came to his senses in a small antechamber, which was lit by luminous mosses. There the soldiers cleaned him up and gave him water and carefully beat him until he was fully awake. Then they escorted him through into the courtroom.

The courtroom had walls of wet soil, held in place by a meshwork of root fibres. Worms and grubs of unnatural size crawled blindly amongst them. High windows made of hardened sap cast a hazy and impure light upon the proceedings.

The court waited in silence as the soldiers hauled the mortal into the open floor at the centre of the chamber. He observed them through bruised and puffy eyes: retainers dressed in silks and mosses; magicians in rough-spun cowls; soldiers with shadowsteel weapons identical to those born by the Black and Crimson Queen's host.

The magicians chalked a circle around the mortal and warded it with spells. There were two other prisoners already bound within the chamber. A hunched, four-armed thing made of black chitin occupied the circle on his left. It had no hands or feet at the ends of its limbs, and its head was shaped like the blade of an axe. The circle to his right contained a pile of loose body-parts connected with loops of wire—more parts than could possibly have come from a single being. Hands and feet and legs and arms. If there was a head or a torso in the collection, the mortal could not see it.

The Queen of the Trees entered on the arm of her King. She wore a dress of green silk and high boots cut from supple brown leather. Her hair was the colour of oak leaves and her skin was as pale as milk. A string of emeralds glittered across her breast. The Queen's features were delicate but her posture was haughty. She was as beautiful as any creature the mortal had ever seen.

The Tree Queen spoke a word, and the King stood aside. The magicians withdrew and she walked right up to the edge of the circle that enclosed her new prisoner.

The mortal fell to his knees. He could no longer stand without assistance.

"Do you speak?" asked the Tree Queen.

He opened his mouth, closed it. Swallowed to wet his constricted throat. "Yes."

"A pity," said the Tree Queen. "Now I must waste further words upon you."

He nodded. It was a struggle to keep his head up.

"What manner of demon are you?"

"I'm a mortal," he said.

"A mortal?"

"From the mortal world."

"A demon," she said. "As I thought."

"I'm a mortal."

"Name yourself as you will," she said, "It will not change your true nature. Who summoned you?"

His head fell, and he did not reply.

"Who summoned you?"

"I was not summoned," he said, addressing the dirt floor.

"Yet you reek of sorcery."

"I…I used…I used an enchanted weapon…when…"

"You were given an enchanted weapon to wield against the Black and Crimson Queen," she said. "Was this the same instrument you used to murder the Queen of the Sea City on the Plains?"

"I did not intend… I was forced to…"

"Who compelled you to commit these crimes?"

"No one. I…please, Majesty, let me explain…"

"No," said the Tree Queen, and in that moment she was ugly. She was not the one he sought. "I'm tired of this dialogue. You will forever be bound to this circle, never to speak again, nor wreak your evil upon the Land, nor return to the hell from which you crept."

The coven of green-robed magicians set busily about

completing their spells. The Tree Queen rejoined her King and stood, watching them work, with her arms folded and contempt plain upon her face. The Tree King's face showed nothing more expressive than wood-grain.

The mortal sagged forwards in despair. He didn't know if he could be bound as a demon. He didn't know if he deserved to be or not. But he was determined to prove what he was, and what he was not...to himself, if not to the Tree Queen.

On his hands and knees, the mortal lurched to the boundary of the circle. He reached out to it, and the chalk-marks yielded beneath his fingers.

The magicians reeled as their spellcraft was torn asunder.

The mortal raised his head to beg his innocence once more, but he had not the strength. He sprawled out of the circle, and one of his splayed legs breached the markings that contained the severed-limb demon.

The court cried out in horror as the demon arose to its full twenty feet of height. It sorted itself into the shape of a huge and hideous thing: a head without a torso, but with far too many limbs; strung together with gleaming strands of metal. It laughed and whirled about and fell upon its captors; flying apart and spiralling back together, slicing to ribbons anything caught within its looping, spooling wires. It did not stop until the court entire—the magicians, the courtiers, the guards, the King, and the Queen—had been slashed into shreds.

He lay prone on the floor and watched the severed-limb demon reel itself back together. It saw him there, and came to crouch down beside him; its joints lolling on their wires. "Thank you," it said. It stood up, made a rippling bow, and then swept out of the chamber, away into the day.

Somehow, the mortal managed to crawl out of the courtroom, through the moist piles of meat and entrails. In the antechamber he hauled himself up onto a low wooden bench and sat there, panting. He closed his eyes and tried to summon some further strength, but he had none left. The mortal drank every drop of the water in his canteen. Then he slid down to the floor and closed his eyes.

When the mortal awoke he felt well enough to stand, though he was still thirsty and unsteady. The stairs looked steep and taxing to climb, so he went back through the archway into the courtroom chamber in search of his belongings.

The butchered remains of the Tree Queen's court lay yet upon the ground, still wet and reeking and fresh. The obsidian demon remained unmoving amongst the carnage, still bound to its circle. The mortal's things lay in a pile at the far side of the room. He did not want to cross that floor, but his boots led him steadily across the blood-slick ground without regard for the viscera upon which he trod.

The mortal took up his rucksack and then went to the place where the Tree Queen had fallen. Her face had been sliced off in a single piece: forehead and brows, nose and lips and lashes. An emerald from her necklace had been embedded in her cheek. Her flesh was still warm beneath his fingers when he prised the gem from it.

The mortal turned his gaze upon the obsidian demon, which remained in its place, silent and unmoving. If it had perceived the events that had passed before its eyeless gaze, it gave no sign. He limped over to it and scuffed a gap in its circle, but it remained motionless. The mortal could not bring himself to touch it. He left it to discover on its own that it had been freed, if it still had the capacity do so.

18. The Storm Front

He tramped through the woods until he found the river again. There he stopped to fill his canteen and eat the last of the food the farm folk had given him before he followed the river out of the forest.

For many weeks more he wandered the hill country, stealing food from any farms or hamlets he passed near. He avoided the cities and villages and company of any sort. He kept well clear of all but the merest groves of trees.

Late one afternoon a strange grey washed away the sky. The bright hot ball that served this particular Realm as a sun disappeared, although the light it shed remained, pallid and thin. Two great storm-fronts roiled over the hills, one from the direction the mortal reckoned to be east and the other from the west. Lightning crackled between the cloud masses and the thunder rolled like war drums.

The mortal stared up into the clouds and he saw that this was not weather, as he knew it; this was indeed a war. Each thunderhead was ridden by a squadron of storm folk, who piloted its course and cast its lightning and strove against their enemies. The mortal could not tell which side was which, once the battle was joined, but he was certain that he saw the same banners on both sides.

Surely these folk had a queen to command them. Were they fighting for her attention? Or had she set her own people against each other, for her own amusement?

The mortal considered the question, and found that he

did not care. He had no desire to meet this Storm Queen, however beautiful she might be. He had failed in his quest and now he did not care to complete it.

"All you faerie folk be damned," he said. "Your fancy queens and your whimsical beasts and your flesh-sucking monsters. All of you be damned."

Rain from the storm trickled into his mouth as he spoke. It was sweet and a little salty, and left the taste of iron on his lips. He stood like that, letting it spatter against his cheeks, and found that he did not mind the cold of it as it ran down into his beard.

When the storm cleared, night had fallen. There was no moon, and it was dark but for the light of a strange rainbow, banded with purple and violet and indigo.

"Is that for me?" he said, addressing anyone or anything that cared to listen. "A night rainbow? Are you fucking kidding me?"

The mortal laughed and laughed until the effort of it hurt his face. By that time the rainbow had dissipated and there remained no light whatsoever.

19. The Black Thing

When the dawn came a stripe of black smudged the horizon to the east. A forest of bare, black-skinned trees stood there like an army forming up near a battlefield. Could he possibly have missed it the day before? Or had the black forest marched here to meet him under cover of night?

Regardless, he knew that the Tree of Indeterminate Species lay on the far side of the forest. That was his destination now. He was done with all this nonsense and it was time to go home.

He walked towards it all day, without stopping for rest, and by the time he reached the tree line the withered grey moon had risen to its place in the sky. The black forest did not look any more inviting by night than it had during the day.

The mortal built a small campfire to warm himself, but he ate his food cold. He did not pitch his tent. After the meal he sat before the blaze, sweating from the heat and staring into the flames. When he looked up again the moon had vanished, although the sky remained clear and the stars continued to shine.

A chittering drew his attention back to ground.

Just beyond the circle of firelight, a group of small, black-skinned beings crouched in the thickening darkness. As far as he could tell, they had congealed from the night air itself.

"Please, don't be afraid," said the mortal.

The chittering ceased and the black things vanished liquidly into the darkness.

"Damn it," he said.

"You don't say." It took him a moment to locate the voice.

One of the black things had remained. It stepped brazenly into the flickering light and squatted down across the fire from the mortal. Flames were reflected in its blood-black eyes; in the sheen on its blood-black skin. The black thing's clothes were fashioned from strips of blackened leather and fastened with black iron buckles.

The creature showed him its bloody black teeth and said, "Will you cross the black forest?"

"My destination lies beyond it."

"And what is your destination?"

"Home," said the mortal. "I'm done with this place."

The black thing continued to grin at him. "Do you know the perils of the black forest?"

"No," he said, "But I will face whatever foes the forest sends against me; navigate whatever travails."

The black thing laughed. "There are neither foes to be faced, nor 'travails' to be 'navigated'. Black soil and black trees are all you will find there."

"And why is that?"

"Because," said the black thing, "No living thing can survive there."

"Is there no way to safely cross the forest?"

"It can be crossed, but you must not allow the soil or the trees to touch your living skin."

"And if I do?"

"If you do, your skin will live no more." The black thing showed its teeth again and skipped back from the fire. "Enjoy the rest of your trip," it said. "It will soon be over."

He did not see the black thing depart, but he knew that it was gone before it had finished speaking.

20. In the Black Forest

The mortal stayed up all night, stoking the fire and staring into the flames. The moon did not return. At daybreak he packed up his kit and set forth without breaking his fast.

The ground turned black at the very border of the forest. The trees were blacker yet, and at first the mortal thought they had been burnt—but they were in fact perfectly healthy. They were uniform in their bareness and their size. There was no other vegetation, or even humus, upon the forest floor.

The sky above was blue and bright, though he could not locate the sun in it. The air was clean and sweet and still.

The mortal made his way cautiously through the forest, having care not to touch anything. He was worried that a wind would arise to blow traces of the soil or the trees upon him, but he soon abandoned that particular fear. In this forest, even the wind was dead.

He picked up his pace from a trudge to a stride, and before he was aware of it, he had begun to whistle. When he realized that the song he was whistling was Jimi Hendrix's 'Foxy Lady', and finally he began to smile.

"Ha!" he said, and shook his head, and wiped the muck from his eyes. But he found that he was no longer alone.

The King sat upon his burnt-gold stallion in his smoked-silver armour; a battered old lance in one hand and a gleaming bright sword in the other. His warhorse was shod in platinum, though his own feet were bare in the stirrups.

"Oberon," said the mortal.

"Mortal," replied the king. "What manner of evil have you raised around us?"

The mortal frowned. "This place was here when I arrived."

"Aye," said the King, "And it was not here before that."

"I don't understand."

"Then you will die ignorant," replied the King.

"I am unarmed, yet you confront me with your lance and sword and warhorse," said the mortal. "Will you not deign to fight me on equal terms? On your own two feet, with your own two hands?"

The King said "No," and urged his stallion forward.

The mortal stepped aside and kicked up a clod of black dirt, which burst against the horse's unarmoured neck. The King pulled on the reins and the animal reared, but it was already too late. The stallion's shadow rose to meet it, separating from the ground and flowing up to devour the animal's flesh.

The King leapt from the saddle as his mount buckled beneath him, landed lightly on the black earth—but his feet sank immediately into the soil, and he, too, was consumed by his own shadow.

"Jesus," said the mortal. Of all the horrors he had witnessed, this one disturbed him the most.

Light flared, and the mortal had to turn away and cover his eyes. When his vision returned, he found that another being hovered before him, suspended on a pair of gossamer wings. He looked up through the haze at her and knew immediately that she was a Queen of the Faerie.

"Titania," he said.

She was as tall as Oberon; as fine-boned and slender as her husband was rangy and lithe. She had small, sharp breasts and long, pointed ears. A heart-shaped face rested atop the pillar of her neck. Her hair was as lustrous as mirror-glass. Her gown was spun from liquid gold and laced with naked fire.

The Queen knelt down upon the black soil, where her husband, the King, had perished. Weeping, Titania reached down to the darkness, as she had once long ago reached for Oberon. A shadow reached up to her, and they were drawn together until neither of them remained.

She was not the Queen he had sought.

21. A Kiss Beneath the Tree

The mortal passed out of the black forest and worked his way back along its perimeter until he spied the hills where the market village nestled. He went towards it until he spotted the river, and from there he was able to triangulate the location of the Tree of Indeterminate Species. He came upon it in the late afternoon.

The mortal stood facing the Tree until the twilight sun bled. He considered all that had befallen him and all that he had done in his travels through the Realms of the Land. He considered the life he had led before he had begun his quest, when he had lived in the real world. He considered the Folk he had met here amongst the Faerie, and he knew that he was not like them, and could never be. He would be just as lonely here as he had always been.

"Right, then," said the mortal. "I give up." He adjusted his burdens across his shoulders and walked around the Tree, looking for the opening in the trunk…but there was none.

He jogged around it again, but there was still no way inside.

The mortal circled a third time, more carefully. Previously, the tree had required three circuits before the entrance had manifested.

He ran around the tree a fourth time, frantic, but there was still no opening. Staggering, gasping for breath, he turned his back on the tree and covered his face. The mortal wiped the hair from his eyes, smoothed his beard against his chin. Calm. He must be calm. There was a solution. Perhaps he would climb the tree a second time…

"Hello, master." The mortal whirled around so fast that he stumbled. It took him three steps to right his balance—three steps closer to the voice.

The dog-man stood pissing against the tree. It glanced over its shoulder and grinned at him.

"The exit is gone," said the mortal, trying to regain some dignity.

"You can't go home until you've completed your quest," said the dog-man, securing its trousers and turning to face him. "Or until you lie dead—which I suppose is a homecoming, of a different sort."

"I've already met you three times," said the mortal. "Does this fourth encounter not contravene the…the law of the Land?"

The dog-man grunted. "There are no laws," it said. "Not really. It's true that the various fates and powers favour certain patterns, but they are not stringent about enforcing them. Imbalances in those patterns must regulate themselves, if they are to be regulated at all."

"I don't understand."

"You have encountered me four times; there is likely some other fated being whom you will encounter only twice. If you live long enough." The dog-man drew its cutlass.

The mortal dropped his backpack and the spent Uzi machinegun and backed away. "Here, take my possessions," he said. "Most of them are worthless, but some are treasures. You saved my life; I owe you nothing less."

"I don't want your bag of trophies," said the dog-man, advancing. "I want your bones, to polish my teeth."

"Why are you suddenly my enemy?"

"The not-falcon was my friend," said the dog-man, "And you would not help him."

"You yourself killed and ate him."

"But you are the one who refused to save him." The dog-man grinned as it continued to advance.

"Is this because I would not be your master?"

"You flatter yourself," said the dog-man.

"I'm sorry," said the mortal.

"Your apologies will not restore my friend," said the dog-man. It pointed its cutlass and came on.

The mortal raised his fists and wished for a weapon, but he knew that, armed or not, he was no match for his foe.

The dog-man swung the cutlass in a lazy, overhand stroke. The mortal lurched out of the way, lost his footing, and fell. He rolled clumsily and came to a half-kneel; and raised an arm in a pathetic attempt to ward off the deathblow he expected to follow…but it did not. The clang of metal on metal rang in his ears, and the battle was joined.

A warrior stepped between him and the dog-man. She had a loop of chain in one hand and a bastard sword in the other.

"Well, well," said the dog-man, "If it isn't Dolly Dagger."

The mortal scrambled away from the combatants until his back was jammed up against the tree. It did not surprise him to hear the dog-man quoting Jimi Hendrix nearly as much as it should have.

He recognized the warrior, now. It was she who had saved him from the lithophage.

The dog-man laughed its growl-bark-laugh and closed with his opponent. The warrior's chain flickered outwards and looped around its wrist. She swung it over the dog-man's head, spun it and yanked it tight, lashing the dog-man's captive arm to its side. The dog-man's laughter ceased as the warrior reeled it onto her sword.

She wrenched the blade free and spun the carcass loose of the chain. The dog-man did not resume its dog form in death.

The warrior thrust her sword into the dirt and coiled the chain around her forearm with a flick of the wrist. "I just saved your life, pig-fucker," she said, white teeth flashing behind her lips.

The mortal smiled back at her. Her brown hair was fine and soft. Her skin was like silk, and the lobes of her small and unusually shaped ears were tender and unpierced and perfect. Her eyes were brown and plain, and they did not need to be anything else at all.

He drew himself to his feet slowly, using the tree for support. He stared so hard he thought his eyes would shrivel and die in their sockets. His heart was lodged hard in his neck.

She was the most beautiful thing in all the worlds.

The warrior came towards him with her hands empty, and he said to her, "What's your name?"

"I am called Zelioliah."

The mortal took her in his arms, and he put his lips to hers; and gently, weeping for joy, he took the straight-razor from his pocket and opened her throat from one perfect earlobe to the other.

When he laid her body upon the ground a doorway opened for him in the side of the tree. A doorway through which only three kinds of mortal were admitted: lovers, poets, and madmen. And he was most certainly counted amongst their number, for though there was neither poetry nor love in him, there was madness aplenty.

He, who had come to the Faerie Realms seeking the most beautiful thing in the world.

Book 2
The Magus

1. City of Angels

The magus sipped his bourbon and watched the flock of demons circling above the smog-shrouded towers of Los Angeles. Dark-winged, dark-limbed beasts held formation above the looping expressways, waiting for the ground forces to take their positions. He slammed back the remains of his drink and grunted. The magus hated bourbon.

The Conclave had carefully calculated the resources required to destroy him; factoring in his prowess, his power, his tactical aptitude, his temper. By their mathematics, the sum of twenty winged bloodfiends and a platoon of combat sorcerers was more than sufficient for the task.

"Bunch of fucken accountants," said the magus. He was not in the least bit afraid to pit his magic against their book-keeping.

The magus poured himself another drink while the bloodfiends strafed his house with arcane incendiaries. A string of flat, concussive booms followed as the phalanx of sorcerers scoured the hillside with eldritch mortars. Burning gases blew the house to matchwood.

The magus shook the ice around in his glass and took a couple of swallows. He grimaced and poured the rest of his drink onto the ground, where it immediately caught fire. The magus paid it no heed.

His foes had him surrounded. Lightning crackled from their fingers; napalm guttered in their eyes. Their wings creaked in the scorched air and their scalding breath hissed and steamed from between their teeth. Guns and blades glinted in their gloved and taloned hands.

The magus scratched an armpit and spoke a casual string of four-letter obscenities. He called for hell and perdition, for doom and death and bloody damnation, and for other things besides. They came smartly at his summons.

The landscape warped and buckled as a wave of burnt darkness swept over it. When the tide receded, scores of hell-born soldiers had washed up on the blasted hillside. They clambered to their feet, shrieking and roaring, and set upon the Conclave's troops with hatred and with glee.

The magus watched the hell-tide ripple down out of the hills, surging towards the glittering city below. He did not know how long it would take the Conclave to stop the destruction he had loosed.

There was no chance for an armistice, now that he had attempted to consign the City of Angels to hell. Los Angeles was only his latest residence, but he hated it as much as he hated every other place he had once called home. The magus spat. It seemed like a good time for him to take a permanent vacation.

The magus turned his attention to a new spell. Twice he tore the working down, unquickened, but the third time he knew he had it right.

A Door appeared before him: an unframed, two-dimensional rectangle of light. The portal was opaque, for it was a door and not a window, but the magus knew what lay beyond it. This Door did not interface to a hell; it opened instead to a place of dreams and fantasies.

The magus did not then understand how the differing planes lay in relation to each other. He did not know where dream ended and nightmare began; where joy and dread joined or became separate. It did not concern him overmuch. The magus only cared that he was going to another place, where magic flowed like water.

He stepped through into the Land of the Faerie and pulled the Door closed behind him.

2. In the Jungle

The magus emerged in the midst of a verdant jungle. The trees were enormous; their boughs spreading a hundred feet above him. Humus lay thick on the ground. Lianas hung from the branches like intestines looped from a butcher's block. The silence was as thick as the damp, still air. He judged it to be midday, though the layered canopy blocked the sun from his vision. Once the jungle had accustomed itself to the magus' sudden presence the beasts and beings that lived there resumed their scratching, breathing rhythms.

The magus took a moment to recalibrate his occult senses. There was magic all around; in every insect and animal, every bead of water and blade of sunshine. Wild and wasted magic, without a will to direct it.

Once the magus had tuned the distracting wavelengths out, he discovered that a small sorcerous construct was located nearby. He conjured a machete and struck out towards it. The going was hard, but the magus relished the heft of the blade, the bite of its edge; the way that severed vegetation fell behind every slice. Sometimes the simplest pleasures were the most satisfying.

The construct was a spherical silver cage that hung suspended from the trees by some invisible force. The mangy, purple-furred creature imprisoned within it had been there for so long that its bones had warped to accommodate it to the space. Its face was drawn with misery, and its spiked and spiny joints jutted uncomfortably from between the bars. The purple thing turned its head towards the magus as best it could and said: "I beg you, sir, free me from this prison."

"Why should I?" the magus replied

"If you must ask such a question, you yourself can never have been imprisoned so."

The magus grunted. His father had learned most of what he knew about parenting in the Japanese POW camp where he was interned during the Second World War, and had been quite enthusiastic in his reapplication of that learning. The magus was no stranger to confinement.

"Free me," said the purple thing, "and I shall grant you whatever is in my power to grant."

"Power?" asked the magus. "What power?"

"I can grow you a pelt of fine purple fur," said the thing in the cage. "Replace that stringy yellow stuff you wear upon your head. No mere glamour! A true magic, that will not ever fade!"

"What else you got?"

"That is my only ability," the purple thing admitted, disconsolate.

"Have you got any *proper* sorcery?"

"My master is a most puissant wizard," said the purple thing. "Alas, he has confined me in this cage. I fear that my introduction will do you no service."

"What was your crime?"

"No crime, sir," said the purple thing. "I am here only by my master's caprice." It was lying, but the magus doubted that its crime was of any great magnitude. Most likely its incessant whining had annoyed its master.

The magus examined the spell that kept the cage hanging from the trees. It was nice work. "Who's this master of yours?"

"I serve the Sage of the Sky City."

"Where can I find him?"

"Look for his city, high in the skies. You cannot fail to find it."

"Ta." The magus turned away.

"Would you not like a pelt, like my own?"

"Nuh, mate."

"Will you not free me, as a favour to one less fortunate than yourself?"

"Fortune is relative," said the magus. "I learned the best lessons of my life strapped up in a bamboo box in my old man's back yard."

"What could you possibly have learned from such misery?" asked the purple thing.

"I learned that fear makes you weak and hate makes you strong," said the magus. "And I see that you have plenty of learning still to do."

The purple thing had no answer. It lowered its head and slumped against the bars of its cage. But the magus did not see its despair, for he had already turned his attention to the wild magic of his surroundings. He had spent his own reserves opening a Door into the Realms, but he could surely channel the power that pulsed around him.

The magus spoke some words in the tongue he had crafted for such workings, and quickened it with a rune of his own devising. The magus rose into the air and ascended through the canopy, and gave no further thought to the purple thing or its captivity.

3. The Sage of the Sky City

The simple spell that bore him aloft was causing the magus a number of unexpected problems. The ambient magical field of the Faerie Realms was rich and easy to tap, but it pulsed through the circuit unevenly. Sometimes the power levels surged enough to warp the logical fabric of the spell; other times they felt so weak that the weave started to fray. The magus had to attend to it constantly or risk falling back under the power of whatever force approximated gravity in this Land.

The sky above the jungle was milky-green and streaked with white vapour. The Sky City was easy to spot, although naming it a city seemed to be overstating the matter. It was more like a village: two-dozen squat, bulbous buildings blown from coloured glass, huddled together upon a platter that bobbed in the air like a moored vessel. Its shadow lay spread across the uneven green carpet of the jungle below.

The lattice of baroque spells that held the Sky City aloft was a clever bit of work: its shadow had been inverted, so that it reflected the shape that had cast it back towards the sun. Clever, but whimsical. The magus went on towards the Sky City, propelled by his own ragged, bleeding magic.

A small shape rose out of the city and swooped towards him, its hair and beard streaming in the wind. The creature drew up in front of him, spread its knobby hands and said, in a sonorous voice: "I am the Sage of the Sky City."

"Owareya, mate?"

The Sage clasped its hands and considered him. "What is your business here, magus?"

"I come looking for you, actually."

"Then tell me why you have sought me, for I am as puissant as I am wise, and my time is valuable."

"You're a piss-ant, alright. Tell me—you build this all by yourself?"

The Sage looked embarrassed for a moment. Then it intoned: "The Sky City was a gift from the Queen of the Winds, in exchange for advice rendered. I resolved her fierce dispute with the Queen of the Mountains." The Sage puffed up its chest. "I am, after all, a sage; wise and puissant."

The magus grinned. "You stole it, huh?"

"You dare to call me a liar?" The sage waved its spindly arms above its head. "I am the wise and puissant Sage of the Sky City!"

The magus drew a .50 calibre Desert Eagle from the holster he wore beneath his open flannel shirt. He cocked the weapon and pointed it at the sage's face. "What you are, mate, is cactus."

The weapon clicked feebly when he pulled the trigger.

"Fuck," said the magus. He turned the pistol over in his hand and glared at it, but the mechanism just would not work. When he looked up again, he found that the sage had vanished.

"Fuck," said the magus. "Come back here, you little... *Fuck*!"

The bindings that moored the Sky City to the canopy fell away, and the vast structure fled with a velocity that surprised the magus. He holstered his weapon and extended his hands towards the fleeing city...and so did his shadow, reaching across the stippled green roof of the jungle. His black fingers lengthened until they held the city's shadow between them. Then he drew his hands apart.

The Sky City's buildings fell dark as the magus tore its magic. The platter tilted and structures spilled from the sky with a great clattering sound. The jungle below drank down the shattered glass without complaint.

The magus hawked his sinuses clear and spat. Then he called the winds to him once more and flew on, away from the setting sun. His shadow led the way.

4. The Dog-Man and the Barbecue

The magus was trying to light a small gas barbeque when the dog found him.

The Faerie Realms were not subject to the rigors of proper physics, and mortal technology would not function there... but he was a magus, and he felt that it was his right, if not his duty, to violate the natural order as he pleased. Still, the barbeque was proving difficult. Pressurized gas was being correctly administered to the burners, but the magus was unable to make it ignite.

The dog watched him work for some time, although the magus paid it no mind.

Once its patience had been exhausted, the dog began to bark.

"Alright! Alright!" The magus threw up his hands and turned towards the dog.

The dog ceased its barking immediately and sat regarding him. It was an ugly beast: a small terrier with hair that was mostly white, where it showed through the scars and patches of mange.

"What?" demanded the magus, unable to meet its gaze.

The terrier stood up—and continued to rise, until it had taken the form of a much larger bipedal creature.

"Greetings, great magus," said the dog-man. Its voice was coarse and low. It was clad in uncured leathers, and wore a large, rusty cutlass strapped to its back.

The magus' curiosity had been piqued. "What can I do

for ya?" he asked, banishing the barbeque with an absent gesture.

"I belong to you," replied the dog-man. Its diction was perfect, despite the way its tongue lolled out of its open grin. "You tell me."

"You belong to me? Since when?"

"Since now."

"Unless I mistook that last pub for a pet shop, I don't think so," said the magus.

"I am a gift."

"I don't like gifts," said the magus. "So why don't you fuck off back where you came from?"

"I must obey your commands," said the dog-man. "But you must speak them as commands, not questions, if you expect me to carry them out."

"Heh," said the magus. The dog-man was smarter than he had expected. "What good are ya, then?"

"I'm a dog," said the dog-man. "I hunt, guard, and fetch."

"I'm not a pipe and slippers kind of man."

"I'm not the kind of dog you let into the house."

"Fair enough," said the magus, and retired into his tent.

The dog-man resumed its terrier-form and curled up in the warm place where the barbeque had been, and went to sleep.

5. Tavern Games

The countryside grew more rugged as the magus and the dog-man traversed it. The grass thinned to bare soil; the scrub and the trees grew sparse as the pastureland gave way to rocky hills. What little vegetation lay upon them looked stunted and burned.

"This is the Storm Queen's proving ground," said the dog-man. "We should seek shelter before she locates us here."

As the dog-man spoke, a whorl of black clouds coalesced on the horizon. The storm uncoiled across the valley, slashing the terrain anew with razored winds and freezing hail.

"Fuck," said the magus. When he had been a child, a storm had destroyed the city where he and his father had lived. Cyclone Tracy had been bigger, but this storm seemed fiercer. This storm was not some random meteorological fluctuation; it was a manifestation of some malicious will… and it was coming straight towards them.

"It's raining tigers and wolves," said the magus.

"We must take shelter, master," whined the dog-man, pointing towards a crag that stood some distance away. Squinting, the magus was barely able to discern that a rickety building stood upon it. He muttered a cantrip to sharpen his vision and the building resolved into a tavern. It had been constructed from pale stone and dark wood, and its round windows were yellow with the glow of a hearth-fire.

The magus was sceptical that the tavern would stand

before the storm, but he spoke some words and they rose into the air. The dog-man yelped as they accelerated towards it.

"Close your eyes if you're scared," said the magus, "but no more whining if you want to come inside."

The dog-man fell silent.

As they flew towards the tavern, battling furious cross-winds, the magus examined the magic that allowed so fragile a structure to stand firm against the storm. The spell that protected the tavern was in many respects similar to the one that had kept the Sky City aloft: it drew power from the cyclonic storm-winds and used it to push back against the maelstrom. He grunted his admiration of the work.

The magus set them down upon the front porch of the tavern. He shoved through the bat-wing doors and swaggered inside with his thumbs hooked into his belt. The magus liked cowboy movies. He scowled at the dog-man when it paused to shake itself dry in the doorway.

Wooden supports held up the tavern's sagging ceiling. Torches burned in tarnished brass sconces. Some of the floor was boarded-over; some of it was naked rock sprinkled with damp sawdust. The bar was splintered and scarred, and looked as if it had been many times repaired. There were a few other travellers in the tavern, as well as a group in the back corner that the magus took to be regulars.

The regulars were huddled together, betting on a game that involved cards, half a skull, an array of knives, and a collection of ceramic vessels that were suspended from a wooden gantry by a variety of chains and cords. The players were diverse in every way, excepting that they were all of them very large and very, very well-armed.

"Fairies wear boots," said the magus. "What a pearler."

"How may I help you, mortal man?" grunted the bruise-coloured creature that stood behind the bar.

"Schooner of beer, thanks, mate."

"We serve only food and ale here," said the publican.

"Ale," said the magus. The dog-man joined him at the bar. "Water for me dog."

The publican tapped a pint of ale and filled a bowl with water. The magus sampled his beverage and smacked his lips, and the dog-man did likewise.

"What's on the menu?"

"Broth," said the publican, "Or stew. You may determine which it is for yourself."

"What's in it?"

"Dead things."

"Good enough," said the magus. "Two servings, please."

The publican brought them the victuals they had ordered. The magus paid him with a handful of unmarked silver coins.

The magus sniffed the bowl of stew. Then he raised his head and sniffed the air.

"Dog," said the magus, "You smell anything strange?"

"No, master."

"But you're a dog."

"Aye?"

The magus sniffed his bowl again. "I can smell the stew when it's near my nose, but…the *air* doesn't smell like stew."

"Of course not. The air smells like the air."

The magus frowned at him. "Odours are part of the air."

"A thing smells only like itself," said the dog-man. "How can it smell of something else?"

The magus grunted "In my world, one thing can smell like another. Odours are transmitted through the air, where they can…mingle. They can even attach themselves to other objects."

"That does not sound a very sensible way for them to behave," said the dog-man. It sounded a bit offended.

The magus considered that while he consumed his bowl of dead-thing stew-broth, which he found mild to the point of blandness. The dog-man was once again proving to be better informed than he had anticipated. "Tell me," he said, "What do you know about magic?"

"All beings that dwell in the Realms of the Land require it in order to live."

"All faeries?"

"All beings," said the dog-man. "Even mortals."

"I guess that's why so few of us can come here."

"Is there no magic in the mortal realm?"

"There is, but not much. Only a few of us practise it."

"Then how does your world continue to function?"

"It doesn't function, so much as...*exist,* really. For the most part, that's down to science."

"What's that?" asked the dog-man.

The magus took a moment before he replied. "Science is a system of rules that can be used to explain the behaviour of...of every bloody thing," he said. "Excepting magic, of course."

"Oh," said the dog-man, unimpressed. "Here we have rules, but no system. That is why your mortal 'science' will not work."

The publican passed a fresh stein of ale down to the magus. "You should be careful where you discuss such matters, mortal man."

The magus returned his attention to the publican. "And why's that?"

"Science is dangerous," said the publican.

"How can it be dangerous, if it doesn't work?"

"There is one who practices 'science' here, and he has many powerful enemies," said the publican, with obvious reluctance. "Enemies who listen to idle conversations."

"Who's this scientist?"

"A mortal, like yourself."

"And who are his enemies?"

"The Queen of the Trees, the Queen of the Mountains," said the publican. "And others, it is rumoured."

"Who's spreading these rumours?" asked the magus.

The publican's livid brow turned a deeper blue when it frowned. "A troupe of players was here, many seasons ago," it said. "In his cups, the playwright told me the story."

"What did this playwright say?"

"I could not understand most of it," said the publican.

"He was very drunk, and the story was full of mortal words. But it was the usual: wandering, and war, and tragedy, and horror."

"Tell me what you remember," said the magus. "I'll figure out the rest."

"You'd best ask the playwright yourself," said the publican. "I have no head for tales."

"See if I don't," said the magus. "Where can I find this writing fella?"

"He might be anywhere," said the publican. It produced a ragged piece of parchment from under the bar and handed it to him. "But you are most likely to find him here."

The magus smoothed out the parchment on the counter top. It was stained and discoloured, rumpled from having been soaked in all manner of fluids, but the magus could still discern some of the script written upon it. He read it aloud, to the publican and the dog-man: "Nentril Revallo presents a Night's Entertainment like no other. Tales of the Dying Folk, Live Upon the Stage and blahdy-fucken blah."

The magus squinted at the illustration, which showed a short-legged man standing with his arms akimbo. "In Season at the Ore-Lands Theatre, or Whither the Winds of Drama Dictates."

The publican glanced over the magus' shoulder, towards the place where regulars were going about their entertainment. "If you should leave this bar alive, that is where I would seek him." It bustled to the other end of the bar, where it resumed its vain effort to clean the scarred countertop.

A shadow fell upon them. "The game requiresss a sssixxxth player to proceed," said the owner of the shadow, "And it'sss your move."

The dog-man growled. The magus took a long drink from his stein.

A clawed, scaled hand fell upon the magus' shoulder.

"Did you hear me, mortal? I asked you a question."

The magus finished his ale, smacked his lips, and then

turned to see who had addressed him.

The creature was as much reptilian as it was insectoid; armoured with scales and discoloured plates of bone. It had compound eyes and a flickering serpent's tongue. Its breath stank of faeces and rotting meat.

"No," said the magus.

"Yesss," said the inseptile.

"I'm not much for games, mate," said the magus, putting a restraining hand on the dog-man's back. "Can't ever remember the rules. Find someone else."

"The first rule of thissss game isss that admisssssion may not be refussssed." The inseptile smiled, tasted the odourless air with its split tongue. "You are already a part of it, mortal magusss."

"This," said the magus, "is exactly the reason I don't play."

The other regulars rose from their seats; drawing weapons and gathering sorcerous energies about them. The magus observed that the inseptile, which was twice his size, was the smallest of its peers. "You will play, or you will die," it said.

"You first," said the magus. With a snap of his fingers, he disconnected the shield that protected the tavern from the storm.

The building imploded before the Storm Queen's fury. The winds and the rain and the lightning tore it timber from timber, ripping the structure from the rock face and sending the bodies of those it had sheltered spinning out into the night. Debris fell swirling from the hillside; guttering with flames and giving off clouds of wet smoke. Nobody crawled out of the blasted wreckage that settled on the valley floor: not the publican, not the regulars, not any of other travellers.

6. The Storm

The magus and the dog-man rose away from the ruin and, sparking with static electricity, they streaked upwards through the grey vapour of the storm front.

Above the roiling clouds, the Storm Queen's host toiled over a fanciful device constructed of bellows and sails and ropes and glass tubes. With that strange machinery they corralled the screaming winds; directed the slashing rains; discharged forks of lightning.

The Storm Queen's people seemed a miserable lot; bedraggled and wrinkled and scorched. The wings upon their backs had been stripped of their membranes, but they beat feebly as the faeries hunched over their work.

Soon the Storm Folk were exhausted. The lightning that crackled through the glassware flickered out; the hail they cast turned to sleet, and then drizzle; the winds that drove them lessened and turned away.

The magus turned to the dog-man. "Wherever the wind dictates," he said. "You think these poor fuckers will lead us to the playwright?"

"I have no doubt of it," said the dog-man.

The magus spoke some words of sorcery and they turned to follow the waning storm.

7. The Playwright

They followed the storm over the craggy highlands, past the banks of a great river and over a lush and verdant forest. They flew over farmlands, and pastures, and a plain where the tall grass blew before them like the tide of a great green sea.

By the time they reached the amphitheatre, the Storm Queen's host had dispersed, and only the thinnest ribbons of cloud were hung from the twilit orange skies.

The amphitheatre was all that remained of a prettily ruined fortress. The magus, who had an eye for such things, wondered what had destroyed the fortress in such a symmetrical fashion. Magic, he supposed. Perhaps there had never been a fortress there, only ruins erected to lend the place atmosphere.

Dozens of Folk were seated on the stepped stone bleachers and many more were arriving all the time: some on foot and some mounted on beasts; some in carts or in wagons; some rising up from the earth or congealing from out of shadows.

"I think we came to the right place," said the magus to the dog-man.

"I have never been to the theatre before," said the dog-man.

"It's kind of like the cinema, but shit," said the magus.

When the dog-man claimed not to know what a cinema was, the magus ignored him.

They spiralled down to the amphitheatre and landed

in an unsteady stumble. The magus had flown all through the day and, even with such plentiful magic to power his way, he felt drained. There were some magi who could turn themselves into birds, or bats, or, it was rumoured, dragons. That would surely have been an easier way to travel—but the magus had never had the knack for it. He was as he was, and he had neither the ability nor the inclination to change.

They joined the back of a line of other folk seeking admission to the performance. The dog-man was so excited that it could not remain in its place. It kept darting away to try to find a new vantage of the amphitheatre, or the queue, or perhaps overhear something about the performance. Then it would return to the magus' side and wait, fidgeting and panting, until it could wait no more and had to dart away again.

"You see a candy bar?" asked the magus.

"A what?" said the dog-man, keen for some service to perform.

"A place that sells snacks," said the magus. "Popcorn, chocolate…that kinda stuff."

The dog-man shook its head. "I could fetch you some squirrels," it said. "Or perhaps a rabbit, if you are hungry."

"Maybe another time," said the magus. "What I could really use is a beer."

At the head of the queue, a long-armed creature wearing a rolled up conical hat sat behind a stone slab. "Admission is one two coin each," said the cashier, holding out a metal jar, which it shook to indicate what they should do with the coins.

"What kind of coins?" said the magus.

"Whatever kind you carry in your pocket."

The magus turned over his hand and revealed four gold coins. "I do not carry them in my pockets," he said. "But I hope these will suffice?"

"No!" A rangy being with a protuberant chin and beady, intelligent eyes came rushing up, a black cape fluttering behind it. It pushed the cashier's pot away from the magus.

"The punters must pay their way, Revallo," said the cashier. One of its ears, which was long and pointed and hairy, twitched out from underneath its cap. "How else are we to eat?"

The playwright kept its eyes fixed on the magus. "You are no punter, are you?" he said. "You are a mortal, a-questing in these Realms."

"I just come to see the show," said the magus.

"And see it you shall!" declared the playwright, reaching out and folding the magus' hand closed upon the four one-dollar coins he had offered. "But we will take no payment from you here."

"Well, isn't that generous of ya," said the magus.

"It's a trap, master," said the dog-man. "Agree to no bargain before you have asked the price." It turned to the playwright, hackles raised, and grabbed the playwright by its collar. "What will you have from my master in another place, that you will not take his gold here?"

"That's no gold," said the playwright, wrenching himself free of the dog-man's grip. "Not if I am any judge. What I desire is something far more valuable: I want his stories."

The magus considered. "I'm not much of a *raconteur,*" he replied.

"You are something even better," said the playwright. "You are a source of stories. You just tell me the events—I will find the drama in them."

"Alright," said the magus. "Two stories—one for my admission, one for the dog's."

"Three," said the playwright. "Because I know you did not come here to watch the show, and I know you desire something else from me."

"Alight," said the magus. "It's a deal."

The playwright shook his hand with far too much enthusiasm. "Enjoy the show, my mortal friend. We will meet afterwards to complete our business."

"I'm not your friend," said the magus, to the playwright's retreating back.

The magus and the dog-man sat at the back of the amphitheatre, but the view down to the stage was excellent. The players voices carried to them without difficulty, and the moon above provided a spotlight that tracked the action across the rickety boards.

The magus had not expected the show to be an anthology, but there were two supporting dramas before the main feature.

The first was a slapstick called Thomas and Jeremiah. It was a pair of rival homunculi—one fashioned into the shape of a cat, the other a mouse—who caused havoc in the house of their ever-absent master. The magus quite enjoyed it, but it was over very quickly.

The second was a situation comedy called Different Folks. It was about a pair of mortal children who were adopted by a Faerie noble and brought to live in his tower. The children's poor comprehension of the customs of the Land was supposed to provide humour, but the magus did not understand the jokes which the rest of the audience found uproarious. The noble concluded the episode by lecturing the children about the danger of traveling about the Realms without a guardian.

The third play was called The Day the Realms Stood Still. It was about a mortal who came to the Land aboard a falling star. This frightened the monarch of the Realm in which he had set down and she set her army upon him, but the mortal was protected by a demon who destroyed her forces. The mortal wandered the Land, making friends and enemies alike until finally he was tricked and slain by the monarch's agents.

But the mortal possessed a soul, unlike the denizens of the Realms, and the demon brought him back to deliver a warning to the Folk: let mortals be about their business unmolested, or the demon would summon others of its kind, who would burn the Realms to a cinder.

At the end of the play, Nentril Revallo descended upon the magus, his fingers clutching with eagerness and his black cloak billowing like the wings of some great carrion bird.

Revallo herded the magus and the dog-man from the amphitheatre into a ring of covered wagons, where a great fire blazed. The players they had seen strutting upon the stage were there, gossiping and bickering and carousing in celebration of the night's performance, which by consensus seemed to have gone well. When they saw the playwright approaching with his two companions, however, they fell silent and retreated back into their accommodations.

"Pay them no mind, no mind at all," said the playwright. "They are weary from the night's exertions."

"And they fear my master's presence," said the dog-man.

"Well, perhaps," said the playwright. "He is not the first mortal they have known."

"So I've heard," said the magus. "Tell me about this other bloke."

Revallo waggled a finger. "Oh no," he said. "First you must repay my earlier generosity."

Even depleted as he was, the magus had little doubt that he could destroy the entire encampment. The dog-man looked at him, the flames from the firepit reflected in its eyes, and he could tell that it was ready to fight if he so commanded it. But the magus was curious, and the playwright had answers.

The playwright produced a wineskin and two stemless glasses. "May I pour you a drink?"

"Yeah, why not," said the magus. He was not much of a wine drinker, but then, he was never one to turn down free booze.

Revallo poured the two glasses and proposed a toast, but the magus had already consumed most of his drink. The playwright toasted the night by himself and the dog-man barked its amusement.

"Alright," said the magus. "What stories would you like?"

"Your own, of course, said the playwright. "You are obviously a man of power. Your story must be filled with adventure and marvels and wondrous deeds and, if I may be so bold, no little amount of darkness."

The magus looked away. He thought about his childhood, and his schooling, and his wandering. He thought about his brief time in the army, and his time in the gangs, and his time in prison. He thought his awakening to magic, and his conflict with the Conclave. But mostly he thought about his father, and again he considered destroying the place.

When Revallo saw his face, he raised his hands and leaned away. "You would be a hero. Everyone would know of your bravery and your power—"

"I'm not any kind of hero," said the magus, "and you're a fool if you think otherwise. My story is a horror show. Nobody wants want to hear all that."

"You might be surprised," said the playwright.

"I doubt it," replied the magus. "Those stories you put on tonight—I know them all. They're what people want. The same, happy bullshit, again and again."

"That is why I want your story," said the playwright. "So I may give them something new."

"Are you sure?" said the magus. "The show you put on tonight—those are all stories from my world. You nicked them off that other mortal."

"He gave them to me," said the playwright. "We were friends, once."

"I bet he thought so," said the magus. "But you were just a thief, weren't you?"

The playwright's eyes grew cold. "They were not his stories, in the first place," it said. "In any case, stories are wherever you find them. The art is all in the telling."

"I guess that's why you're so keen to steal some new ones," said the magus.

"I am waiting for what I am owed, mortal magus," said

the playwright. "If you will not give me your own then you must give me someone else's."

The dog-man put his hand on the pommel of his cutlass, but the magus just laughed and pushed the hair from his face. "I'm just joking with ya," he said, to the playwright. "Pour me some more wine and I'll tell you some fucken stories."

The playwright inclined its head. "That would be most kind of you," it said, pouring another two glasses.

The magus took a long draught from his glass. "And then," he said, smacking his lips, "If you don't tell me what I want to know about this other mortal, I'm going to burn you and your players and this entire goddamned amphitheatre to a cinder."

"If there is one thing you can be sure about me," said the playwright, "It's that I tell a good story. I only hope that you can live up to your end of the deal."

"Well," said the magus, "First thing you have to understand is the stories this other mortal gave you are rubbish." He spat on the ground. "Sci fi bullshit. Men in rubber suits and cardboard space ships? No fucken way."

"You prefer a different genre," said Revallo, his eyes alight with greed.

"Abso-fucken-lutely," said the magus. "The only real fucken stories you need to know are Westerns."

He went on to describe two of his favourites, quoting lines in imitation of the various actors, making sound effects with his mouth for the horses and explosions and gunplay. When he was done, the magus sat back and folded his arms. "What do you think?"

Revallo had tears in his eyes and a smile on his face more genuine than anything the magus had seen on the playwright's stage. "I think you have delivered *admirably,*" said the playwright. "Now ask me whatever questions you would."

"Tell me about this other mortal," said the magus.

Revallo looked up at the skies and closed his eyes. He

cleared his throat and his sinuses, inhaled deeply, and then began to speak, in a voice that was deeper and plumier than the one he employed for conversation:

"Times were harder, in the days when I met the mortal. My troupe was a ragged bunch, and our productions were just as threadbare. We had taken up with a group of wandering Tinker Folk, for there is some protection in numbers."

"You don't have to tell it fancy," said the magus. "Just tell me about this mortal."

"The mortal came here from the mortal realm, seeking employment for his mortal skills."

"A scientist," said the magus.

"His name was Duncan."

"Duncan," repeated the magus.

"Just so. But there is no place for such as Duncan in this Land. That is how we came to find him, wandering the hills, delirious and dying for lack of nutrition. We took him in, and tended to his health…"

"The tinkers did, you mean," said the magus, who felt he had the playwright's measure.

The playwright did not appreciate being interrupted. "The tinkers fed him and tended to him, aye, but Duncan was also stricken with a malaise of the spirit. I was the one who helped him through that."

"Don't care," said the magus. "I'm not a fucken shrink. What happened next?"

"The Tinker Folk are seldom welcome anywhere they put down stakes. Soon after the mortal joined us, the Tree Queen took particular umbrage at our presence and sent a war party to exterminate us. The very woods marched upon us, then; the foliage bristling with anger; tree trunks creaking with fury…"

"Yeah, yeah," said the magus. "I told you, you don't have to make it fancy. What did you do?"

"We, the players, had been preparing some new material, and we had recently found an engagement in the court of a Queen," said the playwright. "We are not warriors, any more than the tinkers."

"You ran away."

"Aye, and the tinkers would have, too," said the playwright, "But Duncan persuaded them otherwise."

"He had some tricks up his sleeve, eh?"

"The mortal orchestrated the Tinkers' defence, and they defeated the Tree Queen's forces…but the cost was high.

"They had won a battle, but they could not win a war, even with the mortal's terrible weapons, for the Tinkers' numbers have always been few. They retreated into the mountains, and they have remained there ever since."

"So the Tinker Folk no longer travel the Realms?"

"The Tinker Folk are no more," said the playwright. "Duncan's power has perverted them into something other. Their traditions are gone—their customs, their foods, their music. Now they are but slaves in the mortal's machine kingdom."

"Where is this kingdom?" said the magus.

The Playwright turned and pointed, and the moon shone a helpful beam to show the magus where to go. "You will find Duncan and his territory on the far side of the mountains, where the river winds down into the Ore-Lands."

The magus looked around for the dog-man. "Tomorrow," he said. "We'll leave at first light, unless I'm hung over. In which case we'll leave whenever I fucken feel like it."

"But first, you owe me another story," said Revallo.

"Alright," he said. "This one is about the same guy as the other two."

"The gunfighter?" said the playwright. "Does he have a name?"

"Well, they call him different things in each story, but you never really do get his name," said the magus.

"Go on," said the Playwright. The magus was happy to oblige.

In the end, the magus rose at noon. The dog-man was already awake, and he found it sitting beside him, watching over him where he lay by the ashes of the bonfire.

The troupe was in the midst of breaking camp, so there was no breakfast to be had and there was no point in tarrying.

When the playwright saw them making preparations, he approached them with a dignity he had not shown the night before.

"Not now, writer-man," said the magus. "My head feels like a battalion of marines took a shit in it."

"I just wanted to say goodbye," said the playwright, "and to make you one final offer."

"Just so long as it means you'll stop talking," said the magus.

"Once your business with my old friend Duncan is completed, if you should reconsider my offer, I would still like to know your story. Come and see me at my theatre in the City of the Ore-Lands and I'll make a hero of you yet."

"Never been a one for the theatre," said the magus. "But if you want to give me something, I'll have some more of that wine, if you got any."

"Certainly, certainly," said Revallo. He produced a skin from under his cape. "Let me just fetch some clean glasses, and we'll toast to the success of your current enterprise."

"Nah mate," said the magus. "I'll just take the bottle."

8. The Queen of the Mountains

They flew all through the day, heading in the direction the playwright had indicated, but the distance was greater than the magus had reckoned. All too soon the setting sun had bloodied the snow-covered peaks, and the magus grew wary of his exertions.

The magus and the dog-man alit on the shadowed western face of one of the smaller mountains, where the wind was less.

"This is territory of the Queen of the Mountains," said the dog-man. "And she is poorly disposed towards trespassers."

"What does she care if we camp here for a night?" asked the magus, rubbing an aching spot in his neck.

"Would you permit itinerant travellers to camp in your home?" said the dog-man.

"It's just a fucken mountain. I don't see so much as a mud hut, much less a palace."

"The mountains themselves are palace to this Queen," said the dog-man.

The snow was calf-deep, and the wind was bitter, so the magus laid a cantrip to warm himself and the dog-man. They tramped along the slope while the twilight waned, looking for a protected place to pitch their tent.

"Fucken mountains. Fucken snow," said the magus.

"Do they not have such things in your mortal world?" asked the dog-man, surprised to consider the notion.

"Oh, we have both of them," said the magus, "But the

place where I'm from is all hot wind and sand."

The dog-man made to reply, but instead it fell into a crouch and drew its cutlass. The magus stopped in his tracks, surprised to discover that they had been surrounded by a contingent of warriors.

It was not easy to discern the warriors in the darkness, for they seemed to be made of the very rock from which the mountain grew. Twelve feet tall and armoured with quartz plates, each of them was armed with weapons made from some strange metal that was black and without lustre.

"Dog," said the magus, "How in the name of fuck did these gigantic bastards manage to sneak up on us without you noticing?"

"This is their territory," said the dog-man. "They are not as distinct from it as you might expect, and thus they have no need for stealth."

The magus was not a patient man, and he harboured no desire to engage in a staring contest with a dozen piles of rock. "G'day" he said. "I'm, uh, looking for the Queen of the Mountains."

"That is where we are taking you." He could not tell which of the quartz warriors was speaking, for its voice was like sheetrock cracking, and seemed to come from all sides. Perhaps the mountain itself was addressing him. "After your audience, you will be taken to the gaol, where you will reside with those others who have trespassed upon our sovereign territory, and there you will remain until your mortal span is ended."

"Steady on," said the magus. "All I wanted was to borrow a cup of sugar."

At spear-point, the quartz warriors marched the magus and the dog-man up a treacherous slope, along a series of precipitous ledges, and then down into a dark, jagged opening. The magus was certain that the path had not been there before the quartz warriors had appeared.

They went down unlit tunnels too narrow for them to stand abreast. They navigated a rickety suspension bridge that swayed wildly beneath their weight. They marched through cavernous, marbled antechambers and up a grand staircase; through a series of increasingly large vestibules and atriums; and finally, they were delivered into the enormous chamber where the Queen of the Mountains held court.

The ceiling of the throne-room was conical, so the magus reckoned they were near the top of the mountain. He found the idea that a mountain might be hollow disturbing.

Courtiers and politicians milled about, as in any court, gossiping and intriguing amongst themselves. Orderly rows of stalactites and stalagmites gave the vertiginous impression of soldiers standing at parade rest along both the ceiling and the floor. A double-row of them guarded the path to the throne.

The light was poor, so the magus shifted the spectrum of his vision downwards. In infrared, the stony mountain folk were surprisingly bright. Perhaps they had molten cores, like volcanoes or planets. He wondered if their spilled blood would crystallize into igneous rock.

The Queen of the Mountains sat rigid and unmoving upon her throne. Her pale dress pooled around her like cooling lava; her dark grey skin gleamed with the texture of polished slate. Shards of leucite protruded from her skull in a manner suggestive of hair.

A cluster of foreign dignitaries stood around the foot of the queen's massive throne, engaged in what seemed to be a heated discussion. The quartz warriors stopped well short of the throne: they would not interrupt their Queen's diplomatic business with something as trifling as a pair of trespassers.

"If the Ore Queen will not provide us with soldiers she must at least provide steel to arm our forces," the Queen of the Mountains demanded. She spoke slowly and deeply, like a glacier grinding against a cliff.

"Nay, Majesty," replied the dignitary to whom the queen had spoken: a broad-shouldered being clad in raiment of finely woven metals. "Your foe is a friend to the Ore-lands, and my liege will not give you materials with which to fight him without payment."

A being garbed in dark robes spoke up. Its voice was calm and soft and so deep that it resonated oddly inside the magus' skull. Its face was completely concealed inside its hood. "The Council of the Magi requires Ore-lands steel to manufacture the shadow weapons. No other source will provide metal of the required quality."

A dignitary dressed in a cloak woven from living foliage jabbed a finger angrily. "Our foe is equipped with terrible mortal arms; we cannot wage this war without shadowsteel. The Tree Queen will not stand for this."

"Then the Tree Queen must sit her throne for all her days to come," replied the emissary from the Ore-lands. "My Queen will not help you to make war upon her friends."

The Queen of the Mountains again spoke. "This mortal abomination encroaches upon the Ore-Lands, as he does upon the forests and our own mountains. Surely the Ore Queen would profit from his destruction?"

"The land he occupies has already been mined clean," said the Ore-lands' emissary. "He is a peaceable neighbour and a reliable customer."

"Peaceable?" shrilled the emissary of the Tree Queen. "He has enslaved the entire Tinker nation."

"The Tinkers were squatting in our territories long before the mortal ever came along," said the Ore-lands' emissary. "As I recall, the Tree Queen was hardly a friend to them, either."

"They were good, honest faerie folk—"

"And the Tree Queen did her very best to exterminate them," said the Ore-lands' emissary. "That is how this mortal came to rule them in the first place."

"Yet faerie folk they were. Now, they are—"

"The Queen of the Ore-Lands considers that the mortal has greatly improved the Tinkers."

The magus stepped between a pair of quartz guards and

elbowed his way through the courtiers and diplomats. "Ey, Queenie," he said. "Queenie. I got a proposition for you."

The Queen of the Mountains tipped her head back, the better to look down her nose at the magus. Her neck cracked visibly as she did so, though the fractures sealed themselves as soon her head was in its new position. "And who is this impudent beast, to address us so?"

"I'm the Grinch that fucked Christmas," said the magus. "I'm looking for this mortal, same as you are. Tell me where I can find him and I'll take care of him for you."

"The mortal is most powerful," said the Tree Queen's emissary. "We are assembling an army. What makes you think that you can defeat him by yourself?"

"Well, I'm not a fucken *elf* who lives down a fucking rabbit hole or up a goddamn tree. I'm a mortal, too—I know how to deal with his tricks and his toys."

"I do not believe that you know anything," said the Tree Queen's emissary.

"I know his name," said the magus. "Do you?"

The robed figure turned its cowl towards him. It raised its hands, which were covered with scars and burns, and the magus felt it drawing magic about itself.

The magus opened his mouth, but his words froze on his tongue. The spells he had palmed slipped between his fingers like sand through the tines of a fork, and the runes he imagined broke apart, unquickened.

The dog-man drew its cutlass and leapt snarling to his aid, but its blade had no effect on the warriors' rocky hides. They subdued it easily. The magus was too stunned to give any fight. The quartz warriors did not need to restrain him while they divested him of the considerable number of weapons he carried upon his person.

"What manner of beast are you?" demanded the Queen of the Mountains, when the magus had recovered his senses.

"The worst kind," said the magus, unable to turn his face towards her because a quartz warrior was kneeling on his head. "A human."

"He is as he claims, your Majesty," said the cowled figure. "He is a mortal, like the one we seek to destroy."

"Is he now, Councillor?"

"Indeed. He is a magus of no mean skill, and a practitioner of the vilest of arts. He is a necromancer. He traffics with demons."

"Can he be trusted?"

"No, your Majesty. His crimes against the faerie folk are numerous already. If he remains free to travel the Realms I cannot divine how great the consequent destruction will be."

"You forgot to say about me heart of gold," said the magus.

"Take this beast from our presence," said the Queen of the Mountains. "At dawn, he will be lowered into the canyons. We will personally supervise the mountains as they grind his meat from his bones."

A quartz warrior struck a blow to the magus' head, and his senses fled once more.

9. Gaol

The magus awoke in a cell that was six feet deep, three feet wide and five feet high. The walls were cut from stone that had been polished as smooth as glass. He sat up and felt the bruises on the back of his head. The magus winced, grunted and pushed his hair from his eyes. He'd been in jail before, and did not enjoy the experience.

The dog-man assumed its human form when it saw that he was awake. It drew its knees to its chest and looked at him with sympathy. "Are you intact?"

"I've suffered worse from a slab of beer."

"That must be a formidable foe," said the dog-man.

"Not as formidable as you'd hope," said the magus, leaning back against a wall. "Tell me: who's the bastard in the hood?"

"He serves the Council of the Magi," said the dog-man.

"The Council of the Magi?"

"They govern the use of magic throughout all the Realms of the Land."

"I know the kind," said the magus.

"The thirteen who comprise the council are of many kinds," said the dog-man. "Folk from all over the Realms, from every nation and territory and species."

"All the most boring assholes from throughout the Land in one boring fucken place," said the magus. "I'd rather be in jail."

He rose and went to inspect the bars that sealed him

inside the cell. They were made of black steel, and they went into the stone of the floor and ceiling without any seams or joins. They were too narrowly spaced for the dog-man to pass through, even in its diminished, canine form.

The magus took the bars in his fists, but found that he could not channel any power. The Councillor had set an enchantment upon him that would not allow him to build any spells. He could perceive the construct that constrained his abilities—dimly—but that was all that remained to him of his art.

The magus let go of the bars and retreated back into the cell.

"Dog," said the magus, considering, "When you change shape, you also change size. Right?"

"Aye," said the dog-man.

"Do you have to?"

The dog-man looked at him quizzically. "Aye, for a dog is smaller than a man."

"Well, yes, but…can you shift your mass without changing your shape?"

"No," it said. "I cannot."

The magus rubbed the bridge of his nose. Lank blonde hair fell across his shadowed eyes. "Become a dog again."

The dog-man complied, unquestioning.

"Now," said the magus, "Become a man, but maintain your current mass size."

The two-foot tall dog-man grinned at him in its human form.

"How old are you, dog?"

"I have no way of reckoning that would be meaningful in mortal terms."

"Oh," said the magus, disappointed that he had lost the opportunity to cite a cliché. The dog-man just stared at him blankly.

"Now," said the magus, "Go find that motherfucker in the black robe and fetch me his spleen."

Tail wagging, the dog-man slid between the bars. It set

off down the corridor at a lope, becoming a terrier the size of a bullock in four strides.

Before long, the magus felt his sorcerous perceptions sharpening. The spell that restrained his magic loosened, and the magus brushed it away like cobwebs from an old suit of clothes. He rose and went straight to the shadowsteel bars that kept him inside the cell. No amount of heat would soften them; no force would bend them; but the rock walls that held them in place gave no such resistance. The magus cracked the bars right out of the walls and stepped out into the corridor.

As he walked through the halls, he found the corpses of the wardens, savagely mauled or smashed to rubble. "Good dog," he said.

The magus drew a pair of summoning circles on the glass-smooth floor, using the plentiful supply of fresh blood to mark them out. He worked with care, because the things he intended to summon into them were as terrible as he could reckon—and that was terrible indeed.

In the first circle he raised a demon that was twenty feet tall and possessed of far too many limbs. It had no joints, but rather was strung together with spools of razor wire. Into the second circle he conjured a demon that looked like an ordinary human man, only covered with hundreds of functioning eyes. The sockets in its skull lay empty.

To the first demon, the magus said: "Find the court of the Tree Queen and kill everyone you see. The Queen, the King, every nob and general and minister and courtier. All of them. Report back to me when you're done."

"Sure thing," said the disconnected demon. The magus scuffed a gap in its containing circle and it set off with a jouncing gait. It jumped through a stone wall and vanished, leaving only a pattern of soot-stains to mark its passing.

To the second demon, the magus said: "The Queen of the Mountains and her lot are yours." He paused a moment. "Make sure you don't hurt me dog."

"Whatever you say, brother," said the eye demon. When

the magus broke its circle the demon sauntered off down the corridor, whistling one of the magus' favourite songs.

The magus slapped together a teleportation spell and vanished in a gasp of sulphur and smoke. He rematerialized in the foothills below the mountains amidst a similar cloud, about two feet above the ground. He fell and turned an ankle.

"Fuck goddamn shit," he swore, though he knew he had been lucky: two feet below the ground would have had far worse consequences. He stood up, spat, and limped away to pitch camp.

10. Beer and Spleen

When he had erected the tent, the magus started a fire and drew a six-pack of German beer out of the foldspace repository he used for an arsenal and a larder. His thirst was such that he drank the first bottle warm. Sated, he tried to figure out a spell to chill the rest of the beers to a more acceptable temperature, but succeeded only in exploding three of the pressurized bottles.

While the magus drank beer by his fire, the eye demon wandered through the halls of the Mountain Queen, harvesting the eyes of every creature it looked upon and collecting them in a pink leather bag. It wandered through the ballrooms and the halls of parliament and the throne room. It wandered through the kitchens and the barracks and the sculleries and the courthouse. Every blinded victim watched itself die from the thousand viewpoints fixed upon the demon's hide. None were spared, for there was no place to hide from a demon with eyes enough to see all that could be seen, and with empty sockets that perceived all that could not.

By and by the dog-man came trotting to the magus' campsite in its terrier form, at its habitual size. It bore its huge cutlass in its teeth, wound about with the intestines of the emissary of the Council of the Magi. Most of the emissary's digestive system trailed behind it in the dirt.

The terrier deposited the cutlass at the magus' feet and resumed its bipedal form. "My apologies," it said. "I was not able to determine which of its organs you might consider its spleen."

"So, you brought them all?"

"Aye."

The magus laughed and slapped the dog-man on the back and said that it could keep the Councillor's innards for itself. The dog-man made a happy noise that was as much laugh as it was a growl and a bark. It cut a spit from a nearby tree and sat down to roast the dirt-caked offal at the magus' fire. The magus declined to share in its meal, claiming that he could subsist on beer alone.

When the eye demon manifested, the dog-man whined and crept behind its master. The demon clasped its orb-encysted hands and bowed. "All dead," it said.

"The Queen of the Mountains and her entire court?"

"There are a few platoons of her soldiers wandering around the slopes, but they're all that's left." It smiled. There were eyes on its teeth and tongue. "Guess I got a bit carried away."

"Ta, mate," said the magus. The demon bowed again and slung the pink leather bag across its back. The magus dismissed it with a wave of his hand.

Hours passed, but the severed-limb demon did not return. The magus stirred the embers of the fire with the toe of a boot and bent to peer into them. He grunted, spat, then finally stood up and swore. Divination was not his strongest magic; he was much better at demons and fire and death. The magus kicked an empty beer bottle into the smoking ashes and smashed it with the heel of his boot. That seemed to do the trick: now, he could indeed see into the Realm of the Tree Queen.

The forests of the Faerie Realms had long been infested with demons and monsters—just as they had been in his own world, in the days when it had lain closer to the Land. The Tree Queen had suffered many such attacks before, and she had her own coven of magi who protected her with wards and spells and traps. They had captured and bound his wire demon before it could wreak any harm upon them.

The magus grunted and swept the ashes away. His destruction of the Mountain Queen would suffice in delaying the action against the one he sought. This other mortal, who had brought science to the Land of the Faerie. The Tree Queen did not herself interest the magus.

He called the dog-man over. "The bloke we're lookin' for lives where the forests, the mountains and the Ore-Lands have a common border. You know where that is?"

"I can find it," said the dog-man.

11. The Machine City

The Machine City erupted from the side of the mountain like a cancer. A great river had been choked into a canal system to feed its growth upon those blighted slopes.

Prefabricated outposts dotted the arid sand flats that had once belonged to the Ore-lands, spreading into a clear-cut area that the magus supposed had once belonged to the Tree Queen. Metal vehicles that looked like APCs and tanks crawled across the terrain closer to the command citadel, weaving amongst trenches and pillboxes. Ornithopters buzzed lethargically through the polluted skies, pregnant with bombs, missiles and other, stranger munitions.

"Is this what the mortal world is like?" asked the dog-man.

"Not all of it," said the magus, with regret.

The border station was garrisoned by a strange kind of folk that were better than halfway to being machines. Guns and blades grew from their hands and torsos; tubes and chips were embedded in their scarred and misshapen craniums. This was not any kind of science that the magus had witnessed before. It looked like mortal technology, but it set his occult senses haywire. The dog-man bristled and growled at them.

The machine folk levelled their guns at the magus and the dog-man. "You will come with us," they said, speaking in unison. Their voices were harsh and synthetic.

The machine folk ushered the magus and the dog-man

into the back of a half-track, which bore them slowly through the secure zone and up into the citadel. They passed through another checkpoint, and then were frog-marched through kilometres of circuitry-fouled corridors and hallways. There were no windows, but diffuse light shone from ceiling fixtures. Cool, stale air hissed into every room through vents in the ceilings. Pipes clanked inside the walls. In some rooms, electricity hummed.

Eventually they came to a high-ceilinged laboratory. Glassware filled with bubbling liquids lined the bench-tops; cathode ray tubes hung, flickering, from wall brackets; rolls of insulated cabling looped all over the floor and walls. There were no chairs.

The dog-man whined and growled. The magus sniffed and wiped his nose: the stink of acid was strong enough to leave his nasal membranes tender. There was definitely another human around.

The machine folk shouldered their weapons and filed out of the room in lockstep, their rubber-soled feet thudding dully on the tiled floor.

"Well, hello, there." The voice was in the baritone register. The magus and the dog-man could not see the speaker until he walked around a low bench and presented himself to them.

The speaker was a dwarf dressed in a white lab coat. His hair was clipped in a military style and his face was clean-shaven. One of his eye-sockets was empty, sealed over with smooth flesh.

"G'day," said the magus. "I'm looking for Douglas."

"I'm Douglas," said the dwarf.

The magus gave him a good, hard look, and noticed that the dwarf was wearing jeans and tennis shoes under his lab coat.

"Yeah, I'm a human, just like you," said the dwarf, angry at the magus' unconcealed scrutiny. "Who the hell are you?"

"Nobody important," said the magus.

"Fine," said the dwarf. "In that case, I'll call you Blondie."

The magus grinned. "Suits me."

The dwarf scowled. It had not intended that as a compliment. "What can I do for you, Blondie?"

"Just come to say hello," said the magus. "See what you're up to. Fellow mortal, and all."

Douglas spread his arms grandly. "Well then, welcome to my humble home. The locals call it the Machine City, but I like to think of it as the Citadel of Reason."

The magus thought about that for a moment. "You built a Citadel of Reason…in Faerie Land?"

"Where better?"

"I'm not sure I understand the point," said the magus.

"If you're going to re-imagine the laws of physics, you need to start in a reality where there aren't many rules."

"Why would you want to do that?"

"Well," said the dwarf, "Back in the old place, I was a scientist." The dwarf looked away as he said it and the magus knew he was lying. "I was a scientist, but after a while I discovered that I didn't much like science."

"Sounds like you had a bit of a problem."

"Well, I liked the idea of science. I liked the scientific method. Validation, verification, falsification—all of that hoo-ha. What I didn't like was the actual physics. I didn't like how the equations fit together. I didn't like the *math*."

"Now that I can understand," said the magus. "And so you came here?"

"Sure did," said the dwarf. "I came here and rewrote the whole thing. Cleaned it up, you might say. The constants are integers; the energy transformations are perfect…" He shrugged. "It may seem a bit whimsical, but, under the covers, this world is a lot more elegant than ours."

The magus cocked his head. His own experience had been the opposite: spells that had been perfectly sound in the mortal realm did not function properly in this inconstant environment. "Really?"

"Really, truly, absolutely," said the dwarf. "Fixing the math makes engineering a whole lot easier. How else could I have built all of this?" The dwarf gestured grandly. "Generators, refineries, factories… All of this, with only a rag-ass band of Tinker elves for labour?"

"Wouldn't know, mate," said the magus. "I never finished high school."

The dwarf looked the magus over a second time. "What's your interest, then?"

"I want to know how all of this works."

"But you're not a scientist."

"I'm a magician."

"A crazy-man, more like," snorted the dwarf. "Everybody knows there's no such a thing as magic."

The magus opened and shut his mouth three times before he found a reply. "We…we're standing waist deep in Fairyland."

"Fairyland, shmairyland," said the dwarf. "It's just some other reality. The facts and rules of how things work together might be different than what you're used to, but that doesn't make it magical."

"You really believe that?"

"Belief is for religious fruitcakes. I know it, because that's how it is. Magic doesn't exist in any possible world."

"This is one of the other kind, mate."

"Logic says otherwise."

"Logic says no such thing."

"I can't believe we're having this argument," said the dwarf. "The only two rational beings in all of fairyland."

"I don't reckon your powers of arithmetic are up to much," said the magus. "But then, you did say you had a problem with math."

The dwarf stamped his foot. "There's no such thing as magic. There wasn't any such thing back home and there sure as hell ain't any such a thing out here."

"You clearly don't know very much about Hell, either."

"Magic is how science appears to the ignorant, *Blondie,*" said the dwarf. "Best case. Worst case? It's plain old coincidence."

"Magic is deeper and stranger than just 'coincidence', *Douglas,*" said the magus. "Magic is not just the things we can't explain. It's the exception that proves every rule."

"Science built all *this,*" said the dwarf, waving his hand to indicate his kingdom. "What did your flim-flammery ever build?"

The magus had no reply to that.

"You say you can do magic, Blondie?" said the dwarf. "I say, show me proof."

"The burden of proof is on science," said the magus. "Magic is magic, no matter what else it appears to be."

"Sophistry," spat the dwarf. "Your magic is nothing but *sophistry.*"

The magus turned his head from left to right, scanning the Citadel with his occult senses. He saw runes where the dwarf had laid diodes and transistors. He saw ley-lines where the dwarf had laid copper wires; rift-farms and spell-wheels where the dwarf had built reactors and dynamos. He bent down to the dwarf and said: "What if I told you that you're a better magician than I am?"

The dwarf took a step back. "What?"

"What if I told you that everything you've built is magical? That you've solved all of the spell-crafting problems I have been unable to? What would you say to me then?" The magus folded his arms. "How could you prove otherwise?"

"Abracadabra, sim sala bim," said the dwarf. "Blondie, that's not even sophistry; it's just god-damned nonsense."

"Alright then, Douglas," said the magus. He jammed a rune into the spell-turbines that provided electricity to the citadel. The lights blinked out and the air-conditioning fell silent as the turbines seized up. The images on the CRT screens blinked away; the chemicals bubbling through the network of glassware cooled and stilled.

The dog-man barked once in the sudden silence.

"Let me demonstrate for you the power of *sophistry.*"

The magus drew a symbol in the air, his fingertip marking a character that glowed with heat. The dwarf lurched away from it, but the rune leapt after him. It struck him directly in the chest.

"Presto change-o," said the magus.

"Ah," said the dwarf, as his bones began to shift. "Aaah."

The dwarf's musculature rippled and stretched as his achondroplastic skeleton elongated to normal proportions. The skin that sealed his empty socket split open and the eye he had been born without formed in the cavity behind it, forcefully wiring itself back into his brain. The scientist who had until-recently been dwarf began to scream.

"Get 'im, boy," said the magus. The dog-man silenced the former dwarf with a single stroke of its cutlass.

The magus raised his hands and cast the citadel's chromium spires to slag. The canals flooded; the trenches collapsed; the pillboxes and outposts puffed apart. Ground vehicles stopped in place. Ornithopters fell out of the sky. There were no explosions: without the dwarf's magic none of the fuel could burn; none of the munitions were live. The Citadel of Reason fell ruin with sound that was closer to a fart than a sigh.

The magus put two fingers in his mouth and whistled. The dog-man emerged from the rubble with a grin on its face. "C'mon, boy," he said. "Let's get out of here."

Together they negotiated their way through the debris on foot, for the magus was too weary to fly. He knew that he could not have managed such feats in the mortal realm. There was power to burn, here, but he was used to working with embers. It would burn him out if he could not learn to channel it properly.

For all its flaws, the dwarf's working had done exactly that.

The dog-man assumed the form of a terrier, and it jumped and gambolled all the way down the mountain with its tail wagging.

12. A Player of Guitars

They made camp deep in the Ore-lands, near the rapid grey river whose waters cut a snaking line down towards the capitol. The sky was as black and empty as wet tar, but even in that starless, moonless night, the city of the Ore-lands somehow contrived to gleam.

By the light of the campfire, the magus inscribed a transformer spell upon the brass oval of his belt buckle. This would serve to regulate the flow of the ambient energies of the faerie world into his sorcerous constructs. The magus was pleased with the spell, which was far simpler than he had expected. He had refactored the dwarf's logic into four symbols and five connecting lines.

The magus conjured a bucket of crushed ice and filled it with bottles of beer. Humming to himself, he dug out a record player and a box of his favourite LPs. While the beer cooled, he set about simulating an electrical current for the record player. Once he had the music cranking, the magus collapsed into a beanbag, popped a cold beer, and settled in to listen to some Hendrix and Sabbath and Zeppelin and Purple.

When he was halfway through the bucket of beer, he asked the dog-man what he thought of the music.

"I have never heard its like before," said the dog-man, who lay curled up at his feet.

"It's not exactly hi-fi, but I'm doing me best," said the magus. "Do you like it?"

"I hear poetry in the words and emotion in the voices, and I feel the rhythms in my marrow," said the dog-man.

"Poetry," spat the magus. "What would a dog know about poetry?"

"I cannot make it, but I know it when I hear it."

"Yeah, you might be right," conceded the magus. "But I listen to it anyway." He raised his bottle to his lips, discovered it was empty. Flung it away and took another from the ice.

The dog-man cocked its head. "What is that sound?" is said, when the music grew stranger and louder.

"Guitars," said the magus. "That sound comes from the guitars."

"I know what a guitar is," said the dog-man, "but I have never heard one to cry and scream and growl so."

"We use electricity...power...to distort the sound," said the magus. He mimed a solo on an imaginary instrument, screwing up his face, waggling the fingers of his left hand and strumming fiercely with his right.

"It excites me," said the dog-man. "But it frightens me, too."

The magus drained his bottle in three gulps and then sent it spinning off into the darkness. The sound of it smashing seemed to come from very far away. "I always wanted to learn the guitar. You know that, dog?"

"Why didn't you learn, master?"

"I was too busy being a bad man," said the magus. "And after that, I was too busy being a magician."

He scowled at the record player, and its arm slipped off the record. The music ended with an abrupt, liquid tearing noise.

The dog-man started, but then calmed itself when it saw that the magus was not angry. He looked sad, if anything. "Where will we go next, master?"

The magus plucked another beer from the ice; ran his thumb around the corrugated edge of the bottle-top. "We're here in the Ore-Lands," he said. "I thought we might visit the playwright."

"Will you tell him your story, after all?" asked the dog-man, panting with enthusiasm.

"You will not," said a voice from the darkness.

The dog-man growled low in its throat and rose fluidly to its feet, its cutlass in hand. The magus lowered his beer bottle and looked over his shoulder.

A dozen soldiers emerged from the darkness. They wore heavy plate armour as if it were ordinary clothing, and were armed with an assortment of beautifully forged swords, axes, and halberds.

Their sergeant came forward with its weapon drawn. "Magus."

"G'day," said the magus, trying—with limited success—to sit up in the beanbag. "There's plenty more beer, but I've only got one left that's cold."

The sergeant shook its head grimly. Metallic scrollwork pressed through the skin of its face in high relief, and its hair shone like an oiled rainbow. "Magus," the sergeant said, "I bear a message from the Queen of the Ore-Lands."

"I'm listening."

"You have destroyed one of her Majesty's allies and slain one of her own emissaries," said the sergeant, "but you have also solved a problem of diplomacy for her. My liege would have you know that she considers the accounts balanced. She hopes that you will proceed on your way without visiting harm upon the people of the Ore-Lands."

"All I want is to visit me old mate, Nentril Revallo."

"And then? You think he will write some new skit about you?"

"I just thought..." The magus had not actually thought any further ahead than that. He just wanted to tell his story to someone who would not judge him.

"You thought he would turn your sordid life into some kind of a heroic adventure? Magus, have you *seen* any of Revallo's works?"

"Three," replied the magus. "I liked the cartoon the best."

"Magus, you are a villain," said the sergeant. "You bring

wanton death and destruction wherever you go. Whatever your intentions, this is the only outcome that pleases you. My liege will not have you inflict yourself upon her people."

The magus knew that it was true. He was unsure how he felt about being turned into some character, to prance and stalk about a stage. Even if the playwright did not in some way displease him, the magus knew he would surely find some other excuse to bring the scenario to a violent end. He could envision it already: the stage; the play; Revallo in his triumph…and then he himself, swooping down from the sky to rain vengeance and destruction upon the theatre.

The magus rose to his feet. His hands were empty now, so were his eyes. "Are you threatening me?"

"Her Majesty fears you," replied the sergeant. "If you endanger her subjects she will not rest until your corpse has been cut into pieces too small for the finest blade to part."

The magus smiled. "Tell this queen of yours I like her," he said. "No bullshit, I mean it. I swear, on my honour, that I won't kill anything in her Realm that doesn't try to kill me first."

The magus had never sworn any such a thing before. He had never considered that honour might be a virtue he possessed—for he certainly possessed no other. Yet he meant what he said.

"Then we will trouble you no more." The sergeant bowed its head and backed away.

The magus watched them go. Once they were out of his sight he grunted and looked for the remaining beer.

"Now what?" asked the dog-man.

The magus stared at his bucket of melting ice for a long, long time. Finally, he looked up slowly and moistened his lips. "I believe it's time I introduced meself to the Council of Magi," he said.

13. The Council of the Magi

The Realm of the Magi was remarkable only for its plainness. Rolling hills, lush meadows, dense woods, rushing rivers, cloudy skies. It reminded the magus of drab Olde England, at first, but something about it felt unnatural. Even in the Land of the Faerie, this place seemed strange.

The trees were too evenly spaced. The hills were too uniform of height. The river cut a near-perfect sine wave through the lowest of the valleys. Even the passage of time seemed oddly metered: the magus could feel the seconds tick by, as though a metronome had replaced his heart as the arbiter of his mortal lifespan.

In the geographic centre of the realm stood the City of the Magi; a carefully planned metropolis that was more beautiful and more hideous as any place the magus had yet laid eyes upon. There was arcane significance in every curve and angle; there was power in every thoroughfare and intersection. The city had not been constructed from stone or wood or mud, or any material harvested from the land: its walls were panes of purest magic, and they glittered like a million television screens.

No walls protected the City of the Magi—no fences or barricades or moats—but there were gateways across all of the roads that led down into it.

"Strewth," said the magus, skidding and sliding carelessly down the scree-slope towards the closest of these. The dog-man followed him down with more care and equal speed.

The gateway took the form of two rune-etched columns, which were cut from some lustreless, rain-coloured material. When the magus put his hands upon them he found the columns warm to the touch. There was no actual gate hanging between them, but some unseen force barred the way.

The magus examined the spells that protected the gates, and found them to be intricate, robust, and obscure. It took him all of two minutes to determine that the puzzle was beyond his abilities to solve. He could not fathom the meaning of any of the runes, nor could he make sense of the way they were connected. He could not even determine where the spell drew its power from.

"Dog," he said. "You've been here before, right?"

The dog-man looked at him, but it was not able to respond.

"Any clues?" he asked. "Is there a party-trick door knocker or something I should be looking for?"

The dog-man regarded him mutely.

"Ah, fuck it," said the magus. He drew a key upon the palm of his left hand and jammed his fingers into the gate-spell without regard for the interface it offered. Then he pumped as much power as he could into it until, finally, the lock broke. The gateway yielded, and the magus and the dog-man passed through into the City of the Magi.

Although there was tremendous variation in the size, species, and gender of the black-robed folk who dwelled in the city, there was a uniformity about them that the magus instantly disliked. Their hands were scarred and blackened from the frequent handling of unnatural energies, and they carried themselves with a slightly hunched posture not unlike the magus' own.

The folk paused in their business as the magus and the dog-man passed amongst them. Although he could not see their faces inside their hoods, he could feel their distaste. They knew him for what he was: a vagrant mortal, staggering about in a cloud of his own stinking magic.

The magus did smell pretty ripe, he supposed. He had not bathed since leaving the Ore-Lands.

"Take me to your leader," he demanded. Before he had finished the sentence, he found that he had been transported to another location. The teleport had been so swift that he had not detected any magic acting upon him. Perhaps the Realm of the Magi itself had shifted around him, and he himself had not moved at all.

The council chamber was a vast, polyhedral room walled with mirrors. Those mirrors reflected only abstractions of the events that occurred between them: the councillors' speech notated as music for some impossible orchestra; vector drawings showing the eddying currents of time; mathematical constructs that represented the contents of the room in greater resolution than reality itself.

The Council sat around a large table, shaped like a rimless wheel. Each Councillor sat in a heavy marble throne at the end of its thirteen spokes.

The magus scratched an armpit and cleared his throat. "G'day."

"Magus," said the Speaker for the Council. "We welcome you to our session. If you have a petition to submit or a grievance to voice, you may speak it now."

The magus drew back his shoulders and folded his arms. "Well, I do. Are you the ones who sent me the dog?"

"The circumstances under which you sought refuge in this world are known to us," said the Speaker. "We thought a friend would help you settle into this new place."

"Charity," spat the magus. The dog-man stood proud at his side, cutlass in hand, glowering at the Councillors. It did not growl; its master was speaking.

"It was a welcoming gift to a new colleague."

"You were trying to placate me."

"That was our mistake," said the Speaker. "For you are known to be an implacable foe. But, friend magus, we bear you no enmity."

"Course you don't."

"Have you any further business, now that you have thanked us for our hospitality?" asked the Speaker.

"I do," said the magus, hooking his thumbs in his belt. "I'm told you arseholes are the most powerful sorcerers in the Realms."

"That is true."

"Who's the best among you?"

"I am," said the Speaker.

"Right," said the magus. "Well, if you're that good, you already know that I'm here to kill you."

"Only one who sits on the Council of Magi may challenge the Speaker to duel arcane."

"That's bullshit."

"That is the law."

The magus scowled. "What do I have to do to get a seat?"

"Should a seat become available," said the Speaker, "you must demonstrate to us a form of magic we do not have in our recorded lore."

"Alright," said the magus. "This is something I call 'powdermancy'." He drew back his shirt and drew the Desert Eagle from its holster, cocking, aiming and firing the weapon in the same motion.

The trigger fell; his spell took; the spring caused the hammer to strike the firing pin. The pin and the bullet blipped momentarily into the mortal plane, just long enough for the black powder to ignite. The bullet exploded from the muzzle of the weapon. Gases expelled by the combustion slammed back the slide and chambered a new round. The ejected shell casing spun across the room. The spent spell-rune flickered brightly. The .50 calibre round smashed through the windpipe of the councillor who sat immediately to the Speaker's right.

The room fell quiet as the reverberations of the gunshot faded. The magus vaulted onto the table and strode to the dead councillor's place, the pistol still in his hand. He kicked the councillor's corpse out of its seat and settled himself in its place. The dog-man came to stand behind him.

"Seems there's a place on the council after all," he said. "And a candidate who meets the criteria."

"I cannot fathom your quarrel with us," said the Speaker. "We welcomed you here with anonymous gifts and open arms."

"Well," said the magus, putting his boots on the table, "I come by me magic the hard way. No teachers, no spellbooks, no nothing. When the Conclave back home told me I had to answer to them, I told them where they could shove their Code of Practice and their Annual Fees and their fucken Journal of the Mystical Arts..."

"This Council maintains cordial relations with the Conclave."

"Yeah, I figured," said the magus. "I didn't get on with those bastards, trying to tell me how to do me magic, so I come here to Fairyland...and what do I find? Another bunch of wankers who want to tell me what to do."

"You will find that our governance is far less...invasive... than the Conclave's," said the Speaker.

"Not the point," said the magus. "Fuck you and fuck your Council and fuck your politics and fuck your gifts. I don't care if you were born with more sorcery in one arse-hair than I'll ever have—I hate you and I'm going to fucken kill you."

"Ah," said the Speaker. "Now I truly have your measure."

"Twelve inches," said the magus. "If you start at the base, not the balls."

"You hate us because we were given what you had to work for."

The magus bit his lip. "No," he said. "I hate you because you think it makes you better than me." The magus tried to imitate the Councillors' bassy tones, but fell short by almost a full octave.

The Speaker nodded gravely. "Alright. I am prepared to forgo the ceremonies of investiture and declare you now a full member of the Council of the Magi of the Realms of the Land of the Faerie. Councillor Magus, I accept your challenge to duel arcane."

"Too bloody right."

"Do you require any strictures on the conduct of said duel? Do you want invigilators to adjudicate it or notaries to record the outcome?"

"Nuh," said the magus, grinning. "No rules, no umpires, no cameras. Just you, me, and a big fat arse-kicking."

"Name the place and the time," said the Speaker, "And we will duel to the death."

14. Godzilla

The magus made camp just outside the City of the Magi, but he did not pitch a tent or light a fire. He boiled up some rice, the way his father used to prepare it, and conjured a slab of XXXX lager, which his father used to drink. He devoured the rice with his fingers, and then proceeded to drink his way through the full twenty-four cans of beer.

The dog-man sat in its terrier form and observed this silently. When the magus was so intoxicated that he could neither stand nor see it became a man and addressed him. "Are you sure this is a good idea?"

"Fuck-oath-bloody-*hell* I am!" bellowed the magus. He collapsed onto his back.

"The Speaker for the Council is unmatched anywhere in the Realms of the Land," said the dog-man. "Or in the mortal world."

"Eggs-bloody-zactly!" replied the magus, propping himself up with his hands. Whatever else he tried to say was inaudible over his panting breath.

The dog-man tried another tack. "I don't understand how you expect to profit from this venture, an you prove successful."

"Profit! Loss! Fucken accountants!" roared the magus, swinging his fists at the empty air. He fell over again.

"Do you intend to die?" asked the dog-man. "Is that what you seek?"

The magus, lying flat on his back, grinned like a skull.

"Nuh, mate," he said. His grin parted and his tongue skinned the edges of his teeth. "I don't deserve to be put out of me misery."

"Yet that is the likely outcome of tomorrow's confrontation."

The magus shook his head. "Nah," he said, "Only thing that can kill a monster is a hero or bigger monster… But there's no such things as heroes, and I'm the biggest fucken monster there is."

"Aye?" said the dog-man.

"I'm the god of monsters," said the magus. "I'm God-fucken-zilla."

The magus began to laugh. His guffaws shook his frame, flexed his skinny chest like a blacksmith's bellows. He laughed and laughed, and he did not stop until his mouth filled with spit and he spluttered and choked. The magus rolled onto his distended belly, threw up, and fell unconscious.

The magus had scheduled the duel for dawn the following morning, but the Speaker had to wait until mid-afternoon for him to rouse himself.

The magus had already divested himself of his previous night's dinner, but he still found reserves of food to vomit. When the magus spat a final mouthful of bile and wiped his chin on his sleeve the Speaker approached him. "You look poorly. Would you like to postpone the combat?"

"Course not." The magus cleared the grot from his throat and repeated himself more clearly. "Course not." He smoothed the sweaty hair back from his face and shaded his eyes with one hand.

"Are you certain?" asked the Speaker.

"Yes, I'm bloody well certain!" The magus shambled to his feet and drew a knife from under his vomit-stained t-shirt.

"Are you ready, then?" asked the Speaker.

"Yeah," said the magus, the knife hanging loose in his fingers. The runes he had scratched onto the blade the night before showed silver through the black tungsten coating. He spread his feet to steady himself, wobbled at the knees, and adjusted his stance again. The magus spat one more time. "Let's get the show on the road."

"Very well," said the Speaker, lowering its head and extending its hands from its sleeves. Its fists opened until its improbably long and supple fingers were fully extended.

Whitelight mojo crackled about the Speaker as it drew power to itself. Ley-lines snapped taut and ruptured. The Speaker had his offense already prepared, and his spell leapt to life as soon as the circuit was complete.

The magus stood his ground.

The skies clouded over, groaning with thunder; slashing at him with lightning and pounding him with ice. Screaming winds bludgeoned and clawed at him. A phalanx of armoured demons swept down upon him on hellburnt wings, and the Land itself yawned open a rock-toothed, soil-dripping maw.

The magus stood, transfixed by the huge and intricate network of spell structures the Speaker had built. The Speaker wanted him to look at it; wanted to show him the extent of its power, the depth and breadth of its art.

It was a sight to behold.

The magus squinted at the spells and raised his puny dagger. He made no effort to understand the Speaker's working. It was too much for him to comprehend at once. He let his eyes lose focus, let the components blur together until all he could see was the broadest shape of the system.

The Speaker held its burning hands out wide. Cords of power writhed like serpents from its fingers. The magus closed one eye, aimed, and threw the knife.

The blade sailed over the Speaker, past its protective shields, and lodged in the heart of its showcase spell.

The storm collapsed. The forks of lightning earthed-out harmlessly; the razored hail melted to slush; the wind howled impotently as it gusted away. The demons tumbled out of formation as their own wings set them alight. The fissure in the ground fell in on itself, coming apart in great damp chunks.

The Speaker tripped on the hem of its robes as it stumbled backwards. Its hood fell back, revealing to the magus a bald head with tiny, unlined features.

The magus allowed the Speaker to scrabble to its knees before he swung a boot heel into its face. Its jaw shattered. Teeth and bone splinters and pulped flesh hung from its ruined face, but there was not a lot of blood.

The magus extended his right hand and the black knife flew into his waiting fingers. He knelt beside the Speaker, held it down with one hand, and put the point of the blade against its sternum. He pushed down on the weapon until the hilt lay square against the Speaker's breastbone.

It was like sticking a fork into a toaster. The Speaker's art coursed up the magus' arm and into his brain like electricity. His back arched and his head snapped back as the current of pure knowledge oscillated through him. The buckle of his belt glowed red hot.

It was too much for the magus to absorb entire, but he held onto the knife until his fingers were blistered and cracked. The magus slumped over, his breath shuddering in his chest. The Speaker for the Council of the Magi lay dead before him, a plume of smoke rising from inside its hood.

The magus arose, blood dripping from his spasming fingers. He turned his back on the City of the Magi and closed his eyes.

The dog-man crept up behind him. "You are victorious, master."

The magus did not turn to look at the dog-man. "I'm not your master."

"You are my master, now and forevermore."

"I'm not your master," said the magus. "Fuck off."

"I am a dog, and I must have a master."

"I told you to fuck off."

"Please. I must have a human master, and there is no other to be had in all the Realms."

When the magus raised his head, his blue eyes had turned black. The dog-man shrank to the form of the terrier.

"If a dog has no master it must have a pack," whined the terrier, "but I am the only dog in all the Realms."

"Go," said the magus.

The terrier crawled towards him on its belly.

"*Go,*" said the magus.

The terrier looked up at him with wide, white-rimmed eyes.

The magus swung his foot at it. It squealed as his boot connected with its ribs.

The terrier picked itself up and turned to face the magus again; growling, then whining, then growling as different instincts seized it.

"*GO!*" shouted the magus, swinging another kick.

The terrier yelped and scooted out of the way. It turned to regard him one more time before it fled.

15. The Poison Sea

The magus had the power to instantly relocate himself to anywhere he desired. He had the power to walk between the seconds. He had the power to travel to any world he could imagine. He had the power to fly. But there was no place that he wanted to go.

Alone and on foot he wandered the Realms, for days or months or years—the magus did not care to count them. Nor did he care to count the miles: The Land was a continent unbounded by ocean; a planet unconstrained by the geometry of a sphere; a world where distance was every bit as relative as time. He walked for years or decades or centuries; and his deeds grew ever darker and stranger, and ever more bereft of meaning.

In time, the magus tired of wanton destruction, and sought some new endeavour to occupy himself. Something difficult and hideous and contrary to the natural state of the world he inhabited. Something that was beyond reason; even there, on the wild fringes of the most impossible of Realms. Some feat that could not possibly succeed.

The magus planned his new enterprise carefully. His project would require massive amounts of power as well as a degree of skill that he knew was beyond him. Still, he had nothing better to do, and his heart had become set upon it. The magus had never considered that his heart could do anything more than its nominal function of pumping blood through his veins, so he took this as an omen.

The magus began by tearing a hole in the Faerie world; rending the Land so deeply that the Abyss itself gazed up at him through the gap—but he did not have time for staring contests. Deftly, he cut and fitted a new piece of real estate over the wound. He pinned it down with jagged black cliffs and stitched the new Realm into place, kneading it into a vast basin and sealing it with molten rock.

Once he was satisfied that there were no gaps, the magus filled the basin with a poisonous black brine. He drove rivers outwards from it and joined them to the rivers that ran through the true Realms of the Land.

The magus paused for a beer and a cigarette. He stood upon the razored cliffs and looked down about his filthy new sea. "Fuck," he said. "Fuck you all."

The Poison Sea did not respond. It lay quiescent and flat in its bed, reflecting nothing up to the bruised and bloodied sky that the magus had cruelly stretched over it.

The magus flicked away the cigarette butt and bent to draw some runes upon the surface of the water.

The brine rippled and frothed as the magus taught it to ebb and flow. It was not an easy lesson to teach, for the water had to make its own tides in the absence of a proper moon. Still, the magus was adamant, and eventually the Poison Sea learned to do as he bade.

The magus cultivated blind and ravenous things to live beneath those uncertain waves. Hideous fish creatures, all jaws and spines and tendrils, abhorred of light and land and air. In the poisoned depths they thrived; preying upon each other; breeding greater horrors yet.

The magus felt something alien, then. Something that was not like hate or loathing or jealousy. Something greater than satisfaction, but less than joy. Pride, he supposed. He swore and spat and retired to his tent to finish the six-pack he had started at breakfast.

When he awoke, the magus found that his mind was racing with designs for merfolk and sea goblins, corals and ships and submarine cities. Even through the hangover he could barely contain his excitement. He stumbled back out to the edge of the cliffs to gaze once more upon the thing that he had made.

But the sea was gone.

While the magus had rested, the rivers had turned away from his island of water, and the Land choked down its poisoned contents. The sky had split and parted and the suns and stars of the true Realms had claimed the remaining night. Nothing remained of the magus' work but salt-cracked wastes and crumbling bones.

The magus surveyed the ruins of his work in silence. He had nothing left to say.

On the cliffs above that dried-out seabed, the magus raised a tower. He did not build it from stone and wood and mortar, but cast it whole from rune and ritual and will. And the tower rose up; dark and jagged; so slimed with evil that it stained the very skies it broached.

The magus sealed himself inside the tower and there he remained, with only his hatred of all things to sustain him. And though he did not age another day in all the countless years that remained of his life, the magus remained mortal forever.

Book 3
Kith and Kin

1. Legacy

The mortal thought that she was the last of the line, until she heard him mentioned in her father's will. She had an uncle, and he was still alive.

She had inherited everything, with only one proviso: the estate would continue to pay a monthly stipend for the treatment of this mysterious relative. Bank records showed that her father had paid the fee every month for twenty years, and that he had taken on that responsibility once his own father had died.

She spent the rest of the week in her father's old Grimsby flat, sifting through piles of ancient paper documents. Her search yielded but a single piece of evidence that this uncle did, in fact exist: an old colour photograph showing her father's extended family standing in front of the Tower of London. The family smiled stiffly, squinting into the sun, the Traitor's Gate standing in its arch behind them.

Her father knelt in the front of the photograph with the other children. He was wearing a school uniform: short pants, knee socks, and a collared shirt. His tie was askew. On the back of the photograph, which was dated 1994, someone had written the names of everyone in the shot. All of them were now dead; and their children, and their grandchildren. All of them, except for this uncle of hers.

He stood in the back row and to the left of the others, slightly detached from the group. He looked to be in his late twenties, although he might have been eighteen and he might have been thirty-eight. Average height and build. Clean-shaven and handsome, though he owed his looks more to a lack of blemishes than to pleasingly formed features. He seemed pale, though he was no fairer than the others; shadowed, though the sun shone as directly upon him.

There was nothing else.

The mortal made a call to the hospice and asked to speak with her uncle, who she identified with his patient number. She could not bring herself to speak his name aloud.

The receptionist also referred to him by his number when she replied that he was not available. She asked that he return her call when he became so. The receptionist informed her it might be a while—he had been in a coma for almost three decades and showed no sign of rousing. She had to ask twice before the receptionist would admit that her uncle was permitted visitors.

The mortal took the tube to Victoria Station, and then a train out to Bournemouth. She hired a flyer from an agent near the pier and took it up. It was a cheap, new model Suzuki: zippy and economical and a little rough on the stick. She swung east, buzzing over the Old Harry Rocks and then dropping into the steady stream of traffic heading north. Salisbury and Stonehenge were up that way. Her destination lay somewhere beyond them.

The hospice had originally been housed in a big-windowed and be-chimneyed Victorian mansion. The old building itself was now used exclusively by the administration, while the medical facilities and housing had been moved into the newer structures that had bloomed up around it like fat concrete toadstools.

The mortal introduced herself at the front desk. After about forty-five minutes, an orderly in a white uniform came to escort her to a toadstool at the far north-western corner of the complex. The air outside smelled of ozone and clipped grass. She saw nobody coming or going from any of the buildings.

The orderly opened the airlock-style entryway to her uncle's ward and led her inside. Handrails embedded with fluorescent strips ran along each wall. Lines on the floor marked out routes to the rec room, the dining hall, the therapy suites, and the showers. There were no signs indicating the way out.

The orderly located the correct dormitory and they moved down amongst the rows of skeletal steel beds, until they came to her uncle. The orderly said: "I hope you brought something to read. I'll be back for you in half an hour."

Her uncle lay on his back. The blankets had been pulled up to his armpits and his arms lay exposed. Tubes were needled into his veins. Monitors showed his vital signs to be measured and steady. The bedclothes were neat and unrumpled; the bed had been made over him and he had not moved since.

He had not aged visibly since the photograph had been taken, nearly thirty years earlier. He looked well, for a man who had been in a coma for most of that time. Thin, but not emaciated. He looked rested.

"Hi," she said, coming to stand beside him. "I'm your niece."

She was not surprised when he opened his eyes. He sat up and turned his head towards her smoothly. "Hello," he said, with not even a hint of sleep congestion in his voice. "I'm your uncle."

"Your brother's dead," she said.

"I expect so," he replied. "He must have been quite old."

She stared at him. "I didn't know you even existed."

"I barely did."

"You haven't aged at all."

"I can explain that," he said. "If you're truly interested."

"I am."

Her uncle plucked the catheters from his arm and freed himself of the life support machinery, which immediately began to bleep with alarm. He drew back the blanket, swung his feet off the bed, and stood up. He did not stretch.

He looked around the room at the beds, the machinery, the other patients. When his eyes fell on the cabinet beside his bed, he bent and opened it. Inside was a set of pressed but musty clothes, a pair of scuffed old army boots, and a small canvas rucksack. He looked inside the bag and smiled.

The orderly came sprinting back into the room. Her uncle looked up at him and smiled. "Hello."

The orderly skidded to a stop. "Did you…were you… weren't you just—"

"I have risen."

"But…you were…"

"My great niece and I require a place in which to discuss some family matters. Would you be so kind as to find us an empty room?"

"I, uh, yes…" said the orderly. "I should call a doctor."

Her uncle reached out and shut off the bleating life support machinery.

"You should find us a quiet room," he said.

The orderly took them to an unused examination room. It was furnished with two chairs, a desk, and a high bed. A bench with a sink lay against one wall. Her uncle sat on the chair beside the desk; she sat on the bed.

She had a lot to ask him. She wanted to know about her family and her father. She wanted to know why she had never heard his name before. But the question she asked was: "Tell me your story."

"It'll take some time."

"If I'm bored I'll stop you."

"No," he said. "Once I have begun you will not interrupt me. Afterwards, I will permit you no questions."

"Fine," she said. "Whatever."

And so the mortal told his mortal niece how he had sought the most beautiful thing in all the worlds. He explained his sojourn in the forest and his transition into the Land of the Faerie. He spoke of the beasts and beings he had met; of the wonders and horrors that he had witnessed. He told her of the magus, and the dog-man. He told her how he had come to find that Zelioliah, the Queen of the Warriors, was the most beautiful thing in all of the worlds. His voice remained low and calm and without emotion, though his eyes shone with pride when he told his niece how he had made the Queen his own.

As he spoke, the mortal showed her the souvenirs he had kept, which he had carelessly tipped out of the rucksack and onto the bed: the skull of a badger-like animal; a small silver lighter; an artificial hand made of glass and sprung steel; a ring of purple metal; an obsidian mask; an emerald embedded in a sliver of impossibly soft leather; a straight razor.

"What'll you do now?" she asked him.

"I will remain here," he said, carefully packing his trophies back into the rucksack. "It's your turn to quest."

"What am I supposed to quest for?"

"I can't determine that for you."

"Well, I can't think of anything."

"Surely there is something you desire," he replied. "A truth, a vision, a weapon. A queendom. A cause. Wealth. Power. Love. Justice. Vengeance."

"There's nothing I want that I won't get eventually," she replied. "If I work hard. If I meet my obligations."

"Some would envy you your life," he said.

"And you?"

"I do not stand in judgment."

"But you think I need to go on a quest."

"Even if you don't know what you are seeking, if you do not seek it you may as well lie cold upon a slab." He looked at the door, in the direction of the bed he had occupied for so many comatose years.

"Yeah, I've been meaning to ask you about that," she said. "What exactly drove you to run off to Never-Never Land intent on killing the prettiest fairy queen you could find?"

"I told you I would answer no questions," he said. "You must find your own answers. You must take your own quest."

"Are you actually *listening* to what you're saying?"

"Certainly. Are you?"

She made a noise in her throat. "I'll…I'll think about it."

"You will indeed."

"What about you? Are you going to go back into…into the world? This world, I mean. Or…the other?"

"There are many other worlds," he said. "Although the Faerie Land is, perhaps, the most popular."

"You know what I meant."

"My quest is over," he said. "Return to me when your quest is done…if ever you complete it. I would like to hear of it. In the meantime, I think I will sleep again."

"Pleasant dreams," she said. She wished him anything but.

2. Raising the Tree

The mortal returned to her quarters in the East End and retired to her sleeping web without taking a meal. The alarm woke her at 0600, cleaned, clothed, and rested. She left the house without breaking her fast and rode the tube to the office.

The inertia compensators on the lifts were still broken—or they had fallen into disrepair again while she had been away—so she took the stairs up to her floor. She did not trust the old-fashioned cable elevators.

At 0823 the mortal emerged from the dank stairwell into the artificial brilliance of the cube farm. She was early; her workmates would not arrive until 0900. Blinking, she went directly to her workspace. She sat down at her node, spread her hands on the interface plates, and got to work.

First, she raised a forest; allowing the system to populate it with random species of trees, spaced at a medium density. Then she swept an empty blue sky above it. She set the climate to British-Standard, and all other parameters to Earth-Normal. She filled the forest with British-Native fauna, and she cleared a narrow path through the trees. At the end of the path, in the middle of the forest, she drew up the bedrock and cut the vegetation and topsoil away from it.

The software she was using did not have sufficient intelligence to model for her a tree of indeterminate species. Reckoning that her deficit of botanical knowledge was all she needed, she set about manufacturing one from scratch.

She began with an upright cylinder, from which she extended limbs using a fractal branching algorithm. She truncated the structure when she judged that the out-growing bulb was of sufficient size, and applied a variety of transforms and filters to warp the hard-edged shape into a more natural one. She coloured it brown, mapped the first tree-bark texture in the library, and finished by scattering tiny green diamond shapes upon it to give the semblance of foliage.

It was 0833. Her stomach growled. She hadn't eaten since she'd left for the hospice on the previous day.

She pressed down hard onto the interface plates and they yielded beneath her fingers. Machinery gently enveloped her hands; sensor coils crept up her arms and over her shoulders. Spider-tendrils settled in place over her spinal column, her cranium. The tendrils of the virtual immersion apparatus had been warmed to body temperature, but she nonetheless shivered as she closed her eyes…

…and found herself high in the foliage of a virtual forest, looking down upon the crude shape of her avatar. Virtual birds sung to her in surround-sound. When she moved her avatar, virtual critters fled before its virtual footsteps. Maintaining a third person viewpoint, she located the pathway quickly and sent her avatar jogging along it. It did not take long to reach the fractal tree.

The tree looked odd and unnatural, even amongst the virtual trees in the virtual world. She had built it from imagination, not from observation, and she had been clumsy with the tools she had used: she was a programmer, not an artist.

The mortal descended into first person and walked her avatar around the tree three times. On completion of the third circuit she found that a small aperture had opened at the base of it, where two roots had split the trunk around a spur of rock.

She opened her eyes and withdrew from the virtual world, choking on the recycled office air. The apparatus whipped free as she tore her hands out of the interface.

0834. She looked up. The maze of bench-tops and cubicles extended away in all directions, sectioned up with low, blue-carpeted partitions. There was nobody else in the room.

She set her jaw, closed her eyes, and let her hands fall back into the interface. Once more the virtuality enveloped her, and she stood before the distorted and unfinished tree. Its surface was tattooed to look like rough bark, though it was smooth to the touch. Limbs branched from their parents like crystals from a block of salt. The leaves were perfect, two-dimensional green diamonds. They did not grow from twigs, but were embedded in the branches like shrapnel from exploded munitions.

The aperture at the base of the tree was still there.

There were a number of ways in which she could proceed. Like her uncle, she could climb the tree and hope that another opening would appear for her there: a spiralling silver chute that would bear her down into Faerie Land like a slide at a waterpark. But that seemed undignified. She did not fancy the notion of sliding down into another world on her arse.

Of course, if dignity was her greatest worry she could unplug herself, de-allocate the nonsense forest, and get started on the backlog of email that had accumulated while she had been out of the office. After breakfast and half a dozen coffees.

She decided to scale-down her avatar and simply walk through the aperture.

3. The Star Below

The inside of the tree was black. She had not specified any features or sources of illumination inside its trunk, but there should still have been light shining in from behind her. When she turned around, she found that the aperture was gone.

She grunted and added a small, asterisk-shaped beacon to her avatar. It hovered a foot above her virtual head, casting a blue-white light about her in all directions. The ground beneath her was flat, hard stone. No ceiling or walls were visible.

She started walking. Her virtual feet were soundless on the virtual stone floor. Presently she saw a small light in the distance. A tiny flame, such as a candle or a match might give off. Or a small, silver lighter.

She went towards the flame. "Hello, Uncle," she called. "It's me."

The light moved on and she followed it for what seemed like hours, but was probably only minutes. Her Head Up Display showed the date and time in characters she did not recognize. The on-board maps refused to recognize that she had travelled any distance within the Tree of Indeterminate Species.

The flame-light went out.

She stood there, staring towards the place she had last seen it. Soon she heard footsteps; heavy boots clocking towards her on the hard stone. Her uncle's boots, she supposed. She opened her mouth to call out to him again. To her strange uncle, who had gone travelling in an imaginary world, seeking to destroy the most beautiful thing in the world.

Panic seized her. Although she knew that her avatar could not be harmed, she turned and fled. The footsteps followed her, beating out a measured and steady walking gait, neither gaining nor losing ground as she pitched headlong through the darkness.

The asterisk.

No wonder she could not lose her pursuer: he was following the giant glowing star she had set above her head. She extinguished it and turned, and ran on…but not for long. She had gone less than a dozen steps when she spotted a light. It was the aperture in the wall of the tree through which she had entered.

She jogged through the gap and emerged in the sunshine of another land. This was not an environment that she had programmed herself, though she immediately recognized it from her uncle's confabulations.

She stepped down into Faerie Land and wondered, for the first time, if she had actually gone mad.

4. A Surfeit of Wrath

The Warrior Queen had risen through the ranks in the same way as every other warrior, but when her mother was slain there was no question that the Queenship would fall to her. She was the strongest and the most skilled of her peers; the quickest and the most intelligent. She, like her mother before her, was the first among warriors, for blood will out.

Yet the Queen of the Warriors knew that she was fated for more than her mere birthright. Her mother had fought and governed and procreated until she died of violence, but the new Warrior Queen knew that her life had a different shape. Her life was a story, and that story was her own.

For this story, the Warrior Queen would need new tools and traits and knowledge. She did not know exactly where this story would lead her, but she did know that its theme was 'vengeance'.

The Warrior Queen went first to the eldest of her generals for counsel. She thrust a spear into the dirt and sat cross-legged in front of it with her weapons arranged about her, in the way that was proper for the warrior folk. Her pennons snapped and whistled in the wind as she faced him across the campfire.

The General sat beneath his own pennons and inclined his head. "So formal an address, my Queen?"

"Yes," she said. "This kind of story requires a formal beginning."

"The story has already begun," said the General. "But you are the Queen, and so formally we shall proceed."

"Tell me what you know of my mother's death."

"I know only that she was slain by a mortal."

"What do you know of this mortal?"

"Rumours, lies and half-truths," said the General. "There is no good intelligence on this matter."

"The truth can be found amongst rumours and lies," the Warrior Queen replied. "One must not look at the shape of them, but rather, one must discern the shape they obscure."

The General regarded her quietly. "That is not a warrior's wisdom."

"It was not a warrior who murdered my mother."

"True enough."

"I will take whatever wisdom I can, if it will help me find the mortal who brought my mother low. What else do you know?"

"I have heard tell of a mortal magus that once stalked the land, and who slew many creatures, both humble and mighty. He destroyed the Queen of the Mountains, but he failed in his attempt to kill the Tree Queen. The Ore Queen somehow drove him from her Realm without conflict. All of this took place before your mother was murdered. I have heard nothing about any mortal since then."

"A mortal man slew my mother," said the Warrior Queen, "And no reprisal was exacted."

"Yes." The General was known to have been close to the Warrior Queen's mother. He might have been reckoned the new Queen's father, had the warrior people arranged their society in families rather than combat units.

"This must be rectified."

"An you designate the field of battle, my legions and I will be happy to challenge any foes on Majesty's behalf," said the General. "But…locating a single mortal, who has surely returned to his own world? That is beyond my power."

"Whose power, then, extends to the mortal realm?"

"The court ruled by Titania would holiday there in times

past," said the General. "But she was too free with her name, and she is gone now; her people dispersed."

"Who else has power beyond the Realms of the Land?"

"Few, I expect, save the Council of the Magi."

"The mortal I seek was himself a magus," said the Warrior Queen. "It is fitting that I take my grievances before the Council."

"May those who would oppose you fall before your wrath," said the General.

"I hope they will be numerous," said the Warrior Queen, gathering her weapons and rising to her feet. "For I have a surfeit of wrath to spend."

5. The Bad Puppy

Sired by a sailor and born to a whore, El Cachorro Malo reared himself on the streets of San Salvador.

The Bad Little Dog once had another name, but he had forgotten it by the time he was old enough to understand its importance. Malo earned his new appellation by his deeds. He lived in poverty and hunger and ignorance, fighting for every morsel or scrap; and somehow the Bad Little Dog grew to be hardy and strong.

When Malo had grown strong enough…survived long enough…something changed in him. Some desire he did not understand: it was not hunger, or thirst, or lust; it was something that went beyond the scarred flesh in which he lived. Malo wanted knowledge.

Though Malo could not read, he knew how to tell numbers from letters. After some experimentation, he discovered that each numeral corresponded to an ordinal number that he knew by sound and by value. Larger numbers required combinations of numerals to represent them. From his analysis of these combinations he learned to add and subtract, multiply and divide. Numeracy came easily to Malo, but literacy was another matter.

Malo gathered up a pile of advertising leaflets, propaganda flyers, magazines, and newspapers. He made lists of the symbols he found there, and he stared at them for hours. He squinted to blur the letters, trying to glean clues from the shapes of the words and sentences. It did not occur to him that some of the characters might belong to different alphabets. He did not know that there might be languages other than the one he spoke and thought. He did not think to ask for help, for nobody had ever helped him before.

Malo invented one system after another, trying to find the meaning codified in written language. He looked to the passage of the stars, to the flight of birds, to the roll of a die... but no matter how hard he worked at it, his constructions always cancelled down to an empty silence.

Malo did not learn to read, but he learned much about language in the process. Language bound his thoughts to his deeds, his memories to his mind; the world outside to the world within. Malo came to hate it—this structure that interposed itself between his senses and his consciousness. It enslaved him; it concealed its truths from him; it bound him to a life of squalor and misfortune.

Malo turned the full weight of his anger and ignorance and will upon it and he grappled with it until something finally gave way. Finally, he broke the hold that language held over him—but that was not all that was broken.

Malo did not think himself insane. He did not know what insanity was...but his capacity to reason and to speak had been damaged, and so had his ability to distinguish wakefulness with his dreams. Malo needed help, and there was only one person to whom he could turn.

He had not seen his mother for half his lifetime, but he had no difficulty finding her. Malo had a sense for it now: for discerning identity, no matter how hidden in context. He found her living in an alley; diseased and frail, halfway starved and three quarters mad. She looked up at him with recognition and fear, and pity. Mad though she was, she was versed in the secret wisdom of shamans and whores.

He fell to his knees beside her. "Mama," he said. "Mama. Help me."

"What has happened to you, my son?"

"I have broken something."

As she looked upon him she felt it; in her ears; in her

breast. "I see what is wrong with you, Malo, but I cannot cure it."

"Mama. Help me."

"Perhaps your father can help you," she said. "It is unlikely, but I know of no other."

"My father?"

"Your father."

The first time she spoke the word, Malo learned its concept. The second time, he knew that such a one existed, in relationship to his own being. The third time, Malo knew the *man*. His father had come from some faraway place, and, after siring him, had moved on to some place further still. His father had power. His father…maybe…could help him.

Malo rose to his feet.

"Stay with me, son," said his mother. "Stay, just a while."

"Your son," he said.

"Yes, Malo. You are my son."

He thought about it for a while. "What is my name, mama?"

"You are Malo."

"I am called Malo, but what is my real name?"

She bowed her head. "I have forgotten."

"I am not your son."

"You're right, Malo," she said. She looked at him one more time. "You are your father's boy, and you always will be."

6. California

It took Malo a week to scrape together the dollars for a bus fare to Guatemala. From there he went north, to the Mexican border, and crossed that nation on foot. He was a city boy, and it was difficult for him to scavenge in the countryside, but he was used to hunger and privation and utterly immune to misery. He had a goal, now; a quest; and that was more comforting to him than fresh food or a warm embrace.

Malo entered the United States of America through a sewer pipe somewhere outside of El Paso.

North of the border it was easier to survive. He walked; he rode in truck beds; once he even sat inside a car. He slept outside, in ditches and hedges, barns and outhouses, alleys and crawlspaces. Those he met pitied him, but he was fierce enough to elicit fear as well. He made no friends, but he made no enemies, either.

His father's spoor became stronger as he drew closer to California, and so did Malo's own affliction. Bad things followed in his wake: power outages, plagues of madness, outbreaks of disease, sprees of violence. He did not know if this was his fault or his father's, and he did not care. He would just keep on walking until he found what he was looking for.

He was not yet thirteen years old.

7. High in a Tower

Not so far away, in a tower hidden amongst many others like itself, the innermost circle of the Conclave was gathered to assembly. All of its officers were present, in spirit if not in person. When each member had found their place at the oval table, the Chairman called the meeting to order. First, he recapitulated the minutes of their previous meeting, and then he called upon each of the officers to report on their domains.

The Pyromancer spoke of solar cells and volcanoes and satellites and perdition. The Psychopomp told about madness and dreams and rock'n'roll and breakfast cereal. The Captain Above and Below spoke of seabirds and shipping lanes and submarines and stars. The Bitch of the South informed the Conclave about icecaps and ozone and whaling vessels and missile tests. The Greenest Man sang about jungles and forests and drugs and chainsaws. The Shadowed One whispered his thoughts of demons and death and presidents and popes.

When it was his turn to speak, the Prince of the New Worlds clasped his hands across his belly and said: "I have an intruder in my domain, and I believe that he warrants the attention of the Conclave." His voice was rich, and jingled like money.

"An intruder?" demanded the Chairman. "Your domain is peopled entirely by intruders."

"This one's different," said the Prince.

"Show us," bade the Chairman.

They sat in silence while the Prince conjured images and stated his case.

Eventually, the Shadowed One spoke. "He is only a child." His voice was made of sounds stolen from past utterances, issued by other people. "Why should we fear him?"

The Captain examined a strand of seaweed that was entwined in his beard. "There's something familiar about this boy."

"His father," emitted the Psychopomp, without moving his lips.

The Bitch flexed her fingers, which were tipped with icicles. "The Australian."

"You have *got* to be shitting me," said the Prince.

They pondered this for long minutes.

"He must be destroyed," said the Pyromancer, his fiery tongue bright behind his charred and soot-stained teeth.

"As we destroyed his father?" said the Greenest Man, shaking his dreadlocks.

"Our failed action against the Australian cost us many lives and far too much power," said the Chairman. "I would not repeat that mistake."

The Shadowed One hissed by drawing the sound from the room. He had been Chairman when the attack on the Conclave had ordered the Australian's death.

"Yet we succeeded in driving him away," emitted the Psychopomp. "Can we not send his spawn after him?"

"The Faerie Council of the Magi is still angry about the damage the Australian has caused to the Realms," said the Chairman. "To send the boy after him would have serious consequences."

"Can we not simply make him whole again?" asked the Greenest Man. "Reassemble the pieces and put him back in his box?"

"No," emitted the Psychopomp. "He was never whole in the first place."

"Then what?" said the Chairman. "What can we do with him?"

"We flush him," said the Captain. "Below the depths, beyond the skies."

"Let us cast him into the abyss that lies between all of the many, many worlds," whispered the Shadowed One. "I second the motion."

"The motion is passed," said the Chairman of the Conclave. "The Abyss will have him."

8. The Abyss

The Abyss was an infinite vacuum that was filled entirely with nothing, but it was not empty.

There was no ground beneath Malo's feet, and no wind on his skin. There was no light in his eyes or sound in his ears. There was no vertigo, no sense of motion or time. There was no air to breathe, but he did not need to breathe it for there was neither life there for him to live, nor death for him to pass into. There was nothing but Malo, alone in the darkness.

There were no referents, no symbols; there was no language to give the world shape and there were no artefacts from which to create one, but Malo did not need language to maintain his consciousness. Language was made of lies, but all was truth to him—and there was one truth that he sought above all others.

His father.

Though his prison had neither walls nor floor nor ceiling, and there was no direction out, there was yet a goal to be attained.

Malo started to climb.

9. The Swordsbeast

When the mortal emerged from the Tree she found that she was no longer located in the simulation she had raised. Meadowlands sloped gently away from her in all directions; a river meandered past on her left. On her right there stood a forest of bare, black-skinned trees.

The Tree of Indeterminate Species itself looked better from this world's vantage. Her version had been a sketch, but this one was a finished painting. Still, it was disconcertingly similar to the approximation she'd built.

A beast came around the tree with an enormous sword in each of its monstrous hands. It wore leather trousers and a coat scaled with metal disks that left its arms bare. Those arms were long and knotty with striated muscle—surely the most frightening pair of arms that the mortal had ever seen. A helmet covered the swordsbeast's entire face, but the mortal could see bloodlust in the eyes that glowed behind its visor. It came on with the shuffling gait of a fencer.

The mortal's avatar was a grey, bipedal shape with a cartoon image of her face plastered across the sphere that served it for a head. Hardly suitable for combat.

"What the hell," she said. "I'll play." With a slight motion of her chin she replaced the avatar with an empty suit of plate armour. She conjured a massive double-handed sword into her virtual hands and stepped towards the swordsbeast. She felt no fear.

"This gateway has not been sealed," said the swordsbeast,

"And it is guarded. You must satisfy my questioning before I may allow you to proceed."

"'Nineveh'," she replied.

"If you continue to speak insensibly, I must strike you down," said the swordsbeast.

So much for Monty Python. The mortal sighed and raised her weapon.

The swordsbeast handled the weapons easily, spun them through a sequence of fanciful guard positions. Its footwork was complicated and nimble, though the beast stood eight feet tall.

The mortal drew her viewpoint up into third person so that she could best observe the combat. She was no fencer. She had never held any kind of weapon before...but she had spent many hours playing video games, and many more hours hacking them into submission. She jacked her attributes to the maximum values their data-types could hold and swung the sword.

The weapon felt weightless. The swordsbeast raised a parry, but her stroke sliced through its blade without resistance—and then all the way through its torso, cleaving it in two.

She was surprised to see that the beast's blood flowed as red as her own, although her uncle had many times described how faeries bled. She had never killed anything before. Not with this degree of realism.

The mortal banished her avatar, leaving only a blinking cursor to stand vigil over the swordsbeast. She stayed there, bodiless, for a long time.

Her uncle had not been in any swordfights during his own quest. He had never even had a sword. She would tell him about this, when she next saw him. She would tell him he'd been doing it wrong. She was proud of her victory, but something rankled.

Her reception into this sandbox world—she assumed it was a sandbox—had been more hostile than she had expected. Certainly more hostile than her uncle's low-key entrance. If this was how the rest of the quest was going to be, she wanted out. She was far too old for hack-slash dungeon crawling. Her uncle had claimed that her quest was for meaning—surely there was more to accomplish here than this?

The mortal cast herself a new avatar, based upon the shape of the body she wore in the real world. She broadened its shoulders, shaved some of the softness from her belly. Added a couple of inches in height. Yeah, that was good. The mortal dressed her avatar in brown trousers, a baggy white tunic, and soft leather shoes. She drew its ears to points and widened its eyes, but quickly let her face snap back to its usual configuration. Pixie ears would fool no one.

The mortal picked up one of the swordsbeast's weapons. It was too big to fasten to her waist or to strap onto her back. Briefly, she considered enlarging her avatar, but that seemed unnecessary. She was infinitely strong; carrying the enormous blade in hand was no encumbrance, and she'd feel bad if she left the spoils of her first combat lying in the dirt.

The mortal followed the river through the meadowlands and into the hills until she came upon the village. Dusk had given way to evening by the time she went down into the cusp where it nestled. She was hoping to find a bed for the night. Once her avatar was asleep she could abandon it in the sandbox and get back to work. She would return to Fairyland in her own time. If she got bored.

10. The Village

In the village marketplace, merchants were packing away their stalls all along the main thoroughfare. The folk ignored her as best they could, but they became timorous in their business when she approached. She supposed that her uncle's past misdeeds were the cause of this.

As the folk took down the market around her, she noticed that one stall remained: a purple tent pitched at the far end of the avenue. In front of it stood an A-frame sign that said, in English, Fortunes Told. The mortal brushed open the door-hangings and went inside, being careful not to damage the fabric with the swordsbeast's weapon.

The tent was also the fortune teller's garment. The walls and floor rose to its neck and curled behind its head as an ornate collar. Its tresses were long and golden, piled on top of its head and secured in an enormous bun. Its eyes were big and bright and blue.

The fortune teller held its fine-boned hands in front of it, fingertips pressed together, and said: "Fortunes read, fates foretold. Lay down your arms and enter, an you desire my services."

The mortal laid the sword near the entrance and knelt before the fortune teller. "What will a reading cost?"

"For most, it costs silver or gold or goods or labour or magic," said the fortune teller. "For you, the only cost will be the burden of the knowledge itself."

"Sounds like a bargain."

"It is no bargain, when one party gives and does not receive," said the fortune teller. "Yet I fear that I have the better end of this transaction."

"Speak my dark fortune, then." The mortal made her avatar smile. The notion that she had a story worth telling—dark or otherwise—was beginning to appeal to her.

The fortune teller's hands came apart and a small, silver globe rose from between its previously empty palms. The globe performed a single orbit around the mortal's head, then the fortune teller's. It divided into two smaller globes, which each sought one of the fortune teller's eye sockets. When the fortune teller raised its head, its blue eyes had become silver.

"You are descending into the darkening sky. Clouds froth about you, churning apart into nothing. The stars come down to look upon you, but when they are close enough to see you true, they take fright and flee.

"But you are not alone, up there in the darkness. A shadow approaches; a vast thing, darker than the night, emptier than the void into which you have been cast."

The fortune teller closed its eyes and lowered its head.

"That's it?"

"Aye."

"That was a lot more…abstract…than I had hoped."

"You have ventured only a symbolic presence into this world," said the fortune teller, blinking the silver from its eyes. "It should come as no surprise that your future is told in similar terms."

The mortal thought about it some more. "Your fortune says that I'm going to die, and there will be no afterlife. I already knew that."

"Death is not the same as fate," said the fortune teller. "To predict that a mortal is fated to die is no prediction at all."

"Lucky you waived your fee, then."

"Luck is a sector of fate," said the fortune teller. "If you believe in such things."

"Now you're just spinning shit," the mortal replied. "Is there somewhere in town I can find a bed for tonight?"

"You will find no welcome here."

"I haven't done anything wrong."

"Once before a mortal scourge walked among us, and he brought harm," said the fortune teller.

"You really believe I'm here to do you ill?"

"I do not," said the fortune teller, "But I would not go so far as to name that belief 'knowledge'."

The mortal stood up. "Well, thanks for nothing."

"That is all that you deserve," said the fortune teller.

The mortal made her way down from the village and out into the foothills. Her virtual form needed neither sleep nor food nor water, though her true flesh did in the real world. She could not tell whether that flesh was hungry or thirsty, and that bothered her a little. She was also puzzled by the fact that nobody had disturbed her yet. Even if her colleagues hadn't noticed that she was playing games at work, the system administrator should have. The corporation did not pay her to daydream in computer-generated fairylands.

Perhaps she was hallucinating. Perhaps she had slipped into madness. That would be alright. If she suffered any ills on the corporation's property, her employer was liable for them. Perhaps she would play for a few minutes more.

She checked the time on her Head Up Display, hoping for a more sensible readout. This time, the data was presented in the Hindu-Arabic numerals she knew, but there were too many of them, and they were inappropriately punctuated.

The mortal went on, following the river away from the town and out into the hills. Night had fallen, and the stars had come out to see what she was.

11. The Council of the Magi

In the Realm of the Magi, the passage of the sun across the sky was visibly articulated. The Warrior Queen could observe every moment elapse as she might watch a column of soldiers marching—but the seconds did not salute as they passed her.

The City of the Magi had no walls, but the folk who dwelt there had raised gateways over every road that led into it. Those gates would only yield to those with craft enough to open them.

Alone, the Warrior Queen stood before one such gateway: two massive columns cast from colourless rock and etched with symbols from a thousand alphabets. "I am the Queen of Warriors, and I demand an audience with the Council of the Magi," she said. "Open the fucking gates."

A hooded figure approached from the far side of the portal. It made a small motion with one burn-scarred hand and drew open the gates. "Come, Majesty," it said, in a stentorian voice that belied its stature.

The cowled figure took the Warrior Queen down into the City of the Magi, where the crystalline buildings were wrought from purest magic. Together they walked down the roadway…but they did not walk very far. Although they did not cross the threshold into any of the buildings, somehow the figure led her into the doorless chamber where the Council of the Magi held session.

The chamber was vast and polyhedral. Every facet reflected the proceedings that occurred within in non-visual terms: as smell, or taste, or thermal energy, or whorls of relative time. Twelve councillors sat around a table that was shaped like a rimless wheel, with a spoke extending from the hub towards each of them. The throne at the end of a thirteenth spoke sat empty.

The Warrior Queen could not tell which, if any, of the Councillors was the one who had transported her there.

"Your Majesty," said the Speaker for the Council. "How may the Council of Magi be of service to you?"

"I seek the mortal magus," said the Warrior Queen. "You know the one I mean."

The Councillors looked to the empty thirteenth place at the table. "Why do you seek him?"

"I would avenge the death of my mother."

The Council was silent, but they turned their heads as though addressing each other; holding a discussion that the Warrior Queen could not otherwise perceive. Eventually, the Speaker said: "The magus is long dead. We keep his seat empty to ensure that he is content to remain thus."

"He was a member of the Council?"

"He still is, though he is dead now, never once having sat in session with us."

"He is dead, but still you fear him?"

"He was a mortal, your Majesty. It is not unknown for such creatures to return from their graves, if they feel themselves slighted."

"You're afraid of dead mortals."

"Not usually," said the Speaker. "But in this case, the Council finds it prudent to be wary."

"Surely an already-dead mortal cannot stand against the Council of the Magi, here in the Realms of the Land of the Faerie?" Weakness was not something the Warrior Queen could abide. Cowardice was not something she would tolerate.

"Surely not," said the Speaker. It hesitated. "But we are faerie; we have no skill with the necromantic arts. In these

Realms, death is rare and final—as you know, Majesty."

"Tell me how he died."

"He was slain by the dog-man."

The Warrior Queen knew who the dog-man was. She knew the heritage and calibre of all warriors that were born in the Realms of the Land, though she did not know their fates.

The Warrior Queen was silent for a time. "How can I be certain?"

The Speaker looked upon her long enough and hard enough that its face became visible in the shadows of its cowl. "Vengeance is not your true end, is it, Majesty?"

"Do you doubt my word?"

"Your words are true," said the Speaker, "But your intentions are not. You do not seek vengeance for the sake of honour or propriety or form; you seek it because you desire a story quest."

She could not deny it.

"You are of the Faerie Folk, Majesty," said the Speaker. "Questing is for mortals."

"I say otherwise."

"With all due respect…this quest of yours is a mistake. It is mistaken on several counts."

"I will have my quest," she said. "And you will assist me as best you can."

"The Council refuses, with regret."

"No," said the Warrior Queen. "You will not deny me. I am the highest ranking military officer in all the Land; I command it."

"We are not your soldiers."

"No," said the Warrior Queen, "but I am still royalty, and I will have my way."

"These are not sufficient grounds for the Council to retract its decision."

"If you will not assist me in this small matter, the Council will have to pit itself against the finest and largest military force in all the Land—and all of those allied with us."

"You would perpetrate a war, across all of the Nations and Realms?"

"Only a short one," replied, the Warrior Queen. "My forces keep the peace amongst the Nations; how many of the Faerie Folk would side with *you* against *me*?"

"The Council provides valuable governance in the use of sorcery and magic."

"The Nations would rather govern their own magic," said the Warrior Queen.

"We are more powerful than any mere Nation," said the Speaker.

"So am I," said the Warrior Queen.

Another silent discussion ensued amongst the Council. Finally they returned their attention to her.

"The Council will assist you in the matter of your vengeance, but not directly," said the Speaker.

"Make me an offer."

"We will train you in the Art Magic so that you may proceed of your own accord."

"That will do."

"But be warned, Majesty—you are acting in error. You are not in possession of all the facts."

"I am a sovereign and a warrior and a questor," she replied. "I will act as I see fit."

"As you wish, Majesty," said the Speaker, drawing the cowl back down over its face. "As you will."

12. The Sage of the Fallen City

Malo climbed from darkness into dream.

He did not know when the transition was made, but after a time he found that he was swimming, not climbing. Soon, he found that he was no longer swimming, but crawling through some place dark and wet. Malo did not care where that place was; he cared only that it was on the way to the place he was headed. In the far distance was a beacon that shone darker than the absence of light. He knew that he would find his father there.

Soon Malo rose up from his crawl. He was on his feet, breathing air that was hot and thick. Green ropes hung before him, obstructing his way. Somewhere distant, the beacon continued to shine, black with evil. Noise rang in his ears, though there was nothing to hear but his own harsh respiration.

Malo stumbled over something he could not see. The darkness shattered and he crashed down into full consciousness.

Malo was in a jungle. All around him stood vast, wet trees, hung about with lianas and thick with deep, wetter shadows. He rose slowly to his feet, which crunched and cracked on the ground. Malo was bleeding from dozens of small wounds. The jungle was bleeding, too: it had been slashed and torn by shards of black glass, which lay scattered across the jungle floor.

He closed his eyes again, found where the emptiness lay,

and struck out towards it. But the signal was fading. Malo had to concentrate hard to keep a sense of where it lay.

After some hours, Malo came across a cage. Its bent and misshapen bars were rotting, rather than rusting, though they were made of a silver metal that still shone in the green-filtered sunlight. The cage contained the remains of a bent and twisted thing; little more of it than a skeleton and a few clumps of purple fur. A sliver of black glass as long as Malo's forearm had impaled it through the chest.

Seeking a weapon, Malo tried to prise one of the bars from the cage, but the metal dissolved in his hands. The skeleton collapsed into pieces.

He stood for a while, regarding the pile of bones. Then, he took the straighter of the two femurs and struck it against his foot. It was good and weighty. He tried to bend it in his fists, but it would not give.

"Hoy there! Ahoy!"

A small being, all hair and beard and spindly arms, came out from behind a jagged sheet of obsidian. Its beard was matted with long-dried blood and its arms were covered with scars and scratches. The being was barely shoulder high to Malo, but it somehow contrived to look down upon him. Perhaps it stood upon its own hubris. "I am the Sage of the Fallen City," it said. "On what business do you interrupt my mourning?"

"I seek my father," said Malo.

The Sage looked him up and down. "Your father," it said. "Yes. I see him in you."

Malo stood over the Sage, the femur hanging from his hand.

"I seek my father," said Malo.

"Your father passed this way many seasons ago," said the Sage. "He cast my Sky City to ruins out of jealousy and spite."

Malo just stared at him.

The Sage folded its arms and drew itself up to its four feet of height. "Help me escape from this jungle and I will ensure that you are well rewarded. I am a great sage, and I will again be as puissant as I am wise. My wealth will grow to match my renown."

"Reward," Malo replied. He could no longer feel the pulse of the dark beacon. The sage's conversation had driven it from his mind.

"A fortune, you may be sure," said the Sage. "Gold and power and wisdom and happiness, forever and for always, in this and any other Land."

Gone. The beacon was gone. Now he was truly lost.

Panicked, Malo struck out with the femur. "No," he said, repeating the word with each stroke until he lost his grasp of its assigned meaning. When his rage was spent, little more than bonemeal and paste remained of the Sage.

Malo stalked through the Fallen City, kicking apart those panels that remained intact. Eventually he found what he sought: a sliver of black glass that was curved and sharp and thick. He strapped the sliver onto the femur and hefted his new sickle. The weapon made him proud. He had never made anything before.

13. The Swamp

For days longer, Malo thrashed his way through the jungle. As he passed out of that territory, the canopy lowered and the humidity rose. Here it was quieter, and the cries of the birds and beasts that lived in this new terrain were hollower, lower, wetter.

Malo wandered through the stagnating water, wading and swimming; clambering through the arching mangrove roots. Startled fowl with gelatinous feathers burst out of the green-brown bog-waters and took flight. Malo's skin became wrinkled and waterlogged and the clothing began to rot off his back.

He began to weaken almost immediately. The water he drank was impure and there were no dry places to sleep. He tried to kill some of the slithering things that swam amongst the bog-waters—neither fish nor rodent nor reptile—but they were too guileful for him.

Malo shivered and sweated. His mother's voice whispered in one ear; a police megaphone bellowed in the other. Neither voice spoke any language he recognized. Colours burst and splattered across his eyes; the silhouetted figure of the father he had never known shambled away from him, muttering and cursing. On the horizon he saw another figure, darker still than his father, and stranger. Truly, a stranger.

Strands of black bled from the stranger's silhouette, thickening and merging until they occluded his vision completely. His others senses were swift to follow.

When Malo awoke he was lying on something flat and hard and dry. He felt weak, but he knew that his fever had broken. Voices that he did not understand spoke to him. Hands helped him to sit up.

He was on a wooden platform. There were two beings sitting with him—nurses or guards; he could not tell. They had amphibious hides that were thick and knobby, and mottled with pale fungi. Hard, transparent membranes protected their yellow eyes, and they were equipped with gills as well as with noses.

Many more of the swamp folk gathered around the platform. Some of them were squatting upon the soft mud islands; others were standing in the brackish waters, immersed up to their snouts. They did not speak.

One of the nurses gave Malo clear, clean water to drink and a meal of stewed and spiced fish, served on some kind of grain. It was the finest meal he had ever eaten. While Malo devoured it, three new figures joined him on the bobbing wooden platform. The first of them bore a short, hooked sword. The second carried a wooden staff, which was inlaid with gemstones and precious metals. The third wore a chain of office around its neck.

"What are you doing here in the swamps, child?" said the official.

"I am lost," Malo replied, looking up with black-ringed eyes.

"Aye," said the official. "And what were you seeking, ere you wandered into our Realms?"

"My father."

"We know your father by reputation," said the official, "But he has never passed through our territory."

"Where is my father?"

"I do not know. But if you seek the Realms that are most benighted, you will surely find the places he has been."

"Benighted."

The official took up a pole and used it to push the platform away from the mangroves. The shaman stood to Malo's left and the man-at-arms stood to his right. The raft cut swiftly through the thick, opaque waters, and soon they arrived at a small wooden dock on the border where the swamp gave way to mudflats.

When Malo stepped off the raft, the warrior handed his blackglass sickle back to him. The official moved to the other end of the raft and poled the vessel away.

14. The Tree Queen's Judgment

Still weak, Malo staggered across the mudflats, which soon gave way to grassy plains. He could see a river in the distance, and beyond it lay forests and foothills. Malo walked beside the river, stopping often to rest.

It was a full day of such travel before he reached the forest, which promised shelter as well as some opportunity to hunt or forage…but as soon as he had broached the tree-line, the foliage disgorged a dozen soldiers and he found himself surrounded.

Some of the tree soldiers were made of skin and blood and muscle and hair, like any ordinary human. Some were of bark and wood and sap and foliage, like any ordinary tree. Some were both, in varying proportions. They were armed with swords and spears forged from black steel, and wore armour made of living wood.

The sergeant among them came forward and said: "You are trespassing in the Tree Queen's Realm. Lay down your weapon."

Malo dropped the sickle and stepped away from it, sullenly.

The tree soldiers led him through the forest at spear-point, until they came to a wide, circular clearing where the sky was visible through the open canopy. The sun above was mottled and fierce.

The Tree Queen came out of the trees on the arm of her King. She was tall and beautiful, with skin as pale as snow and hair as green as the leaves of an oak. The King was dark and dour, with a rough, mahogany hide and a beard that was scaly with lichen.

"Do you speak?" asked the Tree Queen.

Malo grunted his assent.

"Then speak," said the Tree Queen.

He could not. His command of language had deteriorated to the point where he could only answer a direct question or repeat a phrase that had been spoken by another.

"What manner of being are you, that claims it can speak, yet will not do so?"

"I am a man," he said. "A human."

"You are not of these Realms," said the Tree Queen.

Malo said nothing. It was not a question.

"Leave him be," said the Tree King. "He is not the magus who beset us with his demon agent, unprovoked."

"Magus?" said Malo, perking up. Malo knew that 'magus' was another word that denoted his father, although he did not know what it meant.

"It knows the magus," said the Tree Queen. "Could this not be another of his demons?"

"No," said the Tree King, "It can barely speak; it is but a beast."

"The magus is canny," said the Tree Queen. "Perhaps this time he seeks to trick us."

"Whatever you might accuse this one of, trickery is not among its capabilities," said the Tree King. "To our knowledge it has committed no crimes; we have no cause to prosecute him."

The Tree Queen turned once more to Malo. "You are dismissed. Take your weapon and go."

The Tree King took her arm and they strode once more into the trees. The soldiers too receded into the flora, and Malo was alone in the clearing. The sickle of blackglass and bone lay on the ground behind him. He could not determine if the Tree Folk were still observing him when he took up his weapon and crept away.

15. Meat from a Carnivore

The forest darkened as night descended. Malo was hungry, but, try as he might, he could not entice any forest critters near enough to kill. He had no water and he did not know how to find his way back to the river. Malo lay down with only the earth for bedding, and promptly fell sound asleep. When he awoke, something bulky and carnivorous had pinned his legs beneath it and taken his left foot in its jaws.

Malo jerked upright and swung his sickle blindly. The impact that it made when it glanced off the carnivore's braincase jarred the weapon from his hand. The carnivore made an indignant noise and let go of his foot.

Malo found his weapon, adjusted his grip, and swung again. The jagged glass blade found purchase somewhere softer; dug in, scraped over a rippled ridge of bone, then slid free.

"Oh, me," said the carnivore. "I am grievously wounded."

Malo struck out a third time, from a different angle, and something inside the carnivore broke. Blood splashed up Malo's bare arm. He twisted the sickle and wrenched it back towards him. The carnivore's ribs shattered with a series of staccato snaps. It gurgled and choked and fell still.

Malo drew the weapon free and rolled the carnivore off him. Its blood was hot and smelled sweet, like molasses.

He pulled what was left of his shoe off his foot. The

appendage was bruised and oozed blood from a dozen punctures, but the wounds were not severe. He had nothing to dress them with, in any case. He went back to sleep, wondering if the beast's syrupy blood would sate his hunger or poison him.

When Malo awoke, there was daylight enough for him to inspect the remains of the carnivore. He had imagined it to be some kind of bear, but it was more like an outsized badger or a wombat. It had four stubby limbs, a long torso, and a narrow, wedge-shaped head. Its snout was filled with triangular teeth, but it had lips and ears and hands that might have belonged to an adult human. The carnivore was dressed in a cotton shirt and silk britches, and wore a pair of horn-rimmed spectacles.

Malo discarded his remaining shoe, which still had not dried after its immersion in the swamp water. He had stolen those shoes from a Salvation Army store somewhere in New Mexico, and they had been in poor condition even then.

Malo cut some steaks from the carnivore's carcass and tried to eat them uncooked, but he could only manage to swallow down a few mouthfuls of the tough, fatty meat.

Barefoot, he walked through the forest until he found the river again. He searched it for fish, but he was unable to catch them with his bare hands and soon gave up the notion. Malo forded the river and then followed it downstream, through the meadowlands and up into the hills.

The way became more difficult as the hills rose into mountains. The grass abraded to sand, then to naked shale. The landscape seemed to bend and warp as he passed through it. He did not know whether gravity was truly miscalibrated, or whether he was hallucinating due to blood loss. He walked on, though the flesh of his feet had worn through to the bone.

When the mountains receded, Malo found himself in an orchard of sinewy trees, which bore fruits that looked like stillborn babies. The flying things that nested in the tree limbs were more like swine than birds or bats.

There was little meat upon them, but they were plentiful and trusting, and Malo was hungry.

16. The Sea City on the Plains

A river of some opaque, viscous liquid led him out of the Sinewed Forest and down onto a vast, grassy plain. A breeze stirred ripples and waves from the grass, making of it a vast green sea. Malo was on his knees when he came in sight of the city. He crawled towards its bulbous structures, which were more like creatures that lived beneath the ocean than dwellings built for human habitation.

The pastel-skinned folk who dwelled in the Sea City on the Plains wept when they saw Malo's suffering. They took him in and dressed his wounds; bathed him and fed him. They gave him new clothes, made to resemble his old: heavy-stitched, denim-like pants; a kind of t-shirt made of a cottony fabric, a pair of leather boots laced with tough, fibrous leaves. When Malo was healed and rested and as close to presentable as he was likely to get, they took him before their Queen.

The Queen of the Sea City on the Plains reclined upon a throne that was as much an animal as a divan. It shifted to accommodate her every motion, stroking her flesh with rippling cilia and sighing with the pleasure of its service. Malo stared at it, bewildered.

The Queen of the Sea City waved to him to come forward, metal and jewels glittering on her hands. She watched him approach with both love and sorrow plain upon her face.

"Poor child," she said, when it became clear that he did not know to make obeisance before her. "What brings you to our Realm, so weakened and ill? What manner of being has visited such terrible wounds upon you?"

"I seek my father."

"Your father wrought this ill upon you?"

"My father," said Malo.

The Queen squinted at him. "Yes," she said. "I see it now. Your father is the great magus from the mortal realm, who, in his time, visited grievous harm upon this Land."

"Magus," he said, nodding.

"The magus is no longer abroad in the Land as he once was," said the Queen of the Sea City on the Plains. "He has raised a tower and sealed himself within it, and he has remained there ever since."

"Where?" The imperative to know was stronger than Malo's inability to express himself.

"The tower has no fixed location, for the Realms have spurned it. Your father's domain arises in one place and it remains there until it is driven to another place, where it then rises anew."

Malo quit the Sea City of the Plains, and he went forth in search of the dark tower.

Now that knew what to look for, he found that the Tower drew him. It had always been there with him, but now he could identify it, he could properly distinguish its darkness from his own. The signal returned: a shadow upon his mind; a dark, cold place that he could always find, now that he knew its symbol.

As he drew nearer to the tower the signal grew stronger, and so did Malo, the Bad Little Dog.

17. Sympathy

The Art Magic did not come easily to the Warrior Queen. The spells she designed were clever and efficient and syntactically sound, and she possessed ample power with which to quicken them, but they simply would not work. She could not create sympathy between the spell and the reality it modelled. Other students surpassed her quickly and went on to other lessons, while she stayed back with group after group of seekers.

Eventually, the Warrior Queen stopped attending classes. She took to prowling through the boundless libraries, pulling random tomes and flipping through them, then setting them back without reading more than a paragraph. She was unable to ambush any new insights this way, and soon she became too restless to study at all. It was not until she drew her sword that success came to the Warrior Queen.

The library drew a sharp breath as her blade hissed from its scabbard, as if the tomes themselves sensed the violence she intended them. Pages rustled. Leather bindings creaked. Wooden shelving groaned.

"Damn you, books, with all your empty words," said the Warrior Queen. "I wish you all would burn." The angry symbols she spoke glowed as they issued from her lips, and burst into flame when her utterance was complete.

Black-robed librarians rushed up to the Warrior Queen, dowsing her spell, quieting the books and shushing her out of the library. She allowed the indignity, though she could have struck them down without effort or consequence. It didn't matter. She understood it now.

Every problem was a foe to be overcome, and the key to any foe's defeat is to understand them. Sympathy was the key to victory on the battlefield, just as it was the key to successful spellcraft.

Upon this realization, the Warrior Queen's power quickly grew to be as vast as any might have expected, and then it grew vaster still. Soon, she decided that she no longer needed the aid of the Council of the Magi in her quest. And so the Warrior Queen went forth into the wilderness, seeking the next part of her story.

She flew for many leagues as a bird, and then for leagues more in her own form. Sometimes she rode, on horseback or on more exotic beasts and beings. Sometimes she simply willed herself to her subsequent destination. Sometimes she ran, and other times she walked. It was on foot that she came to the stand of trees by the banks of the river, where the magus had finally fallen.

There was no sign that a great magician had perished there. No grave had been dug, no stone had been set. Not even the gossiping winds had anything to say about his passing.

The Warrior Queen squatted down beside the clear-running water and drew a symbol upon it. The rune held its form even though the river continued to flow. On that flickering surface she observed the events that had led to the death of the magus. The Warrior Queen watched him skid down the opposite slope of the riverbank. He walked across the river, treading upon its surface, to confront another mortal. The second mortal had stood where she did now.

The magus threatened the mortal with a weapon she did not recognize, and the weaker mortal begged for mercy. The magus refused, but before he could exact his judgment, the dog-man cut him down from behind.

The Warrior Queen killed the spell.

For all his power, the magus had not been much of a

warrior. None of the Warrior Queen's troops would have allowed a foe to sneak up behind them while they spoke at length with someone they intended to kill.

The Warrior Queen pursed her lips and began to build a new spell. Before it was finished, she scratched it out and began anew. The Warrior Queen examined her second attempt from several angles. She erased a symbol and replaced it, tweaked another, changed the connections on a third. Finally satisfied, she grunted and fired it with her will.

The Warrior Queen had hoped the spell would reveal the spirits of any mortals that remained in the vicinity, but it revealed nothing at all. She could not tell if this was due to some error on her part, or a true absence of dead spirits. The Council of the Magi had admitted themselves to be poor necromancers, but of the Warrior Queen was better acquainted with death than they were.

Most likely the magus' spirit had returned to its own plane. The Warrior Queen would follow it there.

18. The Ruined City on the Plains

The mortal was growing frustrated with the game. There was no hook; no quest; not even the scent of an objective…

But she was not ready to leave. Although nothing was happening, it felt as though she was the centre of attention—the protagonist, or one of them—and she knew that would not be the case when she returned to the office. Here, in the Realms of the Land, she felt powerful and important.

The mortal lengthened the distance her avatar covered with each stride and hastened on her way; following the river through hills and between the mountains, and then down once more onto endless grassy flatlands.

She skirted the ruins of the Sea City on the Plains, where the few remaining buildings had dried to brittleness. Most of the structures had cracked open or collapsed into a burned-looking sludge. A few of the pastel-skinned folk her uncle had described to her milled about, weeping. She hurried on. There would be no welcome for her there.

She followed the great milk-white river through the Sinewed Forest. The trees seemed knobby and arthritic, crackling as they flexed in the wind. They bore no fruit. The distortions in the gravity field she expected did not manifest, though that might have been because her avatar had no true physical presence in the Realms.

None of the pig-birds her uncle had mentioned were in evidence. She smiled to herself as she considered how she would relay that fact to him. "Pigs might once have flown here," she would say, "But not anymore."

The mortal went on. The Sinewed Forest became ordinary woods, and the river ran clear. Soon it began to rain.

19. The Inn

The mortal's avatar felt the rain as a series of tiny digital contacts, but she did not feel cold or wet from it. Still, appearances were important, so she tuned her clothing so that it would appear to be waterlogged. As an afterthought she conjured an umbrella, in order to justify the continued dryness of her hair.

"Oh me, oh my," she said, knowing that she was being observed from concealment, "it's really fucking wet out here."

"Bedraggled," said a bush, though it sounded less than certain of it.

"Beg pardon?" said the mortal. "I could swear I heard a bush talking to me."

"You, madam, are bedraggled, if you don't mind my saying it."

She soon tired of the game. "Come out of there and show yourself," she told the bush. It shook and divested itself of a yellow fox with two bushy tails.

"Madame," said the fox, "you look in sore need of shelter. There is an inn near here with a sturdy roof and a blazing hearth-fire."

"Then why the fuck are you hiding under a bush?" said the mortal. She made an impatient sound and said "Come on, let's go find this inn of yours."

The fox led her through the trees, skirting puddles and skipping over fallen boughs, until they did indeed come to a quaint, gabled building with a thatched roof and the glow of the promised hearth-fire visible through its windows.

"Splendid," said the mortal, and started towards the door, kicking her way through the sucking mud underfoot.

The fox yelped and had to rush to get ahead of her. On the stoop it turned to the mortal with a reproving look, before standing up on its hindquarters and opening the door with its forepaws.

Once the mortal had crossed the threshold of the inn, a matronly creature in a dress, who stood barely three feet tall, bustled up to her. "Come inside, come inside, mortal girlie," said the innkeeper. "Come stand by the hearth, before you take a chill."

"I'm already inside," replied the mortal. She stood there on the threshold and gazed around at the inn and the creatures who were lounging about there, eating or drinking or conversing or playing the fiddle.

"Show me your true selves," she said, and the inhabitants of the inn were revealed to her as ferrets and polecats and stoats. The fox, who was halfway across the room, remained a fox—but it stopped where it was and turned to look at her over its shoulder.

"I, I…we can explain…" said the innkeeper, but the mortal would hear none of it.

"I already know this is a scam." She put her hands on her hips. "My uncle let you off, when he came wise to you, but he's a strange and horrible old man and I think perhaps you set him under some enchantment. I, on the other hand, am a suddenly very angry young woman and I will not allow this to continue."

The weasel-folk cowered but they offered no more excuses. "Get out," said the mortal. "Every one of you, if you value your lives."

They did not need to be told a second time. The weasel-folk bolted for the door, streaming past her on both sides, squealing with fright.

The fox jogged after them, paused in the doorway again,

and then disappeared over the threshold.

The mortal looked at the hearth fire, which had guttered low in the draft from the open door. She could fix that. "Burn," she said, and the flames rose higher, and soon the walls and the floor and the benches were alight and crackling like tinder.

She stood a moment to survey her handiwork, and then turned and stomped her way back outside so she could watch the place come down.

It did not take long before the thatch upon the roof caught fire, and the glass windows shattered with a satisfyingly dramatic explosion.

"Come to me, fox," said the mortal. "We are not done yet."

The fox stepped out from behind a tree and came sauntering towards her—but it came on slowly, and with fear in its eyes. "I am here, mortal."

"Fox, I would better understand your part in all of this."

"I'm just a guide," said the fox. "I guide people to the inn, and there the weasel-folk do as they will."

"That's a pretty sad existence," said the mortal. "Hanging around here, waiting to lead unsuspecting mortals into a trap."

The fox lowered its snout. "It was not always so."

"Oh, indeed?"

"Once I went all about the Realms, and beyond. I travelled to the mortal worlds, guiding your folk among the Ways, helping them to find what they sought. But the world has changed, has it not? Now it is more difficult than ever to cross between the worlds, and few of your kind seek the quest among the Realms. I did not choose these circumstances, mortal. I would have the old days back if I could."

"Time travels in one direction only," said the mortal, wondering why she was wasting so much energy lecturing a non-player character. But perhaps the fox was a player, after all. Surely she was not the only real person awash in this virtuality?

"Not always," said the fox. "But even here it is uncommon for time to reverse itself and I take your point."

"You must adapt to the changed world," said the mortal. "There can be few travellers here if there are no guides to show them the way. Seek them out, if you have the ability. Surely you will find that occupation more rewarding than this one."

The fox regarded the remains of the inn, which smoked and sizzled in the continuing downpour. "You have not left me very much choice in the matter, have you?"

20. A Sorceress

The mortal made her way back to the river and followed it along until she found an iron canoe lying beached upon the riverbank. She pushed the canoe out into the water and climbed into it, taking up the sharp-edged iron paddle. The current did most of the work in bearing her downstream.

The trees thinned as she went, and the soil became dry and grey. The canoe passed out of the forest and into the cratered and barren territory that her uncle had described as the Ore-lands.

The Ore City came into sight. Spires and domes gleamed amidst clouds of steam, which were purged from the many foundries and forges at which the Ore-folk plied their trade.

The mortal drove the canoe aground with the paddle and climbed out. This, she assumed, was the same canoe her uncle had used. It seemed rude for her to leave it there, for it would be difficult for its rightful owner to drag it back upstream.

The mortal looked at the source logic beneath the canoe, and found that it only ever travelled along a single track—down to the city. The fox had said that time was sometimes mutable here—perhaps she could set a loop upon it, so that once the boat had reached the end of its journey, it would automatically reverse back up its set path until it was once more at its original coordinates.

The mortal committed the change and, with a smile on her face, watched the canoe retreat upstream, against the current as well as the arrow of time.

Even had she access to the source code of her home world—or at least its user interface—the mortal would have found such a task more difficult there. In these physics-bereft Realms she could simply apply her logic to the objects around her, for the operating system gave little resistance. She supposed that made her some kind of sorceress. A sourceress. She smiled.

It was certainly a step up from being a code-monkey.

21. The Playwright

The massive iron gates of the Ore City stood open and a caravan of covered wagons was making a hasty exodus through them. The mortal stood aside to let them pass, but a figure in the last carriage called a sudden halt and jumped down from its vehicle.

The caller rushed over to her, bobbling its head and waving its hands in a vain attempt to contain its delight, its ragged black cape fluttering behind it. The mortal regarded it with suspicion, but it showed no obvious threat. It had beady eyes and a protuberant chin; a high forehead and an impossibly mobile pair of brows. "Hello! Hello!" it said.

"Hello, there! You are a mortal, are you not?"

"I am."

"Oh, excellent. Most excellent!" It extended a hand towards her. "I am Nentril Revallo."

"Um, hi." She shook Revallo's hand.

"Mortal, I have met others from your world, and I have found all of them to be quite distinct in their roles. What type of a mortal are you?"

She thought about it, puzzled by his question.

"The first of your fellows that I met was a scientist," said Revallo. "The second was a magus. What, pray tell, are you?"

"I guess, in this place, you'd call me a player."

Revallo clapped his hands. "How wonderful!" he said. "I myself am one of those." He waited a beat for drama, before he leaned in and said: "In truth, I am the playwright—but I often tread the boards with my troupe, in some small role."

"You like to be seen, do you?"

"It is true. I enjoy being recognized. I enjoy being called by name."

The mortal looked at him through narrowed eyes. "I thought that was dangerous," she said. "To be named, among the faerie folk."

"But not so amongst your people, yes?" said the playwright. "A name offers many benefits, to a player. It may lead to a recurring role. It may lead to danger, you are correct, but one who is wise to the traps of Story may profit from joining his fate to such an adventure."

"And you are such a one?"

The playwright bowed.

"Well, congratu-fuck-o-lations."

Revallo tittered with delight. Did he realize she was being rude? Did he simply relish hearing the profanity? The mortal did not care enough to pursue the question. She opened her mouth to speak her goodbyes, but the playwright held out its hands and said: "I would hear your story, mortal, if you would care to share it."

The mortal shook her head. "My story is dull," she said. "I am boring and ordinary. That is why I am here, playing this game."

The playwright's eyes glittered. "I am the playwright," he said. "Let me be the judge of your story, be it dull or otherwise."

The mortal shook her head. "I don't think so," she replied. "My story is not for you."

"I will make you shine," said Revallo. "Like a hero for justice. Like a star in the firmament."

The mortal shivered, though she did not know why. "I have never desired stardom," she replied. "I just want to be entertained, for a little while."

The playwright clutched at her sleeve. "You need not be truthful," it wheedled. "You may lie to me. You may offer a story that you have stolen. I will be in your debt."

The mortal turned to look at him. A faerie did not offer debt lightly. "And how would you repay this debt? I have already refused your offer of fame."

"Sometimes, a sympathetic ear is reward enough," said the playwright. "Sometimes, the act of telling of a story will lead to a revelation that would otherwise remain unknown. You may profit from the exercise as much as I, my friend."

She pried his fingers from her garment. "I'm sorry, Mister Revallo. There are no revelations in my story. There is just a mortal life, with its meagre share of pleasures and its surfeit of pain and horror, and then, at its end, will be my death."

"That is what makes the tale all the sweeter," said the playwright. "The life of the fey folk is a fixed thing, a straight line without a necessary end. It is a ray. But the life of a mortal? Such a life may assume whatever shape it desires, because there is no force pulling it in a single direction."

"And that is why you want my story," replied the mortal. "You believe it will refract your own to some new course."

"That is indeed so," said the playwright.

"Well, you picked a bad day for it, Mister Revallo," said the mortal. "Get the fuck out of here. I'm busy."

"Alright," huffed the playwright. "I shall trouble you no more. Enjoy the rest of your days, mortal woman. Just remember that your name could have lived beyond your death, if you had been more cooperative."

The playwright walked back to its wagon with its chin held high and its cloak swishing limply behind it.

The mortal shrugged to herself as she turned her back on it and strode through the massive iron gates and into the City of the Ore-lands.

22. The Queen of the Ore-lands

The city streets were thronged with metal-clad people who rushed about clanking and clattering. The mortal wondered if they had been so heavily armed when her uncle had visited.

A sergeant with metal hair that gleamed like an oil-slick rainbow demanded to know her business. When the mortal asked to be taken before their Queen, he grunted and gestured for her to follow him. Thus escorted, she made her way through the steel-riven streets and into the chromed-metal palace at the centre of the city.

The mirror-plated throne-room was bustling with soldiers. Clearly, some urgent business was afoot. The sergeant stood at the mortal's shoulder, shifting his weight from foot-to-foot impatiently while he waited for the Queen's attention.

The Queen of the Ore-lands was tall and slender inside her suit of plain, battle-worn armour. Triangular steel teeth glittered through her cheeks, which had been peeled open and secured with wires. Spikes had been pushed through the flesh of her hands and protruded from between her knuckles. This did not appear to have any adverse effect on the function of her digits as she used them to test the soundness of a well-used sword.

The Queen of the Ore-lands did not look up when she addressed the mortal. "You have been granted audience."

The mortal curtsied and said: "Majesty, I thank you for this—"

The Queen squinted down the length of the blade. "I am preparing to go to war," she said. "I have no time for chitchat. Get to the point."

"My uncle was here some time ago, and you rendered him assistance."

"I do not recall," said the Queen of the Ore-lands, sheathing the blade.

"He came seeking the most beautiful thing in all the worlds."

The Queen paused. A smile caught her lips; then split them into a hideous grin. "Oh, yes," she said. "I do remember, after all." She extended her hands, fingers splayed. Attendants came to fit gauntlets over them. The plating locked perfectly over fingers and spikes alike.

"If I may, Majesty, I have some questions about him."

"You may," said the Queen of the Ore-lands. "If you're quick about it."

The mortal took a breath. "I don't understand what it was about my uncle that drew your Majesty's favour."

The Queen of the Ore-lands strapped an articulated metal belt strung with knives about her waist. "He spoke with respect," she said, "but he did not try to flatter me."

"I see," the mortal said. "When my uncle was here, was he followed by the dog-man? Do you know anything about him?"

"Ah, the dog-man." The Queen drew a hooked dagger from a sheath on her belt. "Like all true dogs, it was a mongrel. Its sire was a beast brought to the Realms by a mortal explorer; its dam was a fey creature that yet lives." She replaced the dagger and drew another, straighter one.

"So…the dog-man was half mortal?"

"There is no such a thing as a half-mortal," said the Queen. "Either one is a mortal, or one is not. The dog-man may have had a mortal beast in its ancestry, but it was as immortal and soulless as any other faerie creature."

"Can your Majesty tell me anything about the magus?"

"There are many magi in the Realms," said the Queen.

"But I know the one you mean. He was a mortal scourge of a less discriminate kind than your uncle; one who deliberately set himself to mayhem wherever he went. He passed through my Realm on his travels, but my emissaries were able to turn him away without mischief."

"And the dog-man killed him?"

"Yes," said the Queen of the Ore-lands. "Though his dark tower yet stands."

"There's a dark tower?"

Seeking such a tower was a great and epic quest, and a quest was what she sought. In the absence of a dragon to slay, a princess to free, a talisman to assemble or a kingdom to win, this was the only candidate she had to choose from.

The Queen of the Ore-lands widened her stance so that her attendants could affix spurs to her ankles. "A mortal's sorcery may persist beyond the death of the sorcerer, if that mortal was powerful enough…and the magus was powerful indeed."

The Queen of the Ore-lands stomped each foot to ensure that her spurs were correctly attached and rolled her shoulders. An attendant handed her a poleaxe with a serrated blade on each end of the staff. "Enough questions. I must now do battle with the Tree Queen."

"The Tree Queen? Is my uncle responsible for this conflict, as well?"

"Yes," said the Queen of the Ore-lands. "In part. So, too, is the magus. But there is no love lost between the Ore-lands and the Forests. Our conflict is renewed periodically, with or without mortal intervention."

"I…"

"I have no more time for you," said the Queen of the Ore-lands. "Show yourself out."

23. A Battle

The mortal left the City of the Ore-lands and retreated to a hill with a vantage over the field of battle. On her right, the Ore-Lands host marched out of the city gates to a fanfare of brass and drums. With much ceremony they formed up in columns; foot soldiers flanked by cavalry. Mounted knights rode upon a variety of armoured beasts: horses and jungle cats and elephants and other creatures too strange and monstrous to identify; lumbering about or floating above the Ore Queen's army like dirigible squids.

On her left was the forest. It was difficult to discern where the forest ended and the Tree Queen's host began, for her warriors were themselves trees, to varying degrees. The Tree Queen's army was the larger of the two. Ranks of archers stood in front of spearmen; swordsmen and halberdiers marched on either quarter.

"Salutations."

The mortal turned without alarm to see who had come to watch the battle with her: a hunched and emaciated being clad all in dark robes. Its hands were black with burn-scars, and its face was concealed in the shadows of its cowl.

"Hi," she replied. She thought about asking if the candy bar was open, but decided against it. "Do you happen to know the cause of this conflict?"

"This disagreement is the result of a longstanding chain of grudges," replied her new companion. Its voice was oddly polyphonic, though the bass was the strongest tone.

"What are the most recent links?"

"Some time ago, when the Tree Queen wanted an alliance to bring down one of her enemies, the Queen of the Ore-lands refused to join the coalition. Later, the Queen of the Ore-lands gave aid to a mortal, who caused much harm to the court of the Tree folk. The Tree folk have finally instated a new royal line and restored order to their Realm, and now they are looking for reparations."

"What will happen if one nation is destroyed?"

"Neither nation will be destroyed on this battlefield," said the cowled figure. "Lives will be ended, resources will be squandered. Perhaps a Queen will fall, and thence be replaced…perhaps not. But the dispute will end, leaving only bitterness for both parties. This will slowly fester until it must be lanced by a further act of warfare."

"It sounds rather a waste."

"That is the nature of warfare."

"And you, sir? In what capacity do you witness this battle?"

"I was not dispatched here to observe this conflict. I am here to treat with *you*."

The mortal took a moment to scrutinize her companion. It was remarkably still. Its robes did not shift in the breeze. It cast no shadow. It was like a cheap CGI effect in a B movie. "Well, alright then."

"I bid you welcome, on behalf of the Council of the Magi."

"Thanks."

"The Council recognizes your heritage and your power, and we fear the damage you might cause—but we also recognize that you have committed no crimes since you began your travels in the Realms of the Faerie."

"I'm on my best behaviour."

"Yet the Council is concerned about your wellbeing. We wish to advise you that your deeds here are not without consequence. This Land is a dangerous place, and though you yourself are not malicious, you are yet a dangerous individual."

"Is that so?"

"You should not have come to the Land," said the emissary of the Council of the Magi. "You are only here on the flimsiest wisp of madness; you are ill-equipped to survive in these Realms. Hurry and conclude your journey, before some grievous wrong befalls you."

"I'll keep that in mind."

The emissary drew closer to her without engaging in any actual motion. "You believe this to be a game," it said. "You believe that this world…this fairyland…exists only for your amusement. You believe it is a construct that you have built to resemble the lunatic dreams of your uncle, and you believe that you are the only true sentience here."

She could not deny it.

"You must understand that this Land is as real as you are. You do not believe yourself to be truly present here, but you are mistaken. You are here in every way that counts."

"Then why," the mortal asked, smiling, "can I do this?" Her avatar reached out with impossible speed, and grabbed the emissary with impossible strength. She raised it over her head and tossed it away. The emissary did not resist. Its image spun through the air like a piece of cardboard, vanishing whenever its rotation showed her the back face of it.

"That you have some power over the Land does not make it any less real." The emissary's voice came from behind her. She turned around, but there was no one there. "But you are not the only one with power, and you have more enemies than you know."

The voice remained behind her, no matter how she turned.

"Take your leave of this Land and these Realms. Your welcome has been retracted."

"Yeah, bollocks to you, too," she said.

There was no reply.

On the field of battle before her, the Ore-lands' vanguard, bristling with arrows and spear-shafts, smashed its way through the ranks of the Tree Queen's host. Archers continued to pepper them while halberdiers were rushing in from the flanks. The Ore-lands' bizarre cavalry was waiting for the signal to charge.

The mortal watched folk of both nations die in vast numbers: stabbed, cut down, arrowshot, burned, trampled. She watched them fall, bleeding and screaming, limbs hacked off, guts flopping, skulls crushed, spines snapped. She watched until the horror wore off and the carnage grew boring. It did not take as long as she might have expected.

She could have joined in, she supposed. Perhaps the Ore Queen would like her better if she proved herself in battle. The mortal's avatar was impossibly strong and fast and immune to any form of harm—there was no risk involved. Better yet, she could have hacked the landscape, or manipulated the flow of time to benefit one side or the other.

But wargames had never been her style.

The mortal turned away from the raging battle and considered how next to proceed. Perhaps she would quest for the dark tower, after all. She had nothing better to do.

24. In the Tower

The Tower grew above a basin that had once held a vast sea. Now the seabed was dry and empty, filled only with the cartilaginous remains of the great, vile fish-things that had formerly prowled its depths.

Malo walked through the flats, kicking and stomping his way between the piles of leviathans' bones. The salt crust cracked beneath his every step. He climbed out of the seabed below the tower, scrambling over the razored volcanic rocks, hand over bleeding hand. When at last he came to stand at the base of the tower, his skin was filigreed with wounds both new and old.

Malo had no way to calculate the tower's magnitude. He walked its circumference, but he found no entrance in its twisted and puckered surface. When he laid his hands upon it, the film of slime that coated it oozed between his fingers. The obsidian shaft would not yield to him.

In the highest room in the tower, the magus looked up from his texts. He rose from his desk and went to the window. The tower was the grandest of his achievements, and the vilest, and there was little in the worlds outside of it that concerned him now. Evil was his only abiding interest, and he had yet to encounter anything as talented in that regard as he himself.

The magus looked out of the tower, at the Land he had

blighted, at the Realms he had harmed. He looked at the seabed he had sought to fill and populate. He looked at the skies, whose Queen he was not yet mad enough to contest with. One day, perhaps.

The magus looked down the length of the tower, and saw the mortal man who stood before it, and he knew that man for his son.

The magus considered Malo against the countless abominations he had wrought. He examined the boy's deeds, measured his heart, and rifled through the damaged lobes of his mind.

"Feh," said the magus, disgusted. "Can't even bloody well speak English."

The magus spat on the ichor-slick floor and returned once more to his books and his spellcraft, and he never again thought of his son, the Bad Little Dog.

Malo raged and railed against the tower, but it stood firm beneath his onslaught. He could not harm it, not with his fists, nor with his bizarre and jagged powers. The tower was older than the magus who had raised it, in its present form, and it was infused with an evil that could never be fully expressed with any kind of words or symbols.

Spent and defeated, Malo staggered away from the tower; and what little remained of his ego was finally consumed by rage and despair.

25. Husks

The Warrior Queen stood at the entrance to a small wooden dwelling, in a place where faerie creatures such as she no longer existed.

Plants grew wild all around the house. Birds and insects made soft, unmusical sounds. There was a distinct lack of magic in the humid air, and the stink of death lingered sweetly in its place. Hardy though she was, the Warrior Queen wondered how long she could survive in so desolate a place.

The house stood on stilts, two feet above the ground. Its weatherboard face was grey and sagging. Broken windows were covered over with curling wire mesh. The corrugated iron roof was rusty and lopsided. The Warrior Queen pushed through the listing door and stepped across the threshold.

Inside, the house stank of rot and ashes. The floorboards were water-stained and soft. The husks of dead insects lay everywhere.

The Warrior Queen moved amongst the smashed furnishings, upholstered in fabrics that were neither skins nor weaves. A rectangular altar made of a smooth substance that looked like wood, but was not, stood on a low table. The glass plate in the front of it was broken, and its hollowed-out gut was filled with the sooty remains of some burnt offering.

The Warrior Queen wondered what sort of gods or demons it was dedicated to, but only briefly. Faerie folk were immortal and without souls: religion was of little interest to them.

Books lay stacked on every flat surface. The Warrior Queen took one from the top of a pile and examined its clothbound cover. It had no illustration upon it, and the words were inscribed in a mortal tongue she could not read well. The pages crumbled in her fingers when she tried to turn them.

She kicked her way through to the kitchen and exited the dwelling through the back door. The decking behind the house had long since collapsed, but she leapt lightly down and moved out into the wayward garden.

Some distance from the house stood a metal gantry. A bamboo box hung from it, suspended by fraying ropes and rusted chains.

A boy had lost his childhood in that cage. A boy who had grown into a powerful man; who had ventured to the boundaries of this very world, and beyond. The man had died as far from that box as his power could take him, but the boy…

The boy remained locked inside that box, forever.

There was an unfamiliar, prickling sensation at the base of her neck, accompanied by an emotion that the Warrior Queen thought might be fear.

"Magus," she said. "Will you speak with me?"

Words whispered inside her head. She did not know how the voice had insinuated itself inside her psychic shields. The voice which spoke was that of a child, as well as that of something timeless and filthy.

The magus-child whispered to her that he had never laid his eyes upon her mother, much less sought her out and slain her. That was a different mortal—the one who had caused the magus' own death, and many others besides.

The magus whispered other things, insensible and irrelevant and evil. The Warrior Queen closed her ears, but she could hear the dead thing yet.

She stood for a moment, breathing hard. There was sweat

upon her brow, and her hair was cold against her scalp. The dead thing continued to burble its wordless evil.

The Warrior Queen gathered her magic to her as best she could. It was the most difficult task she had ever attempted. She set the spell slowly, drawing the symbols with only one hand. The other was filled with her sword.

The spell took and her vision flickered as she was transported home, to the Realms of the Land, where death came only as a consequence of violence or accident and magic swirled on every mote.

She was far beyond the reach of the thing in the cage, and yet she could still hear its whispering. The Warrior Queen hoped the whispers were echoes, and would fade, but she feared that her own mind had taken up the chorus.

Madness was a mortal affliction, but if it was a price she must pay for her own story-quest, the Warrior Queen was quite willing to pay it.

26. The Son of the Magus

The Warrior Queen went immediately before the Council of the Magi. "You pig-fuckers deceived me," she said.

The Speaker for the Council shook its head and told her: "No, Majesty. You deceived yourself."

"You knew that the magus was not the mortal who slew my mother."

"We tried to tell you, but you refused to hear our explanation," said the Speaker. "You would not be counselled into some other course of action."

The Warrior Queen was silent for a moment. "You wanted someone independent and expendable to ascertain the whether the magus was truly dead."

The Speaker did not deny it. "If you desire it, we will show you how your mother was slain."

"Show me."

The Speaker conjured an image of a steep-walled mountain pass. Facets of that image were reflected upon all of the surfaces around the room, highlighting one or another detail, motif, or theme.

In the pass, a rainbow-breasted lithophage stood in conversation with a bearded mortal. He was not the magus she had earlier sought. This grinning fool appeared to be charmed by the lithophage, having no sense of the peril it represented. The Warrior Queen's mother, Zelioliah, emerged and slew the lithophage. Zelioliah conversed briefly with the mortal, who acquitted himself poorly.

The scene faded and became another: the bearded mortal facing off against the dog-man in the shadow of an enormous tree. The worldtree. Zelioliah emerged to save the weakling a second time. Once the dog-man had fallen, the mortal took Zelioliah in his arms and showed her his gratitude with a straight-razor.

"I'll find him," said the Warrior Queen. "I'll go back to his world and I'll find him and I'll kill him, and then I will capture his mortal spirit and wear it like a cloak."

The Speaker for the Council shook its head. "This Council has tried many times to do just that, and failed. The mortal is but one soul amongst billions, and he sleeps so deep that we can find no trace of him. You will have no better luck than we."

"How is it that I was able to locate the magus' dead soul, and you cannot find this live one?"

"The magus never hid himself from us."

"Even so. This mortal is no sorcerer."

"We have become estranged from our allies in the mortal realm," said the Speaker. "It is possible that they are protecting him."

"In that case, you should make war upon them."

"This Council cannot start a war between the mortal world and Faerie over the soul of a single miscreant."

"And yet you have searched for him."

The Speaker hesitated. "This mortal is invested with more power than one might expect," it said. "And yet…though his quest here is done…he may one day return."

The Warrior Queen was silent again. At last, she said: "I see what you have made of me."

"You have made yourself," said the Speaker. "You were most insistent."

"You have conjoined our goals so that I must do what you need of me, knowing that I would otherwise deny you."

"It is your duty, as Queen of the Warriors and protector of the Realms of the Land."

"It is, and I must comply with your wishes, but I will

not do so as your vassal. I want the magus' seat upon this council."

"An you prove your skill in the manner of the other Councillors, the seat is yours," said the Speaker.

"I am royalty."

"That is so," said the Speaker, "But the laws of the Council are quite specific."

"Then you had better fucking well change them," said the Warrior Queen.

"We cannot make an exception, even for such as you."

"You are magi. Making exceptions is the whole of your business."

"That is why we cannot; not in the matter of our own governance."

"I will not be attending Council sessions. I have no desire to govern the use of sorcery in the Realms. I have no interest in the civic matters of the territory of the magi. I have real work to do." She put her hand on the hilt of her sword. "But if I must do your work, I will do it as your peer—or as your enemy."

"The laws of the Council—"

"If the Council will not grant me my due I will destroy it. I will see your Realm torn asunder, and your magical repositories burned to ash. Sorcery will go ungoverned in this Land forevermore."

The Councillor on the Speaker's right spoke up, though it did not use its voice. "Can she do that?"

Another Councillor spoke, "She is a faerie, and bound as a faerie to this world and its order."

The Speaker shook its head. "Those bindings have weakened. I fear that they may yet be severed."

"I can *hear* you," said the Warrior Queen. "And you will treat me with respect. Give me my due, or I'll have your severed heads for my battle standard. I'll use your guts to lace my boots. I'll patch my armour with leather from your generative organs."

"That will not be necessary." The Speaker for the Council

of the Magi spoke aloud. "You have treated with the magus' spirit, where none of us dared to. The seat is yours, Councillor-Queen."

The Warrior Queen made a gesture, drawing the first rune of a transportation spell in the air. "Good."

"Councillor-Queen," said the Speaker.

"Yes?" said the Warrior Queen, completing the second rune.

"There is another thing you should know, before your task is underway."

The Warrior Queen was halfway through the third and final rune. "Speak."

"The magus has a son," said the Speaker. "And he is abroad in the Realms of the Land."

27. The Malo

Bereft of what reason he had once possessed, Malo wandered through the Realms like a wild beast; without any intention beyond finding his next meal and shelter from the elements. In that measureless, meaningless time, he roamed from one territory to the next, killing, and ravening, and screaming without cause.

No one moved to end his depredations. Malo was but a single beast, these carefully anonymous forces reasoned, and his capacity for destruction was limited by his intellect. Moreover, he was the son of his father, whose intellect and whose capacity for destruction were not limited at all.

The son of the magus was dismissed and forgotten by all who knew him for who he was. When his father was slain, he did not know it, and nobody thought to inform him. Thus forgotten, he continued to make his savage way in his wildness, and he grew from a boy into a man. And there, he remained, lost in the wastes, until it was time for him to be remembered again.

The Warrior Queen tried first to scry the location of her quarry, but this yielded only pain and frustration. Her spells cracked upon Malo's presence and their shards were turned back upon her. But the Warrior Queen learned much about him from this procedure. Malo could not be scried, he could not be ensorcelled, he could not be enchanted…but she was certain that he could be tracked and tamed.

So the Warrior Queen set after him in the traditional way of her people: seeking with her eyes and ears, travelling on her own two feet, and armed to the teeth.

The Malo was hungry.

He hadn't had a morsel to eat or a mouthful to drink for any of the days or weeks or months he had wandered through the badlands.

The Malo was hungry. The Malo was thirsty. Aside from those two facts, the only other thought in his head was the knowledge that he should be dead. The Malo couldn't survive without food or water. He knew this, though he did not know why.

There was no food or water here; there was nothing but dust and jagged rocks and open, windless skies. There were animals about, but they were either too quick for his hands or too well armoured for his jaws.

The Malo was hungry and thirsty, but he wasn't lost, for there was nowhere he wanted to be. He had neither a home nor a destination. He had memories of other places, where food and water and shelter could be found, but he had not the wit to seek them out.

When the Warrior Queen approached him, the Malo barked with delight and fury. Food, at last. Meat to chew and blood to drink. The Malo raised his sickle and screamed his hunting cry—and then fell, without knowing how he had been struck down.

Malo awoke face down in the dirt. Chains secured him to a tree that was twice as tall as he. The Warrior Queen hunkered nearby, waiting for consciousness to rekindle in him.

Malo rolled over and climbed to his feet. He cast his head about him, snorting and snuffling. When he saw the Warrior

Queen he threw himself at her, snarling his rage. His chains snapped taut and his leap was arrested. He fell heavily to the ground.

Malo picked himself up and moved as close to the Warrior Queen as his bonds would allow. One of the chains encircled his neck: the more he struggled, the more it choked him. Malo strained against it until he choked himself back into unconsciousness.

When Malo again recovered his senses, the Warrior Queen drew her sword and approached him. Malo turned to face her, glowering and growling and twitching, his chains clattering.

The Warrior Queen stopped in front of him, barely an inch beyond the reach of his gnashing teeth.

"You are the son of the magus," she said.

Malo bared his teeth and exhaled hard through his nose. He was unsteady on his feet.

"The magus from the mortal realm."

Malo's breath hissed through his gritted teeth.

"Your father is dead."

Malo threw himself at the Warrior Queen. The chains snapped taut, clenched around his throat. He fell.

"The dog that killed your father is also dead, and its master has long since left these Realms…But I yet live, and so do you."

Coughing and bleeding, Malo rose to his knees, then, swaying, to a half-kneel.

The Warrior Queen stepped close to him, grabbed his chin and turned his face up towards her. "I still live, and I would have a dog of my own."

The Warrior Queen fed and watered Malo, and tended to his wounds. Then she took up his chains and led him out of the badlands. Restoring him to some semblance of self-awareness was not going to be an easy task.

Malo had forgotten how to speak. He had forgotten his

own name. He had barely been rational when he had entered the Realms, and now he was wild as any beast.

So she set about taming him as she would an animal: with the rod and the whip and with harsh words. The Warrior Queen beat him into compliance, and she rewarded him when he did as he was bidden. Soon Malo learned to obey her commands: sit, stay, heel. The discipline was good for him. Those three commands became ten, and then a hundred. Soon Malo could speak again, and understand some language, terse and broken though it was. He was not as damaged as she had first thought.

The Warrior Queen taught Malo how to hunt, how to fight. She was not a healer. She could not make of him a human being, but by the time she was done with him he was a passable soldier and an excellent attack dog.

At last, Malo came to properly understand that his father was dead, and that his thirst for vengeance could never be slaked. But now he had a new purpose: to serve the Warrior Queen. His loyalty to her was absolute, and that grew into something greater yet: a kind of yearning he had no prior experience of. It was not lust, though lust was part of it.

"I'll not lie with you," the Warrior Queen told him. "I will bear you no dog-children. You will sleep by my feet and be grateful for it, for that is the place of a dog."

He knew that he was not truly a dog, but he was no longer sure exactly how dogs were different to his own kind. But it felt good to have a master. It felt good to have somebody who finally cared about him, however small the measure of that regard might be.

28. Mortal Weapons

When the Warrior Queen was satisfied with Malo's progress she took him on a journey. They crossed the plains and trekked over the hills until they came to the juncture where the Ore-lands met the mountains and the forests. Together they reconnoitred the blasted territory that lay there. They climbed amongst spirals of rusted razor-wire, over the ruins of bunkers, between trenches that lay open and oozing. Landmines lay exposed in the dirt, though they did not detonate when Malo kicked them.

The carcasses of some strange, extinct faerie race lay amongst the ruins. Malo and the Warrior Queen sorted through the corpses, finding those that seemed most intact and sawing off the unwieldy metal devices that had been welded onto their limbs.

They laid out the salvage on a hide tarpaulin and sorted the items by size and shape. Malo crouched nearby and watched the Warrior Queen examine them. She went through the collection piece by piece, operating all of the moving parts: slides and levers, triggers and switches.

"These are weapons," she told him. "Fearsome, mortal weapons. But I cannot determine how they are supposed to function."

"Guns," said Malo. He picked out an assault rifle with a barrel that was as long as his arm and popped out the magazine.

"Yes, that's it. Show me."

Malo snapped the banana clip back into place and braced the rifle weapon against his shoulder. He adjusted his grip, aimed it away from the campsite, and pulled the trigger.

There was a single, loud click.

"Bang?" said Malo, confused.

"Machines cannot function in these Realms," said the Warrior Queen. "The mortal who crafted them is dead, and his sorcery has long been broken."

Malo understood most of that. "Guns. Mortal. Dead."

"Yes," said the Warrior Queen. She held out her hand and he passed her the weapon.

The Warrior Queen took the weapon from him. "Most of the runes are still intact, but I cannot follow their logic. Give me your hand."

Scowling, Malo held out his hand. She put it on the breech of the weapon. "We will yet make these weapons function again, Malo," she said. "You and I. Your magic and mine."

Malo shook his head.

"Malo," said the Warrior Queen.

Malo glowered at the Warrior Queen, but he nodded his consent. That was all she needed to harness his power. Malo's mere presence was a strange and dangerous thing.

The Warrior Queen gave Malo a rifle. Once he had taken hold of it, she drew a sigil on the back of his hand, and then covered it with her own. She spoke a syllable that glowed in the air and then took the rifle back.

The Warrior Queen swung the weapon around, looking for a target. About twenty meters away a fallen superstructure lay slumped over a bombed-out signals outpost. She lined up the sights and pulled the trigger.

The weapon issued a staccato bray. Spent runes sparked and flashed in the air amongst the ejected shell casings. Two dozen smoking holes scored the crumbling concrete wall of the bunker. A ricochet zinged off a steel girder.

The Warrior Queen smiled. Malo continued to scowl.

"Come," she said. "Let's repair these others."

When the sun rose, Malo and the Warrior Queen took

their cache of enchanted firearms and went on to their next destination. There was a new mortal loose in the Land, and soon they would have to meet with her.

When the fated hour fell, the Warrior Queen and her man-dog would be there to play their roles.

29. The Farm

The mortal wandered the Realms of the Land looking for the dark tower, but her uncle had not seen it during his journey, and she had no idea where it might be. It did not seem to matter which way she went, or how fast she travelled; every path looped back to a place she had already been. It was becoming monotonous.

After some reflection, the mortal determined that there were two places her uncle had described that she had not yet visited: the farm and the black forest. Perhaps she needed to complete the circuit before she would be allowed to search for the dark tower.

The mortal followed the river back through the Ore-lands, avoiding the battlefield where the Tree Queen and the Queen of the Ore-Lands yet strove for victory. The skies lightened and the river ran clear, and soon she found herself in a rolling pastureland, where crops were cultivated and beasts were penned.

The farm folk put down their labours and offered her their hospitality, which she accepted gratefully. They were quick and furry and grey; as strange as they were homely. They were just as her uncle had described them. Inside a low, thatched dwelling, they bade her take her ease. The eldest of them enquired as to whether she was hungry or thirsty.

"I do not hunger or thirst," she replied.

"You must be tired from the road."

"I do not tire, either."

"That is most curious," said the elder. "Most curious indeed, that one such as yourself should come here without any needs."

"The only need I have is for information."

"You are kin to one that was here before."

"Yes," said the mortal. "It's astute of you to perceive that."

"No," said the elder. "It's perceptive of me, and nothing more. Now tell me what you need to know."

"I'm looking for the dark tower."

"I know of several towers," said the elder, "Some of them are, indeed, dark in appearance."

"It is *the* dark tower," she said. "The darkest one. Not the darkest-*looking* one."

"I know of no tower which was erected for the purpose of being 'dark'."

"It was raised by a mortal," she replied. "An evil magus."

"I know of no such magus," said the elder. "If such a one is abroad in these Realms, he has not found cause to visit his wickedness upon us here."

"He is long dead," she replied. "But I am told that his tower remains."

"Is this your quest?"

"I'd like to see it," she said. "Whether that is my quest or not, I cannot say."

"If you know not what you quest for, you have no quest," said the elder. "If you came to the Realms with no purpose, you will return home just as destitute—if you return at all."

30. The Black Forest

So the mortal went from the farmlands and crossed the Ore-lands yet again, and then the Sinewed Forest, and then the plains of the Sea City. She passed through the mountains and back into the meadowlands, and then down past the village to the black forest that had risen to herald her uncle's arrival.

The mortal spent the afternoon gathering wood for a fire, although her avatar did not feel the effects of the elements upon it. She knew it would draw her uncle's creatures from the darkness.

The mortal did not know how to start a fire without matches, so she crafted a small program to do the work. As the last of the day drained away she flipped the state to 'burn', and soon she had an impressive blaze going.

And sure enough, when the moonless sky was dark, the black things came forth, dressed—or perhaps bound—in leather that was dyed and lacquered and charred. They crouched and capered just beyond the circle of firelight, though they did not cross into it.

"Speak to me," she said.

The leader of the black things came into the circle of light and squatted down across the fire from her. She could barely see it, so thick was the night and so dark was its colouration. The firelight gleamed in its blood-black eyes; glistened on its bleeding black teeth. It made no sound.

"Will you speak with me, as you once did my blood-kin?"

The black thing grinned at her for a while longer, stiller and blacker than the night sky. "Why?" it said. "Do you have anything to tell me?"

"I just want to know what you are."

"Feh," said the black thing. "I am more blood-kin than you are." It hissed impudently and receded into the night.

"Fuck this for a joke." The mortal snatched up her greatsword, and strode out into the black forest in the dead of night.

She walked in silence amongst the bare, black trees, her feet soundless on the dead black soil. The air was still and warm on her skin. The forest was utterly silent: not a breath of wind to stir the dead tree limbs, not a bird or a critter or an insect going about its nocturnal business. She was the only thing that moved there. She was the only thing that lived.

The mortal reminded herself that her avatar had no physical presence, that she could not be harmed in this virtual world, but the reminder gave her no comfort.

The mortal walked on, seeking some being, some presence, some sign, but she found nothing but dying trees and dead soil. Though her avatar was invulnerable, she had not the courage to touch the dirt or the trees with her bare, virtual flesh.

"Fuck!" she screamed. "Just, fuck you all!"

She swung her greatsword about, hacking blindly at the forest. She felled three trees with as many strokes, but many, many more remained standing. No harm came to her from the splinters of wood and the clouds of dust her lumberjacking raised.

"Fuck it," she said. "I'm too fucking old for fucking goddamn fairy stories, anyway."

By the time the sun rose she was out of the black forest. In the distance she could see the Tree of Indeterminate Species.

31. The Tree, The Tower

It was high noon by the time the mortal came to the tree—but by the time she had reached it, it was not a tree anymore.

She stood before a dark and jagged tower; so slimed with evil that it stained the very skies it broached.

Gooseflesh prickled her virtual skin. She turned away and rubbed her eyes. When she looked again the dark tower was gone, and the Tree of Indeterminate Species was again where it was supposed to be.

Cursing, the mortal strode up to the tree, keeping her eyes fixed upon it. It looked as weird and unnatural as she remembered, but it was definitely a tree and not a tower. She walked its circumference, looking for the opening that would permit her to return to her own world—but there was none. She circled it again, and again, but still there was no opening.

The mortal sighed. Some further events must be played out there before she could return to her home, she supposed. Now her true quest would be revealed…or perhaps she would discover that she had unknowingly completed it already. She hoped for the latter; she was tired of fairy tales. She wanted to go home and have a nice cup of tea and a hot bath. She hoped she still had a job.

The mortal waited for a full minute, but nothing happened. "Oh, for fuck's *sake*!" she yelled, stamping in frustration.

"Shut your filthy mouth, pig-fucker." The voice was

smooth and resonant and confident and female.

A warrior dressed in a leather jerkin and breeches stood in the road behind the mortal. Her hair and her eyes were a uniform brown. She had slung about her a variety of swords and sickles and dirks and daggers. In her hands, the warrior held an improbably large machinegun—the sort of weapon that had been popular in the mortal's own world in the late 20th century.

Beside the warrior stood an olive-skinned man with short-cropped black hair. He was tall and lean and held himself with a hunched posture that looked meek, at first...and then it looked aggressive. He was dressed in hand-made jeans and a t-shirt. His eyes were pale; dripping with adoration for the warrior that kept him. A sickle made of bone and obsidian hung from his belt.

"I'm a grown woman and I'll swear as much as I fucking well want to," said the mortal. "What are you, the Warrior Queen?"

"Yes."

"And him?"

"You don't know about him," said the Warrior Queen, "But I will warrant that you know of his father."

"His father is...my uncle?"

"His father was the magus."

"Of course," the mortal replied. "Otherwise it would be too bloody simple, wouldn't it?"

"Yes."

"So...you're Zildjian, or whatever? You're supposed to be dead."

"I am the daughter of Zelioliah."

"Awesome." The mortal hefted the greatsword. "I thought this was D&D, but it turns out to be Happy Families."

The Warrior Queen sneered. "Is that gesture a threat? Are you truly so foolish?"

"You know, you're exactly how my uncle described your mother to me," the mortal said. "But, honestly? I can't understand what he saw in you. Um, I mean, her."

"I am physically identical to my mother," said the Warrior Queen, "But she was the most beautiful thing in all of the worlds, and I am not beautiful at all."

"Oh, you're okay," the mortal replied. "Don't be hard on yourself. Nothing wrong with you that a bit of foundation and maybe some lippy wouldn't fix."

"I may not be beautiful, but I have far more power than my mother ever did," replied the Warrior Queen.

"Have you got a name?" asked the mortal. She looked at the son of the magus. "Does he?"

"Malo," said Malo, shifting uneasily.

"Of course I have a name," said the Warrior Queen. "Do *you*?"

"Oh, what*ever*," the mortal replied. "I've had a gutful and I just want to go home. Tell me what I have to do and let's just get on with it."

"Do?" said Malo.

"Tell me how to complete my hero quest, or whatever bullshit is necessary for me to go home."

"There are no heroes," said the Warrior Queen. "You have no quest. You've come here without a purpose of your own, and there's no way out for you."

"That doesn't make any sense. Of course there's a quest."

"That's true, of course. But it's not your quest. It's mine."

"Great, whatever. I get it. It's all backwards. You're the questor and I'm the questee, that's fucking fabulous. You found me—now tell me what you want from me."

"Justice."

"What?"

"Your kinsman slew mine; now I will slay you."

"That's not justice."

"Justice is whatever I would call by that name."

The mortal brandished her greatsword. "Ok, so, really, you're the Big Bad? If I kill you, that's it, right? This is the last level?"

"I am Queen of the Warriors."

The mortal shook her head. "I copped the cheat codes.

Let's just jump ahead to the final cut-scene and save ourselves the button-mashing, okay? I'll not be playing the sequel."

The Warrior Queen raised her machinegun. "You had power when you came to these Realms," she said, "but, here in the presence of my dog-friend, you do not."

Malo looked up, as though expecting food scraps to be thrown to him.

"You're full of shit," the mortal replied. She raised the greatsword overhead and accelerated her avatar towards the Warrior Queen, intending to deliver a killing stroke in between the gap between virtual seconds...

...but the sword was suddenly heavy in her arms, and the terrain was uneven beneath her feet. Her cut was slow and clumsy, as though her true flesh had swung the weapon. The Warrior Queen avoided the attack easily, stepping outside of the blade's arc and letting it swing harmlessly past.

The mortal staggered as momentum spun her around. The sword fell point-first into the dirt. It had become too heavy for her to lift.

The Warrior Queen cocked the machinegun and raised the muzzle.

"You know what I'm thinking, right?" said the mortal to the Warrior Queen.

"I don't care what you're thinking." The Warrior Queen braced the weapon, aimed low, and squeezed the trigger.

The mortal's ears filled with thunder. Gunfire smashed her legs from under her and she crumpled.

The Warrior Queen shouldered the machinegun and smiled. "Dog?"

"Dog," said Malo, nodding. He came forwards, swinging his sickle.

The mortal rolled onto her stomach and pushed herself up with her hands, willing herself...her avatar...to stand on her...on *its*...mangled legs. She got her hands on the cross-guard of the greatsword and used it to lever herself upright.

Malo closed on her, taking short, bent-kneed steps, just as the Warrior Queen had taught him.

The mortal changed her grip on the hilt of the greatsword, preparing to yank it from the ground and surge upwards; determined to take at least one of these fairy-tale motherfuckers with her before a saviour arrived. Her uncle, perhaps. Or the freak from the Council of the Magi. Or perhaps even the black thing. Or the dog-man, or some other ludicrous creature she was forgetting. These bloody fairy stories always ended the same way.

Malo kicked the greatsword from her hands and swung his sickle. It punched into the mortal's abdomen just below the ribcage. He jerked the blackglass blade upwards even as she fell upon it; shattering one rib after another; tearing through her lungs and piercing her heart.

Malo held her there for a moment, looking down at her. His pale blue eyes were darker than she could comprehend. He pulled the blade free and the mortal slumped at his feet.

The Warrior Queen turned the corpse over with the toe of her boot and inspected it. "Kin for kin, blood for blood. I have wronged the man who wronged my mother."

"Wronged," said Malo.

"Now he will return." The Warrior Queen slung the machinegun behind her and ruffled Malo's hair. "He will return to the Realms of the Land, and we shall be here waiting for him."

Book 4
Black Wings

1. Dreaming Awake

He awoke from a sleep that was closer to death than to dream.

Though he slumbered too deeply for even his subconscious to function, some new information had yet lodged in his mind. Information that drew him back from the abyss; returned him to the worlds of truth and fiction.

She was dead.

The mortal cast off the blankets and swung his legs over the side of the narrow bed.

He had sent her in his footsteps, and she had died because of it.

The mortal stood up and looked each way down the rows of hospital beds. None of the other patients slept as deeply as he, though few of them would return to waking. Intravenous drips fed them; catheters drew away their wastes. Blinking machinery monitored their vital signs.

There were no such devices around his bed. He had been unplugged, but he had failed to die.

The world had aged while he slept, but the mortal had not. Such was the benefit, and the price, of living two lives simultaneously. Mortal and immortal, real and fictive. He was still human, although to a different degree than most.

The mortal found his old pair of patched and faded jeans in the small cabinet beside his bed. He put them on, and then the pale t-shirt that had once been either white or black. Time had bleached or stained it to an indeterminate shade that he wore much more comfortably. He laced up his scuffed old army boots and pulled on the thick nylon jacket.

The cabinet also contained the rucksack in which he had kept his talismans and trophies. He emptied it into the waste paper basket. After a moment's contemplation, he threw the rucksack in as well. He squared his shoulders and walked out of the ward.

As he walked the white-enamelled halls he allowed his vision to lose focus. The phosphorescent strips embedded in the hand rails and the luminous lines painted on the floor blurred until they showed him the direction he sought.

Nobody crossed his path as he followed the flickering lines, for he walked in the interstices between footfalls. His feet fell in the gaps between the seconds; the chasms that yawned between moments.

The lights overhead dimmed and the handrails vanished. The geometrically precise lines on the floor began to bend and twist, and their accompanying directions came to be written in languages no mortal could comprehend. Yet he walked on, and onwards, for the way remained clear to him.

The lines disappeared altogether and the hard, polished flooring changed beneath his feet. It became rock, then bare earth, then grass. Before long he found himself standing atop a hill, looking down upon a village. Three score low, stone buildings were cupped in the valley, which had been cut from the hills by a broad, silvery river. The only road that ran amongst the misaligned buildings was the central thoroughfare, which was presently serving as a marketplace.

"The village," he said, and began his descent.

2. Sequence

The species of the Worldtree could not easily be determined, but the size of it was another matter.

If one were to measure its girth and height, one would surely discover that the Worldtree was *big*. Inside, it was bigger; a maze without walls, with exits into many different worlds. Some of those exits were better used than others. Some were blocked, and some were guarded.

The exit into the Land of the Faerie was not merely guarded; it had been barricaded like a fortress besieged.

In the shadow of those fortifications, the Warrior Queen and her man-dog strove together in combat. The Queen beat the man-dog's weapon away and kicked him to the ground. She sheathed her sword and turned in the direction of the village while he gasped the breath back into his lungs. He was pretty good, for a mortal.

Malo picked up his sickle and got unsteadily to his feet.

The Warrior Queen did not turn to look at him. "He has risen," she said. "He is here."

"How?" said Malo.

"I don't know. He did not pass through the Tree."

The Warrior Queen dispatched a corporal to summon the three special warriors she had reserved for just this contingency. It took longer than she would have liked for them to attend her, although she knew that the three warriors made their bivouac away from the rest of the battalion. Still, there was something insolent about the way they came striding into the shadowy place at the foot of the Worldtree that displeased her. That insolence was among the reasons she had chosen these three for their task.

"The mortal has eluded us already," said the Warrior Queen. "But he's not far away. You will pursue and capture him for me."

"Name a direction, Majesty, and we will chase him down," said the first warrior, who wore a matched pair of scars from the hinges of its jaw to the orbits of its eyes.

"I can do better than that," the Queen replied. "I can tell you his exact route. The village, the grove, the mountain pass. The Sea City on the Plains. Then along the river, over the mountains, and through the Sinewed Forest to the Ore-lands. From there he will proceed through the pastures into the Tree Queen's realm. Then he will cut through the black forest and return to the Worldtree."

"If his route is known to us, Majesty, why do we not lay an ambush?" asked the second warrior, who carried dozens of blades upon its person–though none of them was larger than a dagger.

"This mortal is tricksy," said the Warrior Queen. "But so am I. Let me worry about traps and ambushes; your orders are to pursue."

"And when we find him, Majesty?" asked the third warrior, whose leather jerkin was wet with the blood of the many foes it had slain. "What then?"

"You will bring him to me," said the Warrior Queen. "Alive."

The Warrior Queen dispatched her three chosen warriors and doubled the watch she had set. Then she retired to her tent. She sat down upon the bare ground and drew her magic to her. She muttered a word, waved a gesture, and suddenly she was no longer alone.

The semblances of twelve black-robed, hooded beings surrounded her. Their circle was larger than the interior of the tent, but they were all nonetheless visible to her. A gap in the perimeter of the circle indicated her own seat on the

Council of the Magi. As usual, she sat in the centre of the ring.

The Speaker for the Council said: "What is it that concerns you, Councillor-Queen?"

"The mortal has returned."

The Councillors were still and silent.

Eventually, the Speaker said: "That cannot be so."

"It is so."

"None of our wards indicate this to be the case."

"He has returned," said the Warrior Queen. "I feel it in my marrow."

"You *feel* it, Councillor Queen?" asked the Speaker. "Do you *feel* your intuition to be more powerful than our divinations?"

"In this matter, yes," she replied. "I *feel* his mortality upon the Land. My bones are hungry for it."

"Bones do not hunger, Councillor-Queen."

"You would know otherwise, if you had a full complement of them."

The insult did not give the Speaker pause, but it did drive the supercilious tone from its voice. "If this is true…if the mortal is here…why haven't you destroyed him already?"

"He did not make his passage through the Worldtree."

"How else can he have crossed over? He is no magician."

"Perhaps he found a new portal?"

"No," said the Speaker. "He must follow the sequence of his prior expedition."

"He's a mortal, he's not bound by such laws," said the Warrior Queen. "But I don't believe he's changed his game. He's just skipped ahead of the opening gambit."

"You must be sure that he plays through to the end," said the Speaker.

"Aye."

They were silent a moment.

"You knew he would return, but you have never explained to me why," said the Warrior Queen.

"Perhaps he is just repeating his earlier quest. Perhaps he has no reason at all."

"I have sent warriors after him," said the Warrior Queen, "But I will await him here at the Tree."

"Good," said the Speaker. "He is not so terrible a threat as other mortals we have dealt with, but..."

"But what?"

"But this one has a surprising capacity for destruction, and he has aroused the enmity of many. He must not elude us again."

"He will not," said the Warrior Queen. "It is both my chosen and my fated purpose to slay him. He is a weakling and a fool—it will not be difficult."

"This weakling slew many of our kind. He slew one of his own that was far more powerful than he," said the Speaker. "This fool has much harm in him."

"In the past, the dog-man and the Warrior Queen came to his aid. Now, the Warrior Queen and her dog oppose him. He has no one to protect him, this time."

"Even if he does," said the Speaker, "Who can possibly protect him from us?"

3. The Village

It was market day in the village, and the streets were thronged with merchants and clerks, spruikers and vendors; servants and dealers; and spouses and thieves. Slaves and agents and thralls and free folk bustled amongst the stalls. Faeries from every nation, every breed, every fiefdom or republic or army or freehold plied their business there. *Sidhe* from all the Realms of the Land haggled for herbs or glamours, clothing or arms, favours or companionship, knowledge or lies.

The babble of commerce died abruptly. The words of barter seized on their flapping tongues, jammed in their flexing gullets. A figure was coming down the hillside.

It was an unremarkable figure: male; configured with two arms and two legs; neither short nor tall. It was a mortal.

The sun shone bright above him, and his shadow pooled small and stunted at his feet…but the folk in the market froze as if they felt its darkness upon them.

They broke and ran.

Some fled afoot. Others transformed into beasts or birds or fish, and galloped or flew or swam away. Some took to strange mounts and thrashed them with spurs and whips; others clambered into whimsical vehicles and peeled out on clattering wheels. Some of the folk fell into the ground or dissolved into the shadows; others simply vanished. The market was empty by the time the mortal set foot in it.

The mortal walked the length of the deserted boulevard.

He browsed the weapons and foodstuffs and enchantments and talismans, the gewgaws and knick-knacks and treasures and trophies that were displayed in the abandoned stalls, though he did not stop to examine any particular one.

At the far end of the avenue was a purple tent. A sign in front of it showed the words, in English, Fortunes Told.

The mortal bent his head and pushed his way through many layers of drapery until he came to the dark centre of the enclosure, where the fortune teller awaited him. It sat with its hands in its sleeves and its head bowed, swaddled in the garment that was also its dwelling.

The fortune teller raised its head. "Are you going to harm me?"

"Can you not foretell this?" he asked, sitting down with his legs crossed.

"My future is opaque with your shadow," the fortune teller replied, drawing its long-fingered hands out of its sleeves and putting them together, fingertips touching. "Well, *are* you?"

"No. I only came in here because there's nobody else left in the town."

"I am not as mobile as the rest of the villagers," said the fortune teller, gesturing at the tent without separating its hands. The mortal wondered how much of the creature was buried beneath the ground.

"You weren't here last time I came."

"No. You did not need an oracle, then."

"I don't need one now."

"If you are not here to slay me and you do not desire a reading, why do you linger?"

It was a good question. "Did you speak with my kinswoman, when she was here?"

"Aye."

"Thought you might have."

"Her journey was awry afore even she undertook it, and she came to me for guidance. But my guidance went unheeded."

"Did she find what she sought?"

"If she sought a bitter and violent death, then yes, she did."

"There was nothing here for her, after all."

"I told her as much," said the fortune teller. "But someone had already convinced her otherwise."

He looked away. "Can you truly tell fortunes?"

"I can," said the fortune teller. "If I am asked. Have you changed your mind?"

"No," he replied. "But I have another question for you."

"Ask, then."

"Tell me, fortune teller, do fortunes truly unfold as you have seen?"

"If whomever has asked a fortune of me believes in my vision, yes."

"And if the subject does not believe?"

"If they do not, they ought not to ask me."

"Do your visions predict a predetermined future? Or are they just projections that come to pass, due to the beliefs of your subjects?"

"I am of the Faerie Folk," said the fortune teller, recoiling as if from a slap. "We do not imagine; we are the imagined. The truth of my telling is entirely dependent upon the mortal to whom I speak it."

The mortal pulled at his beard. "What is it about your vision that is so special, that it can shape a mortal's future?"

"Nothing. I see on their behalf, through the lens of my own wisdom," replied the fortune teller. "Power lies not in my ability to see, but rather in my ability to perceive."

"I thank you, fortune teller. Your…insight…has been invaluable to me," said the mortal.

"Are you certain you do not desire a reading?" said the fortune teller. "I am most curious to know what will happen next."

"Thank you, but no," said the mortal, backing out through the hanging drapery of the fortune teller's tent. "I prefer to see things through by myself."

4. The Playwright

Nentril Revallo had erected a small stage in the grove by the riverbank. He stood there on the boards, hopping from foot to foot with impatience, waiting for the arrival of the star. Behind him, a velvet curtain hung parted over a backdrop that was painted a solid black. There was no backstage.

Revallo had never suffered from stage fright, but a fear was upon him then. His players had fled, and there was no audience spread before him. The playwright waited alone for the show to begin.

Revallo knew the approach of his lead when the darkness intensified, though the light of the buckled moon remained undimmed.

The mortal ambled through the rows of empty bleachers, looking around him with evident curiosity.

"Welcome, mortal, to centre stage!" the playwright declaimed. He was pleased that his voice betrayed no hint of his trepidation.

The boards creaked as the mortal mounted the stage.

Revallo bowed low. "I am the playwright, Nentril Revallo. Perhaps you have heard of me?"

The mortal regarded him for a moment. "I have not,' he said. "But you remind me of somebody famous."

"You are likewise obscure to me," said the playwright, "though you are the star tonight, and the lights shine full upon you."

"The better to cast my shadow," said the mortal. "If I am truly the star, I am one that has fallen."

"Hero or villain, you are yet the protagonist," said the playwright.

"True enough."

"Tell me, protagonist: why did you first come to the Realms?"

"I came seeking the greatest beauty in all of the worlds."

"An old-fashioned quest," said the playwright. "How noble."

"My quest was as base as any other. I pursued my obsession to the end of sanity and once I possessed what I desired, I destroyed it."

"The experience transformed you."

"It evolved me, playwright, but it did not make of me somebody new. It drew out my true nature."

"Why have you returned to the Realms, mortal? Have you some new quest?"

"My kinswoman travelled here after I told her my story, and she was murdered."

"Ah," said the Revallo. "Revenge. That is always a plentiful source of drama."

"It is an excuse. A storyteller's conceit. I have returned because it is my nature to do so."

"And what is your nature, mortal man?"

"I am a traveller. I seek new places, because I have no place of my own."

The playwright was bold, and wise to the ways of Story. He believed himself a master of such, and he did not fear to navigate any plot; to embroil himself with any narrative. But the placid way the mortal spoke gave the playwright pause. "And why is that, mortal? Was your place destroyed? Were you cast out from it?"

"I just…I changed, and I felt that I did not belong there anymore," said the mortal. "Soon others came to feel the same way. And so I left."

"And so you came here," said the playwright.

"Eventually," said the mortal. "I went to other places, first. Now you answer one for me, playwright.

"That is only fair."

"Tell me," said the mortal, "are all of your stories about mortal travellers in the Realms?"

"They are," said Revallo. "Left to our own devices, we Folk do not change, and our stories are fixed. Mortals are the only true source of new tales here."

The mortal just smiled. "You are a curious one, Nentril Revallo. You are a Faerie creature. Your kind do not dream. And yet here you are, a playwright, seeking stories to make your own."

"My stories are pale and indulgent things. I understand the structures and the strictures, but, unlike a mortal, I cannot create tales that are truly new. Mine are stolen things, retold to the best of my ability and comprehension."

The mortal cocked his head. "The same is true of mortal storytellers; do not let their hubris deceive you. You may find true greatness yet."

"How so?" replied the playwright. "How may I find such a thing, when my fate is prisoner to some mortal's awful story?"

"I am not yet certain," replied the mortal. "But I believe that I can free you, and all of your kind, if you will but believe in me."

"Why should you need such a thing?" asked the playwright. "I wield no magic. I command no armies. I am but a playwright, master only of my own threadbare troupe of players."

"You are a storyteller, Nentril Revallo, and stories are everything in this place. If I am to have my way I need others to see the world as I do. For that, I would have the storytellers on my side."

The playwright was taken aback. "If you would do this for us, you are indeed a hero."

"I fear not, Revallo. The times to come will be harsh, and few will thank me for them."

"Why, then, would you spend your mortal days on such a cause?" said the playwright. "Deny it as you would, your heart is noble indeed."

The mortal laughed. "My heart is just an organ, Revallo—but you are an inveterate flatterer. You ask what's in it for me, and I can tell you only this…" The mortal looked around, suddenly self-conscious. He scratched behind his ear and said "Sometimes I just get sick of hearing the same damn stories, over and over again."

5. In the Pass

The shadowphage did not know exactly what a mortal was, but it knew one when it saw one. Concealed and compressed into its crevice, it watched him clamber up the steepening mountain pass. The shadowphage did not care to correct its ignorance; it cared only that it was hungry.

When it believed itself to be within range of the mortal's senses, the shadowphage seeped out of the darkness and stepped into its proper shape. It was tall and narrow, with skin the colour of old bones. Shadows hung thick in its eye sockets and amongst the cleavage of its breasts.

"Hello," said the mortal.

The shadowphage smiled at him. "Why, hello," it said. "Are you a mortal man?"

"In a manner of speaking."

"Either you are, or you are not," the shadowphage said, as pleasantly as it could.

"I am *a* mortal," came the reply, "Though I am not, exactly, *mortal.*"

"Have you a soul?"

"Yes."

"Then you are a mortal," said the shadowphage, its smile spreading. "I knew it. Are you dangerous?"

"In my own way."

"Of course you are." The shadowphage stroked the hooked, bladed instruments that hung from its belt with twitching fingers.

"You mean me harm," the mortal said. "You would consume my flesh."

"I cannot ingest anything but darkness and shadow," said the shadowphage, its bloodless lips parting. In its mouth there was no tongue, just ring after ring of teeth. "I am a shadowphage."

"Yet still you mean me harm."

"I must open you up, if I am to have the shadows out of you."

"I fear that would be a grievous error."

"Oh, aye?" said the shadowphage, its darksome grin fading.

"Come, then," the mortal replied, touching his sternum. "Look upon me, as I have looked upon you. Let us see whose insides are the darker."

The shadowphage blinked, and looked at him again; and the mortal returned its regard. There was indeed a darkness visible through the holes in the mortal's face, and that darkness was blacker than the shadowphage could stand to look upon, much less to eat.

The shadowphage backed towards its crevice; paling into translucency.

"Stop," said the mortal. "I am not done with you, yet."

"Please," said the shadowphage. "I will give to you all that I possess. I will serve you; I will cherish you. I will please you in any way you desire."

"I don't wish you ill," the mortal said. "In fact, I think you're kind of cool. Recognize that you are mine and promise to attend me when I call for you, and you may remain otherwise free for all your days."

"I am yours, now and forevermore."

"For ever more," the mortal repeated.

"Thank you," said the shadowphage. "Thank you for the gift of your patronage. Thank you, bless you—"

"Nothing is given that cannot also be taken," said the mortal. "Now give me your silence and retract your company, before I reconsider."

The shadowphage drew itself back into the crevice without another word.

6. The Sinewed Forest

The mortal walked down out of the mountains, passing through the regions where the rock-face was marbled with mirror-glass and living meat, and where gravity recast its direction at whim. He walked on through the Sinewed Forest, where the fleshtrees bore rotting, overripe babyfruit. A river of amniotic milk gave nourishment to all the beasts that lived upon the land and in the trees…but those beasts were scarce now.

He saw none of the pigbirds that had so delighted him when first he had ventured here. Perhaps it was the season: the foliage was red and yellow and purple and black, and the trees crackled like arthritic fingers when the wind pushed them. Perhaps it was some doom more permanent than winter.

The mortal walked on, paying the sights little heed. He had passed that way before, and all of his wonder was already spent.

7. The Ruined City on the Plains

Desolate, the Sea People of the Plains lingered amongst the ruins of their fallen city.

Before their Queen had perished, their capitol had been a great, luminous place; risen from waves of verdant grass; set firm against a sky that had flowed blue and ebbed black, as the days and nights made their cycle. Now the grass grew sparse and yellow, and the ocean of sky had receded to a bed of pale silt. Now the city was broken and rotting, rimed with the misery of its inhabitants.

The mortal came over the dunes, his lengthening shadow marching behind him. The Sea People watched him approach with eyes still raw from their protracted grief. Their pastel-hued skins had bleached to the palest of greys; their sun-white hair was stained nicotine-yellow. He could not tell if they recognized him or not.

The mortal went up to one who stood leaning on a rusty halberd. There was no desire for vengeance, nor even justice, in its cracked and clouded eyes.

"I know that I am the cause of your mourning, and I am sorry for that," said the mortal. "But it is a shame to let this glorious place fall to ruin."

"Our Queen is dead," said the halberdier. "What choice do we have?"

"Could you not instate a new Queen?" asked the mortal. "Are there no heirs?"

"They, too, are in mourning," said the halberdier.

"Come now," said the mortal. "The Realms are changing. Soon you will be free from the shackles that have bound your Folk for all these long centuries."

"No freedom can fill the pit of our despair."

"If you would have your Realm restored, all you need do is name yourselves mine."

"We do not wish to be restored," the halberdier said. "Our only wish is that you leave us to our dying."

"You are immortal faerie folk," replied the mortal. "Dying is not a process to which you are subject. You are either alive or you are dead, and you will not perish unless you are slain."

"Thus we are shackled, as you have said. If you can truly free us, you will allow us the death that we desire."

"Grant I your allegiance. Name yourselves for me and I will see to it that you get what you desire."

"Can you grant us mortality?" said the halberdier.

"I cannot give you a mortal soul. That is something you must earn for yourselves," he replied, "But I am certain that I can deliver you a fitting death."

"Then we are yours," said the halberdier. "We are yours until we perish from existence."

Shaking his head, the mortal left the Sea Folk of the Plains to husk out in their washed-up city. He had offered them a sea change, but all they wanted was a slackening tide.

8. The Three Warriors

The three warriors came to the mountains with the dawn. They came swiftly and silently, sweeping every pass, every trail, every way that the mortal could have taken on his way to the Sea City on the Plains.

In the pass between the tallest and the shortest of mountains, the scarred warrior knelt in the dust and examined the mark it found there.

"This boot-print is the mortal's, no question," said the warrior in the bloody jerkin, coming to stand by its scarred companion.

"How?" asked the swordless warrior. "Even without rest, he cannot have passed through these mountains so many hours ahead of us."

"I don't know how, but the spoor is clear," said the bloodied warrior. "It's him."

"We should separate," said the swordless warrior. "We must try to get ahead of him."

"Her Majesty has forbidden it," said the bloodied warrior. "We are only to pursue."

"I believe that some magic is preventing us from catching him, though I cannot fathom its nature."

"That is because you are a warrior, not a magician."

"We cannot succeed if we continue in this way. We should separate. Her Majesty will brook failure worse than insubordination."

"I don't know," said the bloodied warrior. "Our orders were quite explicit."

The scarred warrior finally spoke. "You two go on ahead. I'll continue to follow him."

"Those are not our orders," said the bloodied warrior.

"If I remain on the mortal's trail," said the scarred warrior, "then elements of our unit are still following him, and we are still operating within the parameters of our orders."

"I agree with this plan," said the swordless warrior, making it a consensus of two against one.

The bloodied warrior regarded its comrades quietly. The three of them were special warriors; none of them had rank over the others. "Harm the mortal if you must," it advised, "but remember: it is her Majesty's prerogative to slay him."

"I will wreak harm upon him," said the scarred warrior. "You may rest assured of that."

9. The Magus

The mortal's footfalls were light and his strides were long as he followed the opalescent river through all of its meanderings. It felt as if the gravity of the Land was too weak to keep him properly earthbound. His progress was swifter than he would have credited.

Presently, the river ran clear and gravity resumed its customary direction and intensity. Soon after, the mortal passed through the copse of trees in which he had once taken shelter.

The mortal stood on the riverbank, where he had once knelt to fill his canteen. This time he had no canteen to fill, and he did not kneel. He looked across to the far bank, but there was nobody there. He looked upstream, and watched the water flow towards him. He looked downstream, and watched the water flow away.

The mortal nosed around the copse until he found the tree in which he had slept. It had grown, he was certain. He ran his gaze from its boughs to the base of its trunk, where the roots squirmed their way down into the soil.

The mortal kicked at the dirt until he found something pale buried there. He knelt down and, using his fingers, scraped more of the earth away until the shape of it was revealed. A skull looked up at him; eye-sockets caked with dirt and shadows.

"Did I make your day?" he asked the skull.

It did not reply.

"Alas, poor magus?"

The skull had nothing to say.

The mortal stood up and dusted his hands off on his jeans. The skull continued to look up at him with dark, empty eyes. He put his boot-heel against its forehead; straightened his leg and leaned forwards upon it. The bone splintered quietly; the sod that filled it muting the sound of it cracking.

The mortal spat upon the ground and went on his way. He had no more words for the magus.

10. The Inn

The mortal followed the river downstream, and the woods became denser around him as he went. Soon the sky darkened and it began to rain.

This was not the drizzle he has felt the last time he had come through this territory. This was a great and melodramatic weeping, and the rain was hot and salty on his face.

"Come, now," said the mortal. "I was merciful when last I passed through this territory."

The rain abated to a sullen spitting and the mortal forged on. Soon he came to the wash where weasels' inn had once stood. All that remained of the place was the fallen-in foundation pit and a few blackened timbers. Perhaps the weasel-folk had tried their game on someone rather less forgiving than he.

On his way back to the river he came upon the stump of a hollow tree. When he peered down into it he found that it contained a den, lined with rotting skins. Curled up among them were the skeletons of an assortment of weasels, stoats and polecats

There was no sign of the yellow fox.

11. The Bloodied Warrior

The City of the Ore-lands sprawled like a great iron beast, crouching to drink from the river. The beast's breath whistled as it exhaled the steam and smoke generated by the many smiths and artificers that made their trade there. The mortal approached the gates with his head high and a smile upon his lips, savouring some past memory.

"Surrender yourself, pig-fucker."

The mortal stumbled, but caught himself before he fell.

A warrior in a jerkin that was red with blood stepped between him and the city gates. "Surrender," it repeated. "You're nicked."

The mortal held out his hands to show that they were empty, though the smile remained on his lips. "No."

The bloodied warrior came on with a sword in one hand an axe in the other. "Come quietly," it said. "I have orders not to kill you, but I will hurt you if you resist."

"I'm sorry," replied the mortal, "But I must refuse."

The bloodied warrior took another step forwards and raised its sword. "Do you truly believe that you, of all the swine-sucking mortals that ever crept across the Land, can defeat one of the warrior folk in single combat?"

"No," the mortal replied, "but this combat is the other kind."

The bloodied warrior glanced to either side without moving its head. A platoon of the Ore Queen's soldiers clanked into a loose half-circle behind it. The warrior drew itself into a defensive posture.

The platoon sergeant came forwards. Metallic scrollwork pressed through the skin of its face, and its grey hair was rainbowed with a sheen of oil. "Lay down your weapons," said the sergeant. "This mortal is a friend to the Ore-lands, and our liege will permit no harm to him in her sovereign territory."

"This mortal is nobody's friend," the bloodied warrior told the sergeant. "He is a scourge and a pestilence; a coward and a murderer. The Warrior Queen would see him face justice for his crimes."

The sergeant drew a huge curved blade. "The Queen of the Ore-lands says otherwise," it said. "Stand down."

"I will not," said the bloodied warrior. "Let me have the mortal; it will cost the Ore-lands nothing. Stand against me, and it will cost you many lives."

"So be it," said the sergeant.

The bloodied warrior parried the sergeant's scimitar blow with its axe and riposted with the sword, delivering an effortless cut that split the sergeant's head in half. The sergeant fell in a spray of rainbowed hair and ferrous red blood.

The warrior wiped its sword clean upon its own glistening red jerkin. "Come on, then," it said, to the rest of the sergeant's platoon.

The platoon swiftly enclosed the warrior in a circle of ringing steel. The circle widened as the warrior whirled and spun, cutting down two or three of its foes with each stroke. Blood sprayed, coating its face and legs until they were as red and wet as its jerkin.

Armour split, limbs fell, heads rolled—but the weight of numbers prevailed. The ring of Ore-lands steel contracted once more and the warrior finally fell. Only three Ore-land soldiers remained. Panting and groaning, crimsoned and hurt, they leaned upon each other for support.

When they had recovered themselves sufficiently, the

surviving corporal wiped the gore from its face with the fingers of its gauntlet and turned to face the mortal.

"Come," said the corporal. It spat a mouthful of blood. "The Queen awaits you."

12. The Queen of the Ore-lands

The Queen of the Ore-lands was immediately struck by how much he had changed.

The mortal hadn't aged, and he wore the same clothes, but he seemed bigger than before. There was now a certainty about him, a conviction of purpose that was both new and attractive.

The Queen rose from her throne, metal garments clattering, lips parting to show her silvered teeth. She raised her armoured hands and said, in her crushed-steel voice, "It's good to see you again, mortal man."

"And you, Majesty," he replied, taking a knee and lowering his gaze. "Though I fear your hospitality has cost you dearly."

"It has indeed," said the Queen of the Ore-lands. "But the price needed to be paid. The Warrior Queen oversteps herself in these strange new times, and I will no longer tolerate it."

"Aye."

"I have heard tell of your exploits," she said, "but I would listen to them from your own lips."

"I completed my quest as I had intended," said the mortal, in the careful way that she remembered. "Then I went home."

"You murdered the Warrior Queen Zelioliah with a cheap razor."

He looked up at her and said: "I did."

The Queen of the Ore-lands threw back her head and laughed. Her mirth boomed like the pounding of a kettle drum. When her laughter was spent she flipped her iron-grey hair from her eyes and looked upon him once more. The mortal smiled.

The Queen of the Ore-lands had to look away. She sighed and sat down on the steps before her throne; leaned forwards and put her hands upon her knees. "What service can I offer you, mortal?"

"My niece passed through the Realms of the Land since I was first here," he said. "Did she visit with you?"

"She did," said the Queen of the Ore-lands. "But I fear that my hospitality was lacking. I was girding myself for battle with the Tree Queen at the time."

"Did you win the conflict, Majesty?"

"Yes," said the Queen of the Ore-lands. "I won the battle, but the conflict is not over. The Tree Queen will build a new army and we will surely fight again."

"The Tree Queen lives?"

"Ah, yes," said the Queen of the Ore-Lands. "It is said that you slew the Tree Queen as well."

"I did."

"You slew every Queen that you came upon," said the Queen of the Ore-Lands.

"They all died," he admitted, "whether it was my intention or not."

"Every one of them but me."

"Aye, Majesty."

"Because they were beautiful, and I am not."

"Yes."

"Now I remember why I liked you so well," she said.

The mortal folded his hands together, embarrassed. "Majesty was telling me of the Tree Queen?"

"The current Tree Queen is of a newer lineage than the one you slew," said the Queen of the Ore-lands. "The Tree Folk are as they have ever been: numerous and proud, and known to bear grudges."

"I know there is no new Queen of the Sea City. Do you know the fates of the other queens I slew?"

"I do," she replied. "The Black and Crimson Queen—who had no territories of her own—is likewise ended; her Nation scattered and dispersed; her titles unclaimed."

"Do you know the state of the court of Titania?"

"I know little of Titania's court," said the Queen of the Ore-lands. "She and her nation spent more time abroad—in your world and in others—than they did in the Realms of the Land."

"And the Warrior Queen?" the mortal asked. "What of her people? You mentioned they have been…aggressive."

"Ah," said the Queen of the Ore-lands, grinning. "The Warrior Queen."

"Tell me."

"There is, of course, a new Warrior Queen; more powerful than even her mother before her. She is not to be trifled with."

"I see," said the mortal. He sighed. "You killed one of her warriors to protect me. Will there be repercussions?"

"There are always repercussions. In this Land, for every action there is usually a disproportionately violent reaction—it's good storytelling," said the Queen of the Ore-lands. "But I do not think this will provoke the Warrior Queen into a formal offensive. Her agent was slain on my sovereign territory, in defence of one I had named my guest. There will be no war unless I myself seek it."

"Good."

"You were asking after your kinswoman."

"Do you know where she went?"

"I know that she tarried to observe my battle with the Tree Queen's forces. I also know that the Council of the Magi sent an emissary to treat with her while she stood upon my territory. Then she left. That's all that I know."

"The Council of the Magi?"

"There is a Nation among the Faerie who govern the use of sorcery throughout the Land. They are gathered from all across the Land, from every Realm or Nation or Tribe, but they have no children of their own. Thus, they are ruled by a Council, not a Queen…nor even a King."

"I see."

"No, you don't," said the Queen of the Ore-lands. "You will not see them unless they choose to reveal themselves to you."

"Then I shall remain vigilant for such an occurrence as I go on my way."

"You are searching for your kinswoman, then? I do not know what has become of her."

"I know that she is dead," he replied. "Though not how or why."

"You seek revenge?"

"Revenge, I am sure, will come to me in its way. But it is a niggardly ambition. I seek something more."

"What, then, do you require, and how may I provide for your quest?"

"I would see the folk free to live without the strictures that bind them now," said the mortal. "But I must have allies who believe in my vision, if I am to succeed. Will you declare for me?"

"I am a Queen," she replied. "These strictures are the source of my power."

"You may keep your lands and titles," said the mortal. "I have no interest in politics."

"Even so. There are none in this land of higher station than me. I cannot give you my allegiance." She regarded him for a moment. When she spoke again, her voice was tinny and quiet. "Even you."

"I beg you to reconsider."

The Queen of the Ore-lands looked away from him and put her hands in her lap. "I would have taken you for husband," she said. "I would have made of you a Faerie King. I would have taken you to my bed, if I had thought you would survive my caress. I will take you as an equal, but I will not set you above me."

"I do not desire kingship," the mortal replied. "I must be something greater than that, if I am to prevail."

"Then I am sorry," said the Queen of the Ore-lands. "I refuse."

The mortal looked away. He drew in a long breath, then expelled it raggedly. "The times to follow will not be kind." He raised his eyes and said: "If you survive them, you will serve me yet."

The mortal turned on his heel and walked unescorted from the mirrored throne room.

The Queen of the Ore-lands sat, motionless on the steps before her throne, and watched him go. Tears like quicksilver fell from her ball-bearing eyes.

13. The Scarred Warrior

Through the darkening days and the darker-yet nights the scarred warrior followed the mortal, never pausing to sleep or take sustenance, nor even to rest. The warrior used every hunter's trick it knew, every bit of trail-craft and endurance and lore. Its march through the forests and the plains and the mountains and the badlands was fleeter than any beast upon the ground. Mile by mile, inch by inch, the scarred warrior drew nearer and nearer to its oblivious prey…but it could never quite close the distance.

Always, the scarred warrior remained in his shadow, and the longer it remained there, the blacker it became. Soon there was evil in its every breath, wickedness in every stride. The scarred warrior welcomed the darkness, and was driven on by it. It would find the mortal.

The scarred warrior would find the mortal when it was fated to, though it no longer knew which agency decreed that fate.

14. The Farm

The eldest of the farm folk was the first to see the mortal approaching, for its eyes were yet the keenest. It leaned on its hoe and watched impassively as he climbed over the outer fence. The mortal crossed the crop fields, keeping well away from the cattle pastures. The sun was high, and his shadow walked long behind him, as it had the last time he had come. The elder put down its hoe and went to greet him.

The mortal had changed, although the signs of it were subtle. He bore no possessions with him, no supplies for his journey. There was something else, too: the elder wondered if perhaps if it was 'beauty', but he soon decided that it was not. The mortal came with a truer purpose than that.

The elder fetched the mortal into the low stone farmhouse and called his family to hospitality. They took him to their hearth and fed him the choicest cuts from the most freshly slaughtered of their cattle; the best-ripened produce from their harvests. They gave him the purest well water they had drawn and the smoothest liquor they had fermented (which he refused). For dessert, they fed him sweets made from the rarest-blooming fruits and flowers they had cultivated.

When the mortal had eaten his fill and the table had been cleared, the elder said:

"I remember you. You are the mortal."

"I am a mortal, but I cannot be said to speak for all of my kind."

"Yet speak for them you must," said the elder, "For no other of your fellows is here."

"I doubt that they would approve me as their ambassador," said the mortal. "Best I represent myself, and no other."

"Have you completed the venture you were about when last we met?" asked elder.

"Yes. I have a new enterprise now."

"I can see that something about your person has changed, but I cannot fathom what."

"I have become immortal."

"How is this possible?" said the elder.

"I stole the years and days from one of your kind," the mortal replied. "Though it took me a long time to realize what I had done, for I have retained my essential nature."

"An undying mortal is a paradox," said the elder.

"My nature is split between dreaming and waking," said the mortal. "I am ageless asleep, so now I must dream awake."

"We Faerie folk do not dream," said the elder. It knew about dreams, just as it knew about death, though it was subject to neither.

"You are dreams," the mortal replied. "But I am not. Soon, you will be *my* dreams."

"I do not understand."

"I do not require your understanding—just your allegiance. Will declare for me?"

"Why?" asked the elder. "Are you raising an army?"

"I am not."

"Then what do you need of us?"

"I require neither service nor obeisance from you," the mortal said. "Just your acceptance or refusal."

"Then I and mine are for you," said the elder. "Since we are not presently beholden to any who might contest your sovereignty."

"I am no sovereign."

"Yet you have made me your subject."

"Subject or object, the distinction yet grows weak," the mortal replied.

The elder showed the mortal to the gate, to keep him from walking through the fields. He had already damaged them by his passage. The crops were blighted where he had trodden on them, and the soil was black and dead wherever he had cast his shadow.

15. The Swordless Warrior

The deeper into the woods the mortal ventured, the larger and more twisted grew the trees. Fewer and fewer lancing columns of sunlight penetrated the canopy, and his shadow became indistinct upon the forest floor. The mortal proceeded warily. As fearsome as he had grown, his kind had always feared to travel alone in the woods.

Soon he came to a clearing where the trees were scored with gunfire and magic. The ground was splashed with blood, which lay wet and fresh despite the years that had passed since he had spilled it. He looked around the place, remembering his battle with the Black and Crimson host. They were dead, now; nothing remaining of them but their colours. Black and crimson; blood and shadows.

Something too fast for the mortal to perceive hummed past his left ear. He raised his arms to protect himself and stumbled about comically, confused as to what exactly had transpired and in which direction it had come from. After a few moments he spotted a knife embedded in a tree, its handle still vibrating. The point of the thrown weapon pinned a long strip of his skin to the bark; a curling ribbon that was red on one side, pink on the other. He touched his hand to his face and found that he was bleeding.

"Hello, pig-fucker."

The mortal turned around slowly, his hands in the air. Blood was dripping from his cheek.

A warrior dressed in leathers and chainmail stood

slouching at the far side of the clearing. A dagger hung loosely in each of its hands. "I have orders to bring you back alive," it said.

"I've heard that before," the mortal replied. "Your comrade, who died at the city of the Ore-lands, told me the same."

"I am not my comrade," said the swordless warrior. "Don't try to run—if I disable your legs I will have to drag you all the way back to my queen's headquarters."

"Why would I run?"

"Will you come willingly?"

"No."

"Here, in the forests, you have no allies to safeguard you," said the swordless warrior. "There is no escape. There is nobody here but you, and me, and my many, many blades."

"Somebody always turns up," said the mortal.

The black thing took that as its cue. Smiling, it eased out of the shadows to face the warrior; its black eyes shining as wetly as its black enamel teeth.

The swordless warrior looked it up and down. "This pathetic thing is your protector?"

The mortal seemed equally surprised. "It appears that way."

"Just the one?"

"Yesss," said the black thing. "Jussst the one."

"And how, precisely, are you going to prevent me from doing what I have said?"

"I'm going to kill you, warrior," said the black thing. "In single combat. My knife against yours."

The swordless warrior snorted. "You have but one knife," said the swordless warrior. "And I have many."

"You have but one life," replied the black thing. "And I have many. Shall we see who dies harder, here beneath the mortal's gaze?"

"Once you lie slain I will take his eyes," said the swordless warrior, lowering itself into a fighting crouch and raising its hands. Blades sprouted from between its fingers; three in each hand.

The black thing drew a dagger from a sheath concealed on the inside of its forearm and, grinning, came towards its larger opponent in a knife-fighter's hunch.

The swordless warrior took a step backwards. When it threw the knife, its motion was too fast for the mortal to see—the first he knew of it was the eruption of pain in his leg. He fell backwards; landed hard on his arse.

"I'll not have you flee while I dispose of your *thing*," said the swordless warrior.

The mortal just lay upon the ground, groaning and bleeding.

The black thing moved to its right. The swordless warrior to its left and launched a looping, twisting attack upon the black thing; a whirl of steel and leather. The black thing stepped away, avoiding the feint-feint-slash easily and striking at the warrior's extended hand. Its gleaming black blade skidded off the chainmail that protected the back of the warrior's forearm.

The swordless warrior spun forwards, kicking at the black thing's knife-arm and throwing a dagger from its concealed hand. The black thing let the kick pass it by and plucked the thrown knife out of the air. It ducked another slash and reprised with a cut of its own. The black thing danced away, leaving the warrior's own dagger embedded in its wrist.

The swordless warrior retreated a few steps, drawing its injured left hand to its chest and extending its right. It rolled its remaining knife over its knuckles into a backhand grip.

The black thing lunged and the swordless warrior stepped into the attack, cutting at the black thing's extended hand. The counter-attack was—just barely—too late. The black thing's blade found the armpit gap in the warrior's armour, slid between its ribs, and pierced the warrior's lungs and heart.

The swordless warrior went over backwards. It did not get up.

"Well, that was easy," said the black thing, fingering the glancing cut it had received on its knife-arm. Its blood was as black as its skin.

"How did you do that?" asked the mortal, who was lying prone upon the ground.

"The warrior was trained a swordsman," said the black thing. "Who can say why it chose to fight only with knives?"

The mortal touched the dagger still embedded in his knee. "Help me," he said.

"I have neither healing powers nor medical skills," said the black thing.

"You have functional hands," the mortal replied. "Pull the dagger from my leg."

The black thing capered closer to him. "Your hands are as functional as mine."

"I've lost a lot of blood."

"You haven't the stomach for it," said the black thing, squatting down beside him.

"Yeah, you're right," the mortal conceded. "Now pull the dagger."

The black thing plucked the dagger from the mortal's thigh, spun it in its hand and made it vanish somewhere into its garments. It was pleased with itself: it had killed a warrior, and now it had some of the mortal's blood.

"Give me a strip of your clothing," commanded the mortal.

"You would have the shirt from my back?" said the black thing, feigning insult.

"Give me a strip of your clothing."

The black thing unwound a section of black fabric from its left arm and handed it to the mortal. He wound it tightly around his wound. When he felt it was secure, he tried to stand, but his injured leg caused him far too much pain. "I need a walking stick."

"Full of demands today, aren't we?" said the black thing.

"Cut me a stick."

The black thing tore a low-hanging branch from a nearby

tree and, with a few deft strokes of its black-bladed dagger, trimmed the branch down to a serviceable walking stick.

The mortal hauled himself to his feet using the stick and took a few tentative steps. He could walk, if he used the stick to take some of the weight from his left side. "Thank you," he said.

"Any time," said the black thing, bowing its leave and scampering back into his shadow.

16. The Tree Queen's Domain

The mortal limped onwards through the Tree Queen's domain; breathing the exhalations of her precious trees; spilling his filthy shadow upon her treasured soil. The swordless warrior had failed to destroy him, and the Tree Queen was becoming concerned.

The new Tree Queen had different ideas about governance than her predecessor, whose hubris had resulted in the destruction of her entire court. She knew who and what the mortal was, and she knew that she could not allow him to pass through her territories…but dare she risk confronting him herself? He had slain so many queens already.

The mortal stopped. Leaning heavily on his cane, he cried: "Where is the Tree Queen?"

The trees creaked and groaned before his words.

Leaves began to fall from the shivering trees. Sunlight shimmered down through the thinning canopy. "I'm just a crippled old mortal, unarmed and alone, without a single spell or sorcerous oath to my name. Will you not face me, here in your own territory?"

The bark on the trees began to crack and slough off. The wood beneath was darkening from brown to black, as though burned by the descending sky.

"I ask again: where is the Tree Queen?"

The tree folk broke and ran. From the humblest of dryads to the Tree King himself, the people of the forest took flight; running headlong in any and every direction, so long as it took them *away* from the mortal. But the forest was no longer their territory. The limbs of the trees did not embrace them; the trunks provided no shelter; the boles gave them no succour. Something terrible had happened to the forest.

"I am here." The Tree Queen's voice was ragged.

"Ah," said the mortal, turning to regard her. She looked most unlike her predecessor, who had been beautiful and human-looking; green haired and pale in her silks and her jewels. The new Tree Queen bald and bark-skinned. Her gown was of moss and lichen, and her eyes were the wet amber of hardening sap.

"Where are your soldiers? Your magi?"

"They have fled," she replied. "I am the only one left here."

"Your defenders are cowards," he said. "They were happy to abuse me when I was weak and hurting, but now that I have returned they flee like cravens."

"They are not cowards," said the Tree Queen. "They have defended my domain from all manner of monsters and abominations…but they remember what happened the last time you were among us. They do not know how to fight the likes of you."

"I don't fight. I only dream."

"What horrors have you dreamt of my Realm?" said the Tree Queen. "What have you done to my *trees*?"

"They're my trees, now," he said. "They are mortal, like me…"

Her eyes glistening, the Tree Queen threw her arms about the trunk of the nearest of the blighted black trees.

"…and like me, they bear the contagion of death."

The Tree Queen's skin peeled and shivered off her frame, which was made of wet, green wood. That wood darkened as the black of the trees bled through it, like ink upon paper. With a creak and a sigh, the remains of the Tree Queen collapsed into a puddle of glutinous shadow.

The mortal walked on, alone in the forest of bare, black-skinned trees; his boots falling silently on the dead black soil. Alone but for his shadow, of course, which scampered and cavorted about him, in accordance with the position of the sun.

One more trial remained. One last antagonist, who would be awaiting him at the Worldtree. Then his task would be complete. Then, the Realms of the Land would be irrevocably different.

The mortal found the direction he wanted and went on with a spring in his limping step and a smile upon his bleeding face. Soon he began to whistle.

17. The Council of the Magi

The Council of the Magi had spent many days in session without a single recess; scrying and divining, observing and seeing, invoking and evoking. They had drawn widely upon the power they had stockpiled. The Council needed to be certain of what was occurring before they could table any action.

After all those days and all that expenditure of power, they had located the mortal. They could watch him going about his business, although they could not ascertain exactly what that business was, or how he sought to accomplish it.

"His workings remain opaque," said the Speaker for the Council. "Whatever he is doing, he is doing it without the use of sorcery."

"I do not believe we will be able to properly determine his purpose from afar," said the Councillor on the Speaker's right.

"Then we must bring him before us," said the Speaker.

The Councillor on the Speaker's left seconded the motion.

When the mortal emerged from the black forest, he found himself in some territory he had not seen before.

Here, the landscape was disturbingly regular. The hills and valleys were far too uniform. The river, which was blue as the skies were grey, meandered a near-perfect sine wave through the territory. The rows of trees hardly seemed a forest, for they were perfectly staggered. The lowland plains were indeed planar. Time was divided equally between day and night. The temperature was unvaryingly pleasant.

Having no desire to visit this Realm, the mortal turned in the direction in which he believed that he would find the Worldtree, but the landscape veered with him.

"Alright," he said. "I'll take the hint." It seemed the Realms could surprise him yet. He let his feet lead him, for they seemed to know where to go.

The mortal was drawn down from the hills towards a strange, shimmering city. He passed through an empty, rune-encrusted gateway, to which he paid scant attention: spells and enchantments were of no interest to him. Still, a short way down the track, some instinct bade him turn and look upon them.

Without so much a groan, the gateway fell in upon itself and puffed away into black dust.

The mortal proceeded at a leisurely pace, slowing to look into the shining surfaces of the buildings that lined the streets. Those surfaces did not reflect back the sun or anything of the Land around it: every wall, every merlon, every buttress showed a view into a different place, a different world.

When he had gazed his fill of these other worlds, the mortal discovered that he was no longer alone. A dozen hunched, robed figures stood upon the sidewalks to either side of him, regarding him from within the shadows of their cowls. He did not know when they had arrived. Most likely they had been there all along, and he had simply failed to notice them.

One of the figures approached him. "The Council of the Magi would speak with you," it said, unfolding a pair of blackened, burn-scarred hands in a gesture that might equally have been a greeting or a warding.

"Then I would speak with them," the mortal replied, and suddenly he was somewhere else.

The teleportation was without sensation, but it left him

feeling violated. He had journeyed the length and breadth of the Land on foot: to be transported instantly from place to place seemed wrong. It was not his way.

He stood before a many-spoked table in a large, polyhedral chamber. The mirrored walls reflected nothing back: he had the distinct impression that they had been curtained from his gaze. The mortal's lips tightened. The Council of the Magi had at least partway fathomed his power.

A dozen robed figures—he supposed the same ones who had met him outside—sat around the table, one at the end of each of its spokes. The chair at the end of the thirteenth spoke was empty. He thought he could see bloodstains upon it.

The mortal stood leaning on his stick. "Hello," he said. "Lovely weather we're having."

"You have returned to the Land," said the Speaker for the Council of the Magi.

"I have," replied the mortal. Something flickered on the greyed-out walls of the chamber, vanishing before he could properly see it. Something black. Perhaps there was an image in it; perhaps not.

"You sent your kinswoman ahead of you."

"I sent her on a quest."

"Yet there was no quest for her."

"No," he said. "There wasn't. I suppose I knew as much."

"You sent her to her death."

"You have an unpleasant way of putting it."

The walls flickered again. There was definitely an image in the black. Something jagged. The mortal did not think the Council would have permitted the projection if they had been aware of it.

"You spent her mortal life for your own purposes."

"That is hardly a fair—"

"Fairness is not our concern," said the Speaker. "Nor justice. We are only interested in the facts of the matter."

"Thus far, I've heard nothing but slander."

"Slander is not our purpose," said the Speaker. "But it is your purpose that is subject to question."

"If you have questions then ask me, already." He was starting to discern the image broadcast upon the walls. Black cliffs, he thought, against a night sky.

"What, then, is your purpose?"

"It will be easier to show you than to explain it."

"Then show us."

"If you would be so kind as to open a window? It's quite stuffy in here." Black cliffs against a night sky, jutting over a seething black sea.

The Speaker clenched its fists. "This Council will brook no more of your insolence. Tell us what you desire, and how you intend to achieve it, or there will be consequences."

A dark tower stood over the black cliffs, the shadowed sea. It was visible only because it was blacker still than the sky and sea and land. It was the source of all that darkness. It was the source of the transmission.

The mortal sighed. "For a minute there, I thought you'd worked it out by yourselves," he said. "My...desire...by perception. I travel somewhere, I observe it, and then it belongs to me."

"Sorcery does not work in this way."

There was something familiar about the tower. Some remembered past, some lingering enmity...but also a shared strength. They were magnets, he and the tower: drawn together and repelled apart; casting a field of influence between them.

"It's not sorcery, it's only magic," he replied. "But that's merely a detail. You're missing the crux of the situation."

The tower had drawn him back to the Realms. It had assisted him without his knowledge, and they had both grown the stronger for it.

"Oh, indeed?"

"By bringing me here you have allowed me to perceive you, who once were hidden from me."

"You speak nonsense."

"What else would you expect of a madman, abroad in the Land of dreams and lies?"

"So now you are a poet, as well as a madman," said the Speaker. "But you are no lover, nor ever shall be."

The mortal lowered his gaze. "But I was," he said. He smiled and looked up. "Of course I was. I was a lover, like every other mortal. I loved so much my heart was full to bursting."

"And then your heart burst," said the Speaker.

The tower pulsed darkly.

"You make it sound obvious, but you couldn't see it until I told you," said the mortal. "You couldn't dowse my past, and you still can't divine what I've done to your Realms. And you haven't even noticed what I've done to you while we have stood here chatting."

"You have done nothing but flap your tongue."

"I have flapped my tongue but I have also been observing what is going on around me." The mortal gestured with his stick. "I would encourage you to do the same."

The mirror-paned walls had darkened from grey to black, and the image of the tower was reflected in every facet.

The Speaker had no words.

"Come," he said. "Lead me out of these halls, and I will show you."

"There is no exit," said the Speaker. "Sorcery is the only means by which this chamber can be accessed."

"Bollocks and bullshit," said the mortal. "As bloody usual."

He limped over to one of the mirror-paned walls and struck it with his stick. The council chamber shattered and liquefied; cracking apart and slushing to the ground, panel by panel. The flooring split open beneath their feet, splintering into a fine layer of dust.

Outside, the City of the Magi was nowhere in evidence. Its towers and apartments, cast from purest magic, had vanished as if they never were. The uniform hills and valleys of the Realm that had once contained that city had been captured and occupied by a forest of bare, black-skinned trees.

The trees slouched in staggered file along the banks of the sine wave river; they stood in parade formation upon the planar plains. The soil underfoot was black and dead. The sky above was blue and bright and empty.

The Speaker struck its hands together and stepped forwards. "Enough!" it said. "Your hideous magic has fouled our Land for too long already." It threw its hands out wide. "Council, attend to me. It is time this mortal met the fate of all of his kind."

"Do your worst," said the mortal, leaning on his stick.

The Speaker shook its hands, stiff-fingered, at the mortal. It danced and incanted and invoked and cursed. The other members of the Council stood silent and unmoving, pooling their collective powers for the Speaker's use.

The mortal stood and watched them with a smile on his face. The Speaker continued to wave and chant and jump about, with no visible effect.

"Please stop that. I feel like I'm in a discotheque."

After a while the Speaker became tired from the physical exertion. Panting for breath, it said: "What have you brought upon us?"

"Apocalypse," said the mortal. He altered his grip on his stick and struck it upon the side of his boot.

The black trees and the dead soil receded, forming a depression beneath them. The exposed bedrock itself subsided and the floor sank deeper yet. Cliffs of jagged stone rose from the collapsing earth like opening fingers. And there, surmounting the cliffs, stood the tower.

The mortal looked up at the tower and nodded. "Go on, then."

The fossilized skeletons of great and hideous leviathans arose from the dust; their chap-fallen bones drawing together, twitching and scraping. They jerked and unsteadily came upright, soft tissues spreading between their salt-caked joints before calcifying into armour. The creatures gasped and twitched as black water began to seep out of the ground.

The seabed filled with swirling brine, as dark as blood

or oil. The saltwater swept the magi away, battering them, filling their lungs. The sea-beasts flopped and thrashed until there was enough fluid for them to swim properly. They churned the waters with obscene vigour, hungry from their restoration. In great gulping bites the leviathans consumed the drowned Councillors: their power was gone, but the meat on them was good enough.

18. Beneath the Poisoned Sea

The Poisoned Sea quickly filled to its capacity, driving its waters outwards and joining them to the rivers that flowed into all of the Realms; feeding the Land with loathing and darkness and malice; flooding out the great, grassy plains that had themselves once resembled a sea. The ruined city that stood on those plains grew up anew, restored, but the miserable folk that lived there could not breathe the black waters. Their salt tears were added to the brine.

The mortal did not know whether they wept for joy or for sorrow, but they went weeping to their deaths, and the terrible denizens of the Poisoned Sea consumed their remains.

Limping, he made his way out of the Sea City, with his naked eyes open to the lightless depths. He supposed that he was drowned, technically, but he did not seem to be dead. Fish-things swirled about him. Eyes too big for their sockets stared. Teeth too big for their mouths gnashed. Girning faces and rushing flukes made obeisance to him as they passed. Thus he crossed the sea floor, wending his way between the reefs of carnivorous and phosphorescent coral; walking amongst schools of fish and fiends that were armoured and finned, fanged and envenomed.

The rocks beneath his feet softened as the seabed began to rise. It was difficult to find traction in the sliding sand, but he trudged on. The mortal was a strong swimmer, but today he had to walk.

19. The Tree and the Tower

The mortal emerged from the filthy tide and fell to his knees in the coarse black sand in order to purge the brine from his lungs. It was more painful than he had expected; far worse than the suffocating feeling the vomiting had relieved.

Weak and gasping, he raised his head. He could not see anything beyond the black trees, which grew thickly just beyond the high-water mark. As he knelt there, the night sky rose above him and the stars came out. The mortal wasn't sure why, but somehow he had come to believe those stars to be blind and hungry things, not so different than the fish-beasts that ruled the Poisoned Sea.

The Sea had grown vast indeed, though it would never be a true ocean. The black forest, too, had spread; following the sea's invasion of the rivers. The black had now conquered Realms which the mortal had never seen, or even imagined. This was the tower's doing: mindlessly broadcasting its taroted message the length and breadth of the Realms.

The mortal scrambled over the sharp and porous rocks at the base of the cliffs and began to climb. The way was steep; the footing treacherous. The knife-wound in his leg pained him still. But he climbed on, cursing and muttering as he went. It felt like days or weeks or months, but he knew it was merely hours before he stood before the tower. His jacket was torn in many places, his hands were bloodied, and his jeans hung in tatters about his boots.

The tower had sprouted from the rock like the shoot of some fat plant, shattering the brittle ground when its shaft had burst through. Even now the rubble shifted, unsettled, though the tower stood firm. It was made of an unnatural material that was as much wood as obsidian, as much plant as stone, as much ebony as flesh—some alloy of sorcery and evil that was slick and scabrous and filmed with slime. The mortal fancied that he could see limbs or tendrils or arteries branching from its apex, to vein the sky.

"I should have known," said the mortal, to any that might be listening. The tower was a tree. The tower was the Tree.

He sighed his weariness and began to limp around the base of the tower. There was no opening anywhere along its circumference. After a second circuit he still had not located an entrance, but the wound in his leg was bothering him less. The third circuit was just as fruitless, but his limp was almost gone and his other wounds were starting to scab or scar.

The mortal stood, leaning on his stick, waiting for the enemies he knew were coming. He did not have to wait for long.

"Turn around, pig-fucker," said a resonant, female voice. "I want to see your face before I kill you."

20. A Kiss Beneath the Tree

He turned around slowly.

The Warrior Queen Zelioliah, for whom he had once quested, regarded him down the barrel of an assault rifle. His heart surged, his eyes felt hot. He choked on his own breath.

It wasn't Zelioliah. Dead faeries did not return. This was her daughter, as the Ore Queen had told him.

He looked away. His heart was still wild in his chest.

A young man stood behind the Warrior Queen; shoulders bunched, head hanging forwards. His breath hissed through clenched teeth. The man had olive skin and close-cropped, ragged black hair. Like his mistress, he was armed with an automatic weapon that looked almost as if it had come from the mortal realm.

"You're not ugly," said the Warrior Queen, "But you're not handsome, either. I can't fathom what my mother saw in you, that she gave you her life."

"You look exactly like her," the mortal said, "But she was the most beautiful thing in all the worlds, and you are not beautiful at all."

"That beauty you destroyed forever."

"Yes."

"She went to you willingly," said the Warrior Queen. "Had she known…"

"She knew," the mortal replied. "She knew what she was, and she knew why I sought her."

"If she had known what you intended she would have struck you down," said the Warrior Queen. "My mother was a warrior; she would not have surrendered to any foe."

"People aren't that simple," said the mortal. "Not real ones, anyway."

"My mother was not a person, she was a faerie."

"Perhaps," he replied. "Perhaps she was, until I came looking for her. When she became also a person, and no longer just the Warrior Queen. That was when she knew that she had weakened. When I saw her as beautiful, as the object of my quest, she was diminished. But she knew there would be another Warrior Queen after her; stronger than she had ever been."

"The creed of the warrior is to better oneself," said the Warrior Queen. "To become the mightiest, or to fall trying."

"Aye," the mortal said. "And now the Warrior Queen is mightier than ever. The cost of it was cheap: a single, soulless life...and beauty beyond measure. Cheap as chips."

"No," said the Warrior Queen. "You can dress it up however you like, but in the end, you slew my mother because you wanted to destroy something beautiful."

"That's also true," he replied. "And here's another true fact: without me, you would not be the woman you have become."

The Warrior Queen was silent. Her companion growled and swore at him in Spanish.

"You think that you raised me to greatness, but I was always the scion of the Warrior Queen—and you are still a petty murderer. For that, I'll take your life."

"Will you?" the mortal asked. "Or will your thrall?"

"My mother saved you from the dog-man," replied the Warrior Queen. "It's only fitting that I loose my own dog-man upon you. But this time, who will save you?"

The mortal opened his mouth, but another, smaller voice spoke first.

"That would be my job."

The black thing slid around the curvature of the tower.

It saunter-scampered to the mortal's side and patted him upon the shoulder. Its teeth and eyes and hair and skin and garb shone darkly in the tower's blacklight. "How's that leg of yours doing?" it said.

"Kill it," said the Warrior Queen to her companion. "Whatever it is."

Malo stepped forwards and slung the rifle off his shoulder. He cocked it, flipped the safety, and sighted his target.

The black hissed through its grin. Black-bladed knives slid into its hands from hidden sheathes.

Malo squeezed the trigger. The gun boomed, flat and hollow and staccato. Smoke and flame and rune-light flashed from its muzzle.

The black thing ruptured. Shredded guts and pulped meat sprayed off its splintering skeleton; a thick black mist of gore and shadow.

"Oh, shit," said the mortal.

"Now the human," said the Warrior Queen. Malo swung the gun towards him.

The mortal swallowed hard and said, in English: "Can you understand me?"

"Sí," grunted Malo. He could understand every language, though he did not comprehend it as language at all.

"Are you a man, or are you a dog?"

"Man," said Malo.

"What is your name?"

"I am El Cachorro Malo."

Malo's eyes were a pale, washed-out blue colour. The mortal wondered why he hadn't noticed before. He frowned. "The Bad Puppy?"

"Sí."

The Warrior Queen laughed.

The mortal had worked it out. "You are the son of the magus."

"Sí."

"And you will slay me—another mortal man—here, before your father's tower?"

"Sí."

"At the bidding of this woman? Like a faithful dog?"

Malo hesitated.

"It was a dog that killed your father."

"I will kill you," said Malo, in Spanish.

"I am the only one who can open the tower," the mortal replied. "If you spare me, I'll let you inside and you will have your birthright."

The son of the magus tipped his head, considering.

"This fool cannot breach the Tower," said the Warrior Queen. "He's less of a sorcerer than you are."

The mortal's attention remained on Malo. "Well, what are you, then? Are you the son of a man, or a pet animal?"

Malo hesitated. "I am the son of the magus," he said. "I am a man." He spoke the last sentence in clear, unhalting Spanish.

"And a human," the mortal added.

"I told you to kill him," said the Warrior Queen. "Have you turned on me?"

Malo backed away from the Warrior Queen. "I won't betray you," he said, "But if you want him dead, you must kill him yourself."

The Warrior Queen gave Malo a long, hard look. "I'll brook no disobedience," she said. "Not from a soldier, not from an officer, and certainly not from a dog."

"Then punish me."

"I will," she said. "In good time. But first, I must deal with this pig-fucker."

The Warrior Queen swung her head towards the mortal. He stood, leaning on his stick, before the dark tower. Before the Worldtree. He met her gaze, but he took a step back when she turned square to him.

The Warrior Queen shrugged the machinegun from her shoulders and dropped it at her feet. She drew a pistol from a holster on her belt and cocked it. "A bullet is more than you deserve," she said, "but it's the cheapest death I have for you." The Warrior Queen raised the gun, steadied it with her second hand, drew a bead and squeezed the trigger in a single motion.

"We are agreed on that," said the mortal.

The Warrior Queen squeezed the trigger twice more. The weapon did not fire.

The Warrior Queen checked the pistol, although she knew it hadn't jammed. "Is this your doing?" she asked Malo. "Are you thwarting my sorcery?"

"No," replied the son of the magus.

"Sorcery won't work here," said the mortal. "Not beneath the tower. Not against me."

The Warrior Queen discarded the pistol and drew the bastard sword that hung from her back. "Magic will not protect you from my sword," she said. "And you have no guardians remaining."

The mortal regarded the Warrior Queen impassively. His lips parted for a long moment before he spoke. "I think," he said, "that you are mistaken."

A dark and fell creature came lurching out of the forest. It was clad in leather and chainmail and hung about with a variety weapons, in the manner of the warrior folk. It raised its head and squared its shoulders as it came on. Thick, livid scars ran up each side of its face, from its jaw to its eyes.

"No," said the Warrior Queen. "It is you who are mistaken. This is one of mine."

As the scarred warrior drew nearer to them, its sickness became more apparent. Its clothing was dishevelled and its hair, which had blackened from its natural brown, stood out in spikes and clumps. Veins of darkness writhed under its skin, and the pupils of its eyes had consumed both the irises and the whites.

"Not anymore," said the mortal.

The scarred warrior twitched and jerked and shook. The black marbling in its skin thickened and merged; the veins bleeding together until only the pink ridges of scar tissue on its face retained their original pigmentation. Another fit of spasms brought the scarred warrior to its knees.

"This travesty is your last ally?"

The mortal shrugged apologetically.

The scarred warrior coughed, shook and rose to a half-kneel. Shadows boiled under its skin. Unsteadily it came to stand between the mortal and the Warrior Queen.

The Warrior Queen drew a second sword from a scabbard on her waist.

The scarred warrior flexed its trembling fingers. Its weapons and mail dissolved into black rust; its leathers dripped off as a thick inky sludge. It stood naked before the Warrior Queen and the son of the magus and the mortal, wracked with hate and shuddering with malice.

The scarred warrior raised her black-skinned face and opened her black, black eyes.

The Warrior Queen was unimpressed. "This was the poorest soldier in my army," she said. "This one took pleasure in killing that was unbecoming of a warrior."

"What is becoming and what is not is purely a matter of taste," said the mortal.

The Warrior Queen spat. "You think this paragon of good taste can protect you from me?" she said. "Naked and unarmed?"

"No," he replied, "But she will be neither." He looked into the forest and said: "Armourer."

The metalled, steel-threaded being that had once been the Queen of the Ore-lands came forth. The plating secured to her living flesh was now soot-blackened and dull. Her pierced and pale-skinned features were smudged and the teeth visible through her peeled-open cheeks were jagged and rusty. She did not smile.

"Armourer," the mortal said. "Gird my warrior for combat."

With deft hands the Armourer bound the scarred warrior in garments of black leather. With sure fingers she tied every truss, secured every strap, fastened every black-lacquered buckle, sealed every clasp.

The Armourer drew a pair of shadowsteel swords from her

own scabbards and spun them over to present them. When the scarred warrior drew the swords from the Armourer's forge-calloused hands, the shadowsteel blades slid through her fingers as if they had been sheathed in velvet.

When its work was done, the Armourer went to stand behind its master.

The Warrior Queen laughed. "Is this how you think a warrior prepares for battle, pig-fucker?"

"Perhaps that was overdramatic," he replied, "But this is still Fairyland. For the time being."

Malo backed towards the tower. He threw down the faux-AK47 and let fall his gun-belt. Malo drew a sickle made from a sliver of blackglass and a twisted length of bone from behind him. He let it hang from his fingers, the knob of bone at the bottom of the haft loose in the palm of his hand. "This fight is yours," he said.

The Warrior Queen regarded him sternly. Then her expression softened. "Aye, you've the right of it," she said. "If you behave yourself, you may yet dine on this pig-fucker's bones."

Malo growled, but stayed his ground.

The Warrior Queen fell into a fighting crouch. "Have you nothing to say for yourself, traitor?" she asked the scarred warrior.

"No." The scarred warrior raised her weapons and assumed an identical posture.

"Then your blades must speak for you."

The warriors spun together and apart; the bell-tones of steel on steel sounding for longer than the two warriors were in motion. They gathered themselves and whirled together again.

The scarred warrior was stronger and faster, and her weapons were of better quality that those wielded by the Warrior Queen. The Warrior Queen, however, was more skilled.

After the third engagement, both combatants had been cut. The scarred warrior's blood was as black as her skin and her garments. The Warrior Queen's blood was red.

After the fifth engagement, it was apparent that the Warrior Queen was growing stronger. The scarred warrior came away from their sixth engagement lacking most of her left ear.

"Your lust for my death works against you," said the Warrior Queen. "It makes you predictable. It makes you weak."

"If I'm so pitifully weak, why did you dispatch me on such an important mission?" asked the scarred warrior. "Why pit the likes of me against this terrible scourge of a mortal?"

"I selected the three warriors I valued the least," said the Warrior Queen. "Three fools, who could not be like the rest of my army."

"Why would you send us, if you knew we would fail?" said the scarred warrior.

"I wanted to see what would happen to you," replied the Warrior Queen. "I wanted to see if this pig-fucker could actually fight, or if his only weapons were luck and trickery and horror."

"Those, indeed, are his weapons," said the scarred warrior. "I am all three of them."

"You're a sow who has fallen for a pig-fucker," said the Warrior Queen.

Combat drew the warriors together again. When their motion halted, the scarred warrior bore a cut that ran from her left brow across her forehead and curved over her right temple. She tore away the flap of scalp, wiped away the strands of severed hair clinging to her brow, and reset her grip on her swords. Her skull glistened white where it lay bare. The Warrior Queen was just as fast and as strong as she was now.

"You'll die beneath my next stroke," said the Warrior Queen. It was true. She now held every advantage, for she was yet the Queen of the Warriors, and such was her due.

"No," said the scarred warrior. "I don't think so."

The Warrior Queen opened her mouth to speak, but instead of words, a shard of black glass emerged from between her teeth.

Malo put his second hand on the haft of the sickle and tore the blade sideways from the Warrior Queen's head. The glass blade sliced through her cheek, snapped off part of her jawbone, and then broke. The Warrior Queen fell dead at his feet.

The scarred warrior went to Malo with her arms wide. He took her embrace, put his own arms around her; the broken end of his sickle coming to rest against the nape of her neck. She crossed the guards of her swords between his shoulder-blades. Malo touched her face where the skin and meat had been torn away. They kissed like carnivores, hungry and savage.

The mortal looked away, embarrassed.

The lovers paused to gaze into each other's eyes, to lick the blood and darkness from each other's teeth, and then they kissed again.

The mortal turned once more to the forest. "Shadow-phage," he said.

The Shadowphage unwound itself from the darkness; its pale skin coalescing before its black silk garments did. "Master."

The mortal looked down at the two corpses that lay sprawled upon the ground. "I have a meal for you," he said.

The shadowphage scowled. "I do not take carrion."

"You will this time."

The shadowphage paled until it glowed. "Must I, truly?"

The mortal nodded. "Yes," he said. "I would not have the Warrior Queen's shadow free to roam, nor the—" The mortal paused.

The black thing's corpse had vanished. Not a shred of black leather or a splash of inky blood remained to show where it had lain.

The mortal couldn't help but smile. The black thing had already stolen its freedom. He felt oddly proud of it. He was sure that was not the last thing it would steal.

"I would not have the Warrior Queen's shadow free to roam," he told the shadowphage.

"Yes, master." The shadowphage chose two small knives from those that hung at its belt and bent to its task without relish.

The mortal turned back to the lovers and cleared his throat loudly. With obvious reluctance they broke their kiss and gave him their attention.

"I thought you were going to stay out of it," the mortal said to Malo.

"If you had perished," said Malo, "who would have opened the tower for me?"

"No one."

Malo grunted. "Open it, then."

"I already have."

An opening had appeared at the base of the tower, where the roots met the trunk of the tree. While they watched, it grew to be a dozen feet high. There was movement inside: slick, fleshy tendrils coiled and writhed. Claws clacked, teeth ground and gnashed. The abominations that lived in the tower were massing at the now open portal; crowding together, wanting to see what was outside…and to welcome whoever was coming in.

"They will come forth if you call them," the mortal said. "They will make way if you ascend the tower. They are your father's creatures and they recognize you as his flesh."

"I'm not his," rasped Malo. "I'm my own."

"No," said the scarred warrior. "You are mine."

"And you belong to Malo," the mortal told her. "And all the Realms of the Land belong to both of you, together."

"You'd give it away?" said the scarred warrior. "After all you have done to make it your own?"

"I never wanted to own it; I just wanted to tear it down," replied the mortal. "Rebuilding it will be your task."

"We're not worthy of this," said the scarred warrior.

"I know," the mortal replied. "But that's why it must be

yours. I couldn't have won this without your bravery and skill at arms." He turned to Malo. "And I could not even have attempted it without your power. Without the work of your father, and your response to it."

"I did nothing," said Malo. It no longer seemed to matter what language they spoke, if ever it had.

"You struck the final blow," said the mortal. "But that's not all. Your presence here eroded the…meaning…of this Faerie Land. Without that, I could never have quickened my own dreams here."

"I still do not understand why you would do this," said the scarred warrior; the newly appointed Empress of the Shaedowlands. "Why indulge such effort? Why risk so much?"

"Mortals have been dreaming this place for centuries," he replied. "The same recycled stories, ever more bereft of meaning. Lovers, poets, madmen. Magicians. Far too many have squandered their dreams in these Realms."

Malo, the Emperor of the Shaedowlands, grunted in assent.

"And so you took it upon yourself to ruin it."

"Not just me," said the mortal. He turned to Malo. "I think your father the magus had a similar ambition. He wanted to change the story from something worn into something monstrous. But he failed."

"Such evil has been here as long as your kind have dreamed us," said the scarred warrior. "The Land is well used to it. How did you succeed, where the magus failed?"

"This Land cannot be reshaped by spellcraft," said the mortal. "Only dreams can make the changes true." He blushed, and laughed at himself. "A Disney moral for a Disney fairy-tale, I guess."

"To dream a world anew? That is the work of a god," said the scarred warrior.

The mortal shook his head. "Whatever I have become, I am something far more tawdry than that. I am an unmaker. It is not for me to rule here."

"Come," said the Empress, turning to her Emperor. "Let us consummate our marriage in your father's tower."

The Emperor of the Shaedowlands swept the Empress up in his arms and carried her to the threshold. He stood, looking into the darkness. Then he turned about and looked out at the half-lit Realms. The Land of green trees and blue waters and golden light, now limned in blacks and greys and purples. The mortal who had rendered it thus stood facing them in silhouette—though his embarrassment was plain enough.

"It's a beautiful world," said Malo. "Won't you stay a while longer?"

"No," replied the mortal. A pair of black wings had unfurled behind him, and now they began to beat. "It's time for me to go, and dream of somewhere new."